DON'T ROCK THE GOAT

ELLEN RIGGS

BOUGHT-THE-FARM
MYSTERIES

FREE FUN STORY

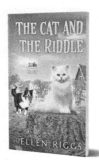

Can this sleuthing sheepdog solve a riddle in time to save a missing cat?

Ivy, Edna and Gertie team up with Keats and Percy to outwit a wily catnapper in this EXCLUSIVE Bought-the-Farm story. Join Ellen Riggs' author newsletter at **Ellenriggs.com** today to receive *The Cat and the Riddle* FREE at Ellenriggs.com

Don't Rock the Goat

ISBN 978-1-989303-68-9 eBook
ISBN 978-1-989303-67-2 Book
ASIN B08NXS79VYKindle
ASIN TBD Paperback
Publisher: Ellen Riggs

www.ellenriggs.com
Cover designer: Lou Harper
Editor: Serena Clarke
2103140714

CHAPTER ONE

The brisk and breezy morning had arrived with a sweet promise of spring. Soon there would be warmth and wildflowers and green meadows. With the snow finally gone, I could walk with my dog through the fields once again, enjoying the serenity Runaway Farm had brought into our lives. Today would be too busy for such indulgences, but tomorrow.

As I stood outside the barn with Keats, the sheepdog in question, he offered one of his conversational mumbles. I expected enthusiasm but it sounded more like, "don't count your chickens before they're hatched."

"There won't be any chickens hatching around here," I told him. "We have too many critters as it is. No babies of any sort, thank you very much."

He gave a little sneeze and I looked down. With Keats, a sneeze was rarely just a sneeze. It was usually code for something else. Something he found amusing. Sometimes a joke at my expense. Only his eyes would tell the tale. If he gazed at me with his warm brown eye, all was good. A stare from his eerie blue one warned me to stay on my toes.

Today he gave me an equal share of both eyes.

"What's that supposed to mean? Should I be worried or not? I don't have time for guessing games, buddy. The guests will be here soon."

He turned to stare down the twisty lane, probably hearing the crunch of wheels on gravel long before I did.

"Already? I wanted to grab a shower first."

He sneezed again and added a happy ha-ha-ha pant for good measure. It wasn't the guests, then. It was someone he liked well enough to put a little extra oomph into the swish of his tail. Normally he wasn't that showy for Kellan, my boyfriend, or Asher, my brother.

"Who ranks high enough for pumping paws?" I asked him. "You're going all dressage horse on me." The answer came a second later and I groaned. "Oh no."

The next mumble was a decided, "Yes. Yes. Yes."

A lime green van rounded the last turn and rolled into the parking area. It belonged to Bridget Linsmore, and no doubt contained Cori Hogan, the expert dog trainer and tiny tyrant who was the object of Keats' esteem. The two women headed a band of vigilante dog rescuers in nearby Dorset Hills. I admired them greatly and enjoyed their company, but so often the doors of that van opened to release more rescue animals. Some I was to house temporarily, others long-term, and the rest were a wait-and-see game. Animals deemed unfit to move on to a regular pet home won a free pass to live out their lives at Runaway Farm.

Everyone urged me to draw the line. Mom. My

brother and five sisters. My best friend, Jilly Blackwood. My neighbor and octogenarian warrior, Edna Evans. And of course, Kellan Harper, Clover Grove's chief of police. Even my brilliant and energetic border collie wanted me to slow things down. While there could never be enough work and adventure for a dog like him, most of these rescue animals were high needs and required more skillful handling than regular livestock. Keats was a master of adapting to the particular requirements of each, but today he rolled his blue eye at me and mumbled a question: "Really? Did we really need another animal?"

We did *not* need another animal, let alone the three goats Bridget, Cori and Remi Malone unloaded from the van despite my protests.

"Ivy, look alive," Cori called, signaling for Keats to join Clem, her own border collie. "Open that gate, and fast. These girls are spark plugs."

"I don't want more goats," I said. "I've got plenty already."

"It's just three," Cori said. "And just temporary."

Temporary. That was almost never true.

Keats trotted over, ready to be deployed. At least when Cori made a deposit in the Runaway Farm bank, she had the decency to bring reinforcements now. Clem was an award winner at herding trials across the country. He and Keats got along like brothers and taught each other new tricks of the trade.

"Two reps," she said, brushing back her short dark hair. Her black wool glove with its trademark orange middle finger left static behind.

"Pardon me?" I watched as she began playing the role

of third sheepdog. She was dodging, weaving, and giving a nudge here and there. These goats were the wildest I'd ever seen, and after eight months in my hometown of Clover Grove, I'd seen quite a few.

"Two repetitions," she called back, signaling Clem to bring in the largest of the goats as the animal started to bolt for the barn. "That's all it takes for a border collie to pick up a new habit. Good or bad. Most dogs take closer to fifty." She glanced over at Remi Malone, who was now cradling Leo, her therapy beagle, in her arms. "In Leo's case, it's a couple of hundred."

"Untrue and unfair," Remi said. "He learned to steal my sandwich out of my lunch bag in a single rep."

"See?" Cori sent Keats after the big goat, too. He normally ignored commands from anyone but me, but Cori was a notable exception. "You've got to be super careful what you do around dogs, especially sheepdogs."

"Or even what you think," I said. Keats regularly read my mind, or at least read my tone and my body language well enough to pass for a mindreader. I personally believed he knew exactly what I was thinking even before I thought it. Sometimes I wondered if my thoughts were actually *his* thoughts and I was the one taking orders.

"Exactly," Cori said. "Ivy, I need you to get those boots moving. Big Mama has a mind of her own and we've got to get her into the pasture before she hurts the dogs or other goats or herself."

"Or us," I said, joining the tiny taskmaster. "I've seen ornery goats before but Big Mama's the worst."

"Cut her some slack," Cori said. "She's got a couple of buns in the oven."

I stopped moving and turned. "What?"

Cori grinned. "She's pregnant and so are the others. We had to get them out of a bad situation before they delivered."

"You're dropping three pregnant goats on me? I can barely handle the animals I have."

She gave a dramatic sweep with her glove to get me running. "You've got plenty of help these days."

I had Charlie, my farm manager, and Poppy, my sister, neither of whom worked fulltime. At best that made a ratio of three to more than 50 animals. Regular farmers might consider that luxury, but my charges were high maintenance.

"Cori, in case you've forgotten, I have an inn to run. In fact, some guests will be arriving shortly. I don't have time for goat midwifery."

Keats and Clem managed to drive the two smaller brown-and-black goats through the gate of my only free pasture. Clem held them there, while Keats came back to help Cori with Big Mama, who was bearded, white and surprisingly agile for a large goat. She was a trio all on her own.

"Your guests will be lucky to witness the miracle of birth," Cori said. "Nothing cuter than a newborn kid." She wasn't even panting, despite running nearly as hard as the dogs. "It never gets old, Ivy. You're going to love it."

"I am so *not* going to love it. The thought makes me queasy."

"Then I guess you're not planning on producing little Chief Hotties," she said. "It's the same thing."

Bridget and Remi laughed, and even I couldn't help smiling. "It is not the same thing at all."

"How would you know if you've never seen a goat deliver?" she asked.

"How would *you* know if you've never seen a human deliver?" None of the Rescue Mafia, a band of about a dozen women, had children. They were all in their early thirties, like me, and most were happily married to wonderful guys. Yet they seemed more committed to saving animals than adding small people to the planet.

Cori laughed and I was happy to hear a hitch in her breath. "Got me there. That is something I hope never to witness."

"Don't say that," Bridget called. "The world needs little Coris. I want to be their godmother."

"We're godmothers to thousands of puppies, kittens, bunnies and assorted livestock," Cori said. "That's plenty of glory."

"Gory, in this case. I don't want to see Big Mama pop." I feinted left and the goat right. She was a smart one. Maybe smarter than me, but hopefully not smarter than Keats. "And I'm tired of being a dumping ground for misfit animals, you guys. There's a limit, and you've reached mine."

"But not Hannah's," Cori called after me. "Hannah's hospitality is limitless."

I flinched as the shot hit home. This farm—this amazing, wonderful place I adored—had fallen into my lap in a huge stroke of luck last summer. Back then, I was living in Boston and had just detonated my corporate career. Hannah Pemberton, a billionaire heiress, saw news coverage of my rescue of Keats from a criminal and decided I was the right person to take over this farm. When family business pulled her to Europe, she had to give up the farm and her plans for an inn. So I came home to Clover Grove and took up where she left off. The Rescue Mafia had backed Hannah as they now backed me, but that support came at the price of never saying no to new arrivals.

"Don't worry," Bridget chimed in. "I've delivered quite a few kids and I'll show you the ropes. When the time comes, all you need to do is call."

I grabbed a broom and started brandishing it in hopes that Big Mama would see me as a bigger threat and decide to join her maternity buddies.

"How exactly will I know when the time comes? What if I'm sleeping? Or hosting dinner? Or running errands?"

"You'll need to scale back on those things for a couple of weeks," Cori said, gesturing for Keats to get between us. "Kids come when they come. There's an empty stall in the barn and I'll get Charlie to put a cot in there."

"I can't sleep in the barn, Cori."

"Why not?" She stretched out her arms and I did the same. "You've done it before."

"Let me rephrase that. I can't sleep in a barn for a couple of weeks when I have guests in the house. It's not fair to Jilly."

"This probably won't take weeks," Cori said. "More like days. And you've got Daisy on board now to cohost."

She had an answer for everything. My eldest sister had started working with us recently and pretty much managed the inn on her own, while Jilly focused on creating fabulous meals, and doing our marketing, which was a far bigger challenge.

"I have a life, you know," I said. "I can't just drop everything and wait for the miracle of goat-birth."

"Sure you can. There's nothing crazy going on right now." Cori waggled her eyebrows. "You haven't had one of your extracurricular crises in weeks."

She was referring to adventures of the murderous variety. My good luck in securing this farm came with plenty of bad luck, too. Within weeks of my arrival, a local dogcatcher turned up dead in my rye field. After that, others had died in suspicious circumstances in Clover Grove and I frequently got dragged into the investigation. Well, sometimes I volunteered. Or even shoved myself in where I wasn't wanted by the police. Kellan far preferred it when Jilly, Keats and I stayed out of trouble. Not to mention Edna Evans, and Percy, my marmalade cat.

"I hope we've seen our last such crisis," I said.

"I don't believe you." Cori's voice took on a singsong lilt.

"You think I want more crises of a homicidal nature? I hope you know me a little better by now."

"Here's what I know," she said. "You and I are like sheepdogs. Which is why we work well *with* sheepdogs." She gestured around. "And *as* sheepdogs."

I glanced at Keats, who was crawling on his belly across the dirt trying to transfix Big Mama with his mesmerizing stare. Clem had dropped to the ground on the other side, while Cori and I closed the circle. We were working together like an expert team... of sheepdogs.

"I'm not a sheepdog," I said. "No offence, Keats."

He mumbled something that sounded like "you could do worse."

Cori laughed. "He's right. We could be the goats in this scenario. Or the llamas. Or the pig."

"Or the emu." I laughed too, in spite of myself.

"Elaine the emu." Cori's voice took on the lilt again. "It's so sweet that Chief Hottie named her after his aunt."

"Can we just stick to the matter at hand?" Discussions about Kellan rarely went well with Cori. The Rescue Mafia was known for breaking rules and laws on behalf of animals, and that rubbed Kellan the wrong way when their work strayed into his jurisdiction. The Mafia had wisely begun feeding him information that helped with his own cases, which made him feel simultaneously grateful and compromised. I knew the discomfort of that position well.

"Which is...? Cori asked.

"The goat maternity ward you're setting up here. All three are due soon?"

"Exact dates unknown," she said. "We extracted them from a dire situation, I'm afraid. If you look closely, Big Mama isn't fat, but malnourished. Everything she scrounged up went to the kids."

"That's awful," I said, as we closed in. "The poor things. All pregnant and starving."

"I'm afraid so. They'll settle down once regular meals start arriving and they feel safe."

"Let's hope she doesn't become an overprotective mother. She's already worse than Drama Llama."

"Hormones and a hard day's night," Cori said. "Glad we got them out of there and into your capable hands."

Cori's praise was as rare as a day off around here, and she dropped the bait at the right moment. "Okay, I'll figure something out," I said. "I'll get Poppy to work more hours while the guests are here."

"Charlie can show her how to do the milking," Cori said.

"Milking? Oh no."

"Lady goats make milk, Ivy. It's time you learned about the birds and the bees."

"You know what would be cool?" Remi called. "An exclusive line of Runaway Farm products, including soaps and lotions."

"And honey," Bridget added. "You could get some beehives."

"No thank you." I gestured as tires crunched over the gravel. "Do you see those cars? They're carrying guests. People who pay real money to stay here while pregnant goats get a free ride."

"The goats will pay in milk," Cori said. "And raise the cute factor."

"Don't worry about the money, Ivy," Bridget said. "We always give Hannah a full accounting of the animals we place here."

"She knows what we do," Remi said. "She used to do what you do."

"That's why your allowance keeps going up," Cori said. "In case you're wondering."

I *had* wondered but was afraid to ask why the stipend Hannah never promised kept increasing. It was a cushion I appreciated as the inn struggled to find its footing. For every person who spread word of the cute factor, many others mentioned the murder factor. I would probably already be looking for a day job again if not for Hannah's generosity. The mayor's backing was valuable, too. She'd asked for my help with my side hustle of sleuthing and paid for it in guests. In fact, the Hill Country Genealogy Society that rolled into the parking lot now was a mayoral referral.

The thought made me turn to the three cars, breaking rank with my fellow sheepdogs.

"Ivy!" Remi called. "Heads up!"

Big Mama saw the breach before the others had time to close it. The big goat could have made a run for it. Instead, she lowered her head and charged after me. I looked over my shoulder and saw her coming.

Keats tried to cut her off. He didn't succeed but he did slow her down. When her head connected with my backside I reeled forward a few steps before crashing face down in one of the many deep puddles the spring rain had filled in the rutted gravel.

"Are you okay?" Remi asked, grabbing my arm.

"Fine," I said, rolling over. "Imagine drowning in your own driveway... So embarrassing."

Remi offered tissues, and when the dirty water cleared from my eyes, I saw that Keats had lost patience. The fun was over and he went after Big Mama like he meant business. Cori and Clem got out of the way, and my brilliant sheepdog did the work of four, swishing, skirting and swooping. Sensing the change in tone, Big Mama gave up the fight abruptly and strolled into the pasture.

"Today's your lucky day, Ivy," Cori called, with another grin.

I reached for more tissues to dab my gravel-grazed nose. "Oh, yeah? How do you figure?"

"Just think about it," Cori said. "She could have horns."

CHAPTER TWO

"Ivy!" Jilly ran down the stairs in high heels and across the pitted driveway to help me. "Cori Hogan, how could you? She has a head injury, remember."

"Then she shouldn't have turned her back," Cori said. "Sheepdogs don't break rank till the job's done."

Jilly helped me up and patted me down to make sure I was whole, and then put her hands on her hips. Cori Hogan didn't intimidate my best friend as she did me. Dealing with high-level corporate sharks in her old career as a headhunter had given Jilly plenty of confidence. "Ivy is not a sheepdog."

"It's a compliment," Cori said. "There is no smarter dog on the planet and we're all like one breed or another. You're a—"

"Stop right there," Jilly said. "I'm not like a dog. Any dog. I'm an innkeeper and chef who wants to welcome her guests inside to a warm fire."

"A Jack Russell," Cori continued. "If I didn't say it,

you'd wake up in the night and wonder. Jacks are spunky, assertive and never give up."

"They're ratters," Jilly said, drawn in despite her indignation.

"And smart and fearless. Before Runaway Farm you were a corporate ratter. Now you're trying to be a golden retriever—everyone's everydog—but inside, you'll always be a Jack, Jilly."

Jilly stared at her with sharp green eyes and shook back her golden curls. "You're annoying. And your timing is terrible."

The guests were climbing out of nearly identical gray sedans and unloading their luggage. I tried to dust myself off before greeting them and succeeded only in distributing grime around my overalls.

"True and true, Jilly," I said. "But Cori's right about my being a sheepdog in human clothing."

There was another clatter of heels on the front stairs and someone else navigated the puddles even more skillfully than Jilly. "Darling! You're addled." Mom took my arm from Jilly and whispered, "Do not say another word, Ivy Rose Galloway. Jilly, you greet the guests and I'll get Ivy sorted."

"Perfect," Jilly said, and backed away.

"Poodle," Cori called. "In case you're wondering."

"Don't give her the satisfaction," Mom said, trying to get me moving faster.

"She's talking to you, Mom."

"She's saying I'm a poodle? Why, I—"

"Don't let her get your goat." The words made me

smile. Big Mama, my new goat, had certainly gotten mine. "Besides, poodles are brilliant."

Despite being nearly a foot shorter than me, Mom practically carried me across the gravel and then frog-marched me up the stairs. After raising six kids, she had all the moves.

At the top, she turned and called, "Get back in that green machine and go, rescue ruffians."

"Cori, please don't leave me with Big Mama," I said.

Mom looked offended. "Excuse me?"

"Not you. *Big* Mama, the vicious goat who's full of babies."

"Oh my goodness, they didn't," Mom said. "You don't know the first thing about delivering babies."

"That's what I said."

She opened the screen door and shoved. "It's no joke, Ivy. Delivering you was like—"

"Passing a set of broken china. I know."

"One day you'll experience that agony firsthand. At least I hope so."

Inside, I let her herd me up the stairs to the second floor. "Mom, can we not go there? I need to get back and greet the guests."

"Not until you've had a shower and changed into something presentable. Jilly and I can hold the fort for now."

Mom loved casing out our guests, ever hopeful that more men of her dreams might arrive. She preferred to date several quality men rather than tie herself down to just one. She called it "rotational dating" and this light-hearted approach worked wonderfully for her. In the past year, she'd become the date of choice among midlife men across hill country. She knew how to dress, loved to get out and had undeniable charms she didn't waste on her offspring. It grieved her greatly that my single sisters—Poppy, Iris and Violet—refused to follow her example.

"Darling, you know I rather like your vigilante friends," she said. "They're strong, committed women. But they keep dumping their animals here and your ark is going to sink."

"Let's talk about it later, Mom."

"You've got to draw the line somewhere. Did I teach you nothing?"

She'd taught me plenty, mostly what *not* to do in any given situation. Also, the teachable moments in our family never included animals. We couldn't keep a pet longer than a couple of weeks before Mom made it magically run away to another good home. Her hands were too full already.

Back then, she hadn't been the powerhouse she was now. My father had left her with a lot of responsibility and precious few skills. Daisy had become the de facto parent while Mom cycled through dead-end jobs. As the last in line, I kept a low profile, either by choice or necessity. I decided young to escape Clover Grove by working hard to win a scholarship and land a big job in the city. It was one of life's ironies that after reaching the corporate goals I'd set, I ended up back in my hometown running a farm, of all things. Yet even after taking a face-plant in front of guests, I didn't regret my choices one bit.

Percy, my marmalade cat, got up from his cozy bed by the fire and strolled over. Normally he graced all the furniture, but when guests were coming Jilly spritzed everything with an essential oil concoction she called "homey inn." It was really meant to be a cat deterrent. No one liked walking around with a fuzzy orange butt except Percy himself.

The cat wove between my legs and purred to offer reassurance. He wasn't always that supportive, but with Keats still outside managing things, he must have felt pressure to pitch in.

"I'm okay, Percy," I said. "Just a bit rattled. But thanks."

"Don't do that," Mom said, pushing me up the stairs.

"Do what?" I knew perfectly well but allowed her to run her script. Mom had a lot of energy and draining it off now meant she'd have less left to be annoying around the guests later.

"Talk to Percy. Talk to Keats. Talk to those big ugly goats who just arrived," she said. "These new guests are a fresh start, Ivy. Don't ruin it by claiming you're a sheepdog and being..."

"Weird?" I asked.

"Eccentric is a nicer word," she said. "I don't know where you got that trait. The rest of us are so normal."

I laughed. "Oh, come on. At least I talk to living, breathing animals. You croon to your sewing machine."

"I do not croon. Sometimes I brainstorm aloud about my work, that's all. My designs are challenging, Ivy. They don't come from patterns."

They came from secondhand stores, actually. We five Galloway Girls took turns driving her up and down the range of small towns and cities to collect her version of rescues—well-made clothing cast off by women who failed to see its potential. Then she ripped the garments apart and put them back together, stitch by stitch, in ways no one else could have envisioned. It led to a one-of-a-kind wardrobe, primarily in shades of red but with enough dashes of other bold colors to keep people guessing. That was Mom in a nutshell: all flash and then even more flash.

I knew a lot about her design work now that she practically lived at the inn. When there were no guests, she took over our best suite so that she could spread out. I normally persuaded her to go back to her apartment in town when paying guests arrived but that was getting harder and harder to do. She was setting down roots here, like the cheeky dandelions invading the lawns.

"That's why Cori called you a poodle," I said, changing the topic. As a former HR exec, I was a professional herder of conversations. Mom, however, was practically unherdable even for someone of my skills. Just as Keats constantly practiced his sheepdog craft on Percy, who foiled him with vertical moves, Mom let me think I was corralling her and then sprang off in a new direction. She kept me on my toes and I rather admired her for it. "You're so much fancier than the average mom. You stand out with your elegance and grace."

"Please." She followed me into my bedroom, where I collected a change of clothes. "I will not be compared to any kind of dog, even the one deemed more intelligent on many scales than border collies."

There was an indignant grumble behind us. Someone

had let Keats into the house to check on me and now he was eavesdropping.

"Don't take it personally, darling." Mom talked to the dog, too, when no one was around. "You're brilliant. Smart enough to know your chitchat makes Ivy look..."

"Weird," I supplied again.

"Eccentric," she countered. "It's time for an image makeover, and Keats can be your greatest ally. Instead of just dropping his opinions whenever he feels like it, he could wait till you're alone." She beamed at the dog. "How about it? Ivy needs to up her game, handsome. Look like a pro."

I walked to the bathroom. "I'm not an old dress waiting to be rebuilt, Mom. I am who I am."

"You weren't like this before, though," she said. "When you left home you were so meek. So sweet. The brightest and quietest of my girls."

"I was seventeen. The human brain doesn't mature fully till twenty-eight, you know. Even then it remains elastic." I tried to close the bathroom door but she stuck a red leather pump in the crack. "My reprogramming started when I rescued Keats. Who knows where it will end up, but I'm going with the flow."

Keats ignored Mom's advice and offered an eloquent observation.

"I like her just the way she is, too," Mom said, perhaps without realizing she was responding directly to the dog. "It's her professional reputation I worry about. This farm is so important to you, Ivy, and I want to help you keep it afloat. That means tamping yourself down sometimes. I know how hard that is, but I try to put the salon first these days."

Before opening Bloomers, she had the longest employment record I'd ever seen, and that was saying something. Mostly she got fired for faults related either to mouthing off or losing focus. Come to think of it, she was like a yappy poodle with plenty of untapped potential.

I looked at Keats and his mouth dropped open in a pant of laughter.

"Mom, how about you do you and I'll do me?"

She reached for my fingers and squeezed them. "Just don't shoot yourself in the foot. I did that for so many years and I'm speaking from experience. Now that I'm finally reaching my potential, I want all my girls to do the same. It's our best revenge on—Well, on our past."

No doubt she meant my father. I never called him Dad, not even silently. I barely knew the man when he abandoned us and he'd contributed nothing to my life except half my genes.

"It's okay, Mom. I do appreciate that you worry about me." Keats fanned his tail and worked his way in between Mom and the door. It was asking a lot of him to get that close to the bathroom, because he considered it a torture chamber. The bravest dog in the world turned into a quivering mess when the tub was full. "Now please go down and work your poodle charms on the guests."

"They're boring," she said, pouting as Keats backed her away. "I can already tell. There wasn't an interesting face among them."

By which she meant there wasn't a handsome face among them.

"Walt Watford, the head of the genealogy society, seems like a decent guy," I said. "He's the one I dealt with in setting up their stay. These people have spent years gathering information about their ancestors and this weekend is about celebrating their success and putting scrapbooks together."

Mom feigned nodding off. "Snoring. People should look ahead, not back."

"Some say you need to know who you were so that you can become who you truly are."

"Nonsense. We make ourselves, just as I was saying." She turned and walked down the hall. "I'll help Jilly and Daisy get everyone settled and then ask Poppy to drive me back to town for a few days."

I noticed she didn't say "home" anymore. Runaway Inn was quickly taking over that role. After more than 15 years on my own, I was living with my mother again.

"This group is exactly what we need here, Mom," I called after her. "It's a great step in our Clover Grove Culture Revival Project. I'll ask Walt to give a talk on genealogy while he's here."

"When are you going to let me offer a seminar in dressmaking?" she called back.

Normally I'd have said, "never," but the white tuft on Keats' tail fluttered. He was asking me to be nice. He had a soft spot for the woman who'd delivered me into this world.

"Soon. If you can come up with a way to appeal to homesteaders. That's something our community should embrace."

She turned and glared. "I won't compromise my art, Ivy."

"You just told me to compromise, didn't you?"

"That was about Bloomers. Sewing is different. Just as innkeeping is different from farming, which I suppose is *your* art, along with sleuthing."

I gave her a strange look. When had my mother started to explore such philosophical questions?

She let Keats keep her moving and turned at the head of the stairs. "Don't look so shocked, darling. You don't know everything about me. It's good to keep a little mystery, isn't it?"

I cracked the door open a little more and nodded. "Here's to more mystery, Mom."

CHAPTER THREE

O ur guests were more reserved than many we'd hosted, but I knew they'd relax once they were alone in the family room talking shop. However, the grand tour of Runaway Farm was a required rite of passage. That's what the experience we offered here was all about. If they never came outside again, that was fine, but they'd leave knowing my animals. Little made me happier than showing off my furry and feathered family.

"Keep them outside for at least fifteen minutes," Jilly muttered as I gathered everyone on the porch. "They're itching to get at their scrapbooks, but I need extra time to set up more tables. They've brought a ton of photos and crafting supplies."

"Done," I said. I beckoned Walt Watford, the taller and older of the two men in the group of six, and we started down the trail to the barn.

Slim and bespectacled, Walt wasn't unattractive at all. It was the comb-over that did him in with Mom, I knew. As a barber, she considered that an unpardonable sin. No doubt she'd mentally deleted him from existence the second she saw it, and he stood zero chance of getting into her good graces now. In her view, comb-overs weren't so much a statement of style as character. A man who couldn't go bald gracefully lacked confidence, she said.

I was less hasty to judge because I made some questionable style statements myself. When I worked in HR, it was all about the suit. A uniform. A disguise. It saved me from decisions in the morning. My hair was a simple bob and my makeup negligible. The point was to evade notice and it worked well. Nowadays I mostly wore baggy overalls and a ponytail. It was just another uniform that allowed me to conserve brain power for animal husbandry and other noble pursuits.

"It's lovely to have you here, Walt," I said. "I'm looking forward to learning more about genealogy. My mom and I were just talking about family roots and how they shape us."

His face lit up. "I'm glad you see it that way. For a while, it seemed like genealogy was a dying art. It used to take so much effort to dig up the facts, but people of my generation considered it a treasure hunt."

"A treasure hunt?" There had been far too many of those in our area lately and some had come to a bad end. I had no interest in treasure or the crazy hunters it brought.

"Absolutely. I can still remember the thrill of finding the deed to my great-great-great-great-grandfather's house near Stratford-upon-Avon in merry old England. He was a neighbor of Shakespeare's, you know. I like to imagine them swapping stories over an ale."

Even with all those "greats," this was a form of treasure I could probably get behind. "Wonderful," I said. "And now you help others make such discoveries."

"It's easier with digital tools at our fingertips. Still, I urge everyone to go in person where they can. There's nothing like the feeling of walking the same earth trodden by your ancestors."

"I can imagine. And this weekend is a special celebration?"

He nodded and I tried to resist watching his hair. Were the strands sprayed down? What would it take to get that comb-over flying on a breezy day? And exactly how long was the hair that did the heavy lifting?

"Once a year we gather everyone together who feels their search is complete. People bring their documents and photos and create digital and physical albums to share with their families. It's a poignant ritual." He stared around as we passed Big Mama and her crew. "Were your ancestors farmers, Ivy?"

"I have no idea." I ushered everyone to the cow pasture to begin the tour. There was no reason to start with the cows, but I always did. "I think Mom's parents ran a store of some kind. I do know I was the first to go to college on her side."

"And your father's...?" His eyebrows rose a little, no doubt letting me know there was much work to be done.

Keats saved me from answering by gently herding the rest of the group closer. The other women ranged from about 55 to 70. Most shared the hairstyle of women of a certain age in our region: short, sensible, salt and pepper. My sister Iris, who was skilled with scissors and dye, tried to encourage innovation but like me, people wanted to blend in.

One guest, however, stood out by choice. Her hair was dark and shiny, with flirty layers. Her makeup was on point and I could see the frilly hem of a fuchsia dress peeking out under a fuchsia coat. I worried she'd stumble on her high-heeled boots but she shared a stiletto super-power with Jilly and Mom.

Walt had earlier introduced the woman as Daphne Newell, who hailed from nearby Dorset Hills. Our more prosperous neighboring city was better known as Dog Town because of clever dog-focused marketing that left Clover Grove's homesteading claim to fame in the dust.

"Ivy, what a lovely place you have here," Daphne said. "It's such a breath of fresh air after Dog Town."

I laughed. "Few people mention my farm and fresh air in the same breath, Daphne. It's a never-ending cycle of manure management, I'm sorry to say."

Manure management was actually my favorite hobby, or at least my favorite stress reliever. Digging and turning was therapeutic and produced fertilizer that was much in demand. This year, I'd see the fruits of my labor, quite literally, in half the booths at the farmer's market.

"Figuratively," she said, with a tinkling laugh. Tinkling laughter normally rubbed me the wrong way and was enough to raise Keats' hackles, but Daphne's didn't bother me. It was a little false, but weren't we all? A comb-over here, a tinkly laugh there... Everyone had some sort of cloaking device. "I just mean that Dog Town has been a shock to my system. It's changed so much since I left as a child."

"What brings you home now?" I asked.

"The same thing that brings all of us home." She gestured to the others with her index finger. "Roots. The desire to know our past. I had planned to retire there, but now I'm not so sure."

"Let the work guide you," Walt said. "Once your family tree is complete you'll transition."

Daphne shuddered. "Walt, really. That term is a metaphor for death."

Walt smiled. "Fans of genealogy don't view death as others do, Daphne."

"He calls us building blocks," another woman said. Joanne Crayton had lively blue eyes, a ready smile and a lovely rich voice. "Just part of the family structure."

"What am I building when I'm the end of my line?" Daphne asked. "I admit to feeling a little sad today. My scrapbook ends with me."

"That's not true at all," Joanne said. "You have cousins and they have children and grandchildren. Your genes will live on and you're giving them such a gift in sharing their family tree."

"Besides, we all turn to dust eventually," Walt said. "Part of the ecosystem Ivy describes."

"Don't you dare call us manure, Walt Watford," Kathleen Nair said. She was the tallest woman and her voice was loud and deep enough to startle Heidi and Clara, the placid cows. Kathleen wore practical slacks and even more practical lace-up shoes that showed her feet were planted firmly on the ground. "My grandchildren will see to it that I end up in the family plot in the Dorset Hills cemetery. None of this newfangled cremation for me. I don't care to be scattered in the hills. Too windy."

"Me either," said Brenda Stayer, the last woman of the group. She was petite and pale, with gray eyes like pebbles and a nasal voice. "People need somewhere to plant geraniums in my memory."

Finn Donnelly, the other man, offered what sounded like a cynical snicker. He was short and stout with a round face that probably should have been jolly but wasn't. His hair was still dark and abundant, but his beard had gone completely gray. "You won't care by that point, ladies," he said. "Dust to dust and all that."

All of the women, including Daphne, gave Finn a frosty stare. It was obvious that only Finn found himself amusing. His voice had a grating quality that would get on my nerves soon enough. I had never particularly noticed voices before moving here. Now I loved all the hoots, whinnies, clucks, and snorts that filled my days, whereas human voices sometimes whisked me back to my old life.

"Finn, beware," Walt said, smiling. "This is a personal choice and I wouldn't dare to comment. All I do is help you grow those family trees as tall as you can and record the story. What you do after that is your own affair."

We toured all the pastures outside the barn, and I introduced Wilma the pig with her new bestie, a gentle giant of a dog that went by the name of Byron. As always, the two llamas and three donkeys got a lot of interest, but nothing compared to Alvina, the dancing alpaca, who shared her space with Elaine, the emu.

I wanted to take them inside to meet the rest of the animals but Daphne shivered and caught my sleeve. "I'm getting chilled, Ivy. Can we pick this up tomorrow?"

"It'll just take a minute," I said. It seemed wrong to neglect Florence, the blind mare, Clippers the miniature horse, and my good pal Bocelli, the singing donkey who rarely raised his voice anymore because he was so happy here. "I want you to know my entire family."

"For us, family is human," Walt said. "Too hard to trace a family tree for an animal."

"You have to draw the line somewhere," Joanne said. It was becoming the phrase of the day.

I hadn't quite given up on them when I noticed an old tan sedan coming up the lane. That wasn't particularly unusual, but Keats' reaction was. His ruff rose and his ears flattened. When that happened, I dropped my agenda and paid attention.

With a flick of my fingers, I told him to take the guests to the house and come back for me. I had a moment of pride that we accomplished that without words. Mom was probably right that I could dispense with some of my chatter with Keats and Percy... but did I want to?

Watching Keats gather everyone with his tail straight and puffy, I pulled out my phone to send a quick text. And then another.

"Tour's over, folks. Jilly wants you all settled in time for lunch," I said. "She's cooked something special to fuel your work this afternoon. Hint... it starts with eggs from my very own coop."

They were already starting back to the house. Daphne was out ahead darting around puddles with ease.

"Was it something I said?" I asked Percy.

He offered an eerie meow that told me the time for jokes was over, at least for now.

CHAPTER FOUR

K eats was a dog of strong opinions, so it was hard to
predict who was arriving in that shabby sedan
with its tinted windows. Come to think of it, he really
didn't like many people outside my immediate family.
Jilly, of course. Kellan. Edna. Gertie. A few other new
friends, like Teri Mason and Hazel Bingham. That was a
mere fraction of the many we'd met since taking over the
farm. So many that names and faces blurred sometimes. I
blamed that on the head injury I'd sustained rescuing
Keats. My memory had been stellar while working in
HR, with everything absorbed into a mental cataloging
system that retrieved instantaneously. Now I frequently
needed prompting from one pet or the other.

A middle-aged man got out of the car and a chill ran
down my spine. There was no need for prompting today.
He was wearing the same suit he wore when he accosted
me at the Valentine's Day gala at the Palais Royale about
six weeks ago. I'd actually expected him to crawl out of
the woodwork sooner.

"Ivy Galloway," he said, gesturing at the barn. "I need a word."

No way was I heading into the barn without Keats, and ideally more backup. This man had grabbed my arm at the dance and only dropped it when I flagged Kellan. The suit that had looked rather nice under the mirror ball was disheveled now, and he was wearing a fedora that had seen better days. It seemed like he couldn't make up his mind whether he wanted to be noticed or not. The car said no, the hat said yes.

"I don't believe we've met," I said. "And I don't introduce my livestock to strangers."

His eyebrows rose at my brusque tone. "We chatted at the Palais Royale. I'm sure you remember."

"That wasn't an introduction. You squeezed my arm so hard I had to call over my boyfriend. The chief of police."

"Typical overreaction of a hysterical woman," he said. "No need to throw your cop boyfriend around."

"Excuse me?" He had some nerve insulting me on my own property.

"Look, I'm here to do you a favor. I would have done it six weeks ago if you hadn't pressed the red alert button."

I glanced around and saw that Keats had dropped to the gravel behind the man. The dog was in position to leap if he had to defend me. The mild panic that fluttered in my belly settled.

"Whatever you want to tell me, you can do it here," I said. "I have guests, as you probably noticed."

"You'll want some privacy unless I'm very much mistaken. It's about your life before Runaway Farm."

Now my stomach sank. I didn't want to think about my life at Flordale Corporation, where I was known as the Grim Reaper because of my talent for clinical detachment in downsizing people. After a retreat here at the farm with my former team ended badly, I didn't hear from them again. That was fine with me. I wanted to slam the door shut on that chapter of my life.

"You can speak right here in the open. I'm a simple farmer now, Mister... What was your name?"

"Moss. Jim Moss." It was probably a name I didn't need to worry about forgetting. A fake. "And your life isn't really that simple, is it?"

I shrugged. "Running a farm and inn can get complicated, I admit. Simple doesn't mean easy."

"I know all about you, Ivy. I've been following your life with great interest."

"You must be hard up for entertainment, Mr. Moss. Because I take great pride in being dull. Up with the chickens and in bed by ten. On a good day I get an hour to turn manure."

"Yet you manage to squeeze in some impressive investigations," he said. "At least, impressive to me, because I'm a private investigator."

"Ah. Well, I do poke around the odd time but as you can imagine, my boyfriend doesn't like that very much. So I'm not for hire, if that's what you're thinking."

He laughed and the sound made Keats creep forward. "I just need information," he said. "And in exchange, I'll give *you* information."

"I don't need information, thanks. Your inquiries are best directed to Chief Harper."

Now a row of stained teeth showed in a smile. "On this matter, I'd choose Officer Galloway."

That got the reaction he wanted. "Asher? Why would you talk to my brother?"

"He's more likely to have the information I need. It's about your father."

A roaring sound began in my head—something that happened right before I fainted. Jilly was forever prompting me to take deep breaths to stave off lightheadedness. Interestingly, it never happened when I was under physical attack, whereas an emotional attack could knock my knees right out.

"Are you okay?" he asked. "You look pale."

"There's a roaring sound," I said. "Do you hear it?"

"Of course I hear it. It's an ATV." He stood on his toes. "And it's going way too fast."

Edna. Thank goodness. I wasn't sure exactly when she'd become my ride or die girl, but I knew that when she was around this girl was less likely to die.

My head cleared about the same moment she leapt off the ATV. That wasn't an exaggeration. The octogenarian came down in one jump, smoothed her fatigues and demanded, "What's going on?"

"Edna Evans, meet Jim Moss, private investigator," I said. "I mentioned him after the dance."

She eyed him up and down and then frowned. "Fedoras have been out for some time, Jim. Even for a cartoon PI."

Color rose in his cheeks and his thin lips pressed together. This wasn't going quite as he'd planned.

"Mr. Moss claims to have information about my father, which I have no interest in hearing."

Edna flicked a camouflage glove. "Be on your way, Jim. No point stirring up old bones. When you've been on the planet as long as I have, you'll believe me."

"It's my job to stir up old bones," he said. "And I think Ivy will want to hear this."

"The lady has spoken. And she said no."

The voice belonged not to Edna but Jilly. She came up beside me and crossed her arms. Edna took up her position on my opposite side and crossed hers. Keats moved around in front of the PI, and Percy climbed up my back to sit on my shoulder.

Many men would have been cowed by this sight, but not Jim Moss. His forehead crinkled but he blundered on. "I need to get in touch with him. Your father. Calvin Galloway."

"Good luck with that," I said. "I haven't seen him since I was a small child."

Jim looked crestfallen, but only for a second. "You will, though." He pulled a card out of his pocket and handed it to me. "Call me."

"Why?" I asked. "I want nothing to do with this Calvin Galloway."

"That's exactly why. I can make this problem go away."

"We deal with our own problems here, Jim," Edna said.

Keats took matters into his own paws and began driving the man away—not toward his car, but the pastures. I tried to catch the dog's eye to redirect him but he was fixated on his "prey." I glanced up at the house to make sure Mom wasn't around. If she heard that my father might be in the vicinity, Jim Moss truly would see a hysterical woman.

"Let me toss him into his car, Ivy," Edna asked. "The sedan says it all, doesn't it? If the fedora hadn't already said it."

"You don't intimidate me, Miss Evans," he said. "I may be the only one in the region who evaded your needles."

That threw her for a second. Edna had taken great pride in letting no child get away during her school vaccination program. "If you want to let avoidable diseases take you down that's your choice, Jim. More food for us when the end comes."

"What?" His eyes widened, and then he shook his head. "Never mind. We were talking about Calvin."

"We weren't," Jilly said. "That's the point. You were getting into your sedan and driving away."

"Look, blondie, I'll be reaching out to your boyfriend next. He'll definitely want to know about his father. About what he's done."

Jilly raised her hand. "That's his choice. Ivy made hers. I suggest you move along."

He shook his head. "I keep hearing about the delightful hospitality at Runaway Farm. But then I hear about people having terrible luck here. Fatal luck."

"Can't always believe what you hear, can you now?"

Edna said. "If you're friends with Calvin Galloway, you've got bigger problems than gossip."

"I'm not friends with Calvin Galloway," he said. "On the contrary, I've been hired to—"

"Cut," I said, slashing at my neck with my finger. "Remember, I don't want to hear anything about him."

"Then you can ask him yourself, because he'll show up here eventually."

"Here? Why?" The alarm in my voice startled Keats and he changed course. It appeared that the dog had been steering Jim Moss to the alpaca enclosure in hopes of Alvina spitting on him. Now, he drove the man against the pen containing the new goats instead. It seemed like a rookie move but Keats was no rookie. These three mamas-in-waiting had already displayed unpredictable and unfriendly behavior.

"Because Calvin wants money," Jim said. He looked relieved that he'd managed to blurt a message past our blockades. "And you're the only one of his kids with that kind of money."

"I don't have money. I'm rich in love and livestock, that's all."

"You can get it from your patron. Hannah Pemberton."

"There's no way I'd jeopardize my standing with Hannah to get money for my so-called father. I don't know him. Don't want to know him. And I most certainly don't want him anywhere near my farm."

"The best way to make sure he never bothers you is to, well, lend him money."

"Mr. Moss, let me make one thing crystal clear. If

that man shows up here, I won't offer him cash. I might offer him to my pig for dinner."

"Now, now, be nice. You barely know the man. Maybe he's changed. All of us mellow with age."

"Take a closer look, Jimbo," Edna said. "Eighty is the new forty. I have no plans to mellow. Ever."

"You do seem to be an exception to the rule, Miss Evans." He stared at her and slid along the fence. Big Mama kept pace inside. There was a wild gleam in the goat's blue eyes, or at least it looked that way. The rectangular pupils were like spooky slots in a coin bank.

Edna crossed her arms. "Ivy, cover your ears if you don't want to hear this. I, for one, am interested to know why Calvin has surfaced after all this time."

"Money, like I said," Jim said. "He owes my client a lot of it and I'm looking forward to brokering peace between them."

"Calvin never was good with money," Edna said. "But I didn't take him for the type to leech off his kids. Especially not when he's been gone for years."

"Decades," I said. "Mr. Moss, I try to look forward, not back. I wish Calvin no ill, but I don't want to see him, either. I have enough on my plate, and it isn't extra cash. You'll need to look elsewhere to help your client."

He straightened and brushed off his suit. "We'll speak again soon, Ivy. I've got a good feeling about this. My instincts never steer me wrong."

Maybe not, but a sheepdog had. "Really?" I said. "Because I suspect you wouldn't even notice if someone picked your pocket."

He gave me a funny look and then frantically patted his jacket. "What the—?"

I gestured behind him to Big Mama. There was a brown leather wallet in her mouth. I was surprised she hadn't swallowed it already because many of my animals ate first and asked questions later.

"Get it," he said.

"I'm not going in there," I said. "She butted me earlier. Almost broke my nose when I fell."

Jilly held up both hands. "Don't look at me!"

Edna leaned against the fence and crossed her arms. "I'm too mellow. It happens when you get old, Jim. You'll see."

"Fine. I'll do it myself." His voice was high now. Squeaky even. He put one loafer on the bottom rung and showed every sign of following through. But then one of the other goats charged the fence and grabbed his fedora. "Stop it! Someone give me a weapon."

Edna started patting her pockets. "What's your pleasure? Daggers? Grenades? Or a sharpened screwdriver?"

"Edna, don't joke about that. He could hurt my new goats."

"Oh for goodness sake, Ivy, you can't keep all these goats. This one's going to pop a dozen like a round of bullets within days."

"Goats don't have litters, Edna." I was struck by a moment of doubt. "Do they?"

She grinned at me. "This one might."

"Ivy," Jilly said. "Maybe it would be better if Keats dealt with this."

I looked at my dog. "Are you up for getting that man's wallet? It means he'll leave sooner."

Keats gave me an eager ha-ha-ha. I opened the gate just a sliver to let him inside. He raced over to Big Mama and circled her quickly. She spun to keep track of him and it was like turning a blimp on a dime.

His strategy worked. She dropped the wallet and he swept in to grab it. I cracked open the fence again and he dropped a slobbery hunk of leather at Jim Moss' feet.

"All yours," I said, rejoining him.

Pulling a crumpled white handkerchief out of his pocket, Jim bent over to wrap up his wallet. He had a decent head of hair and nothing to hide, which meant the fedora was an affectation. Too many old-time detective movies. He probably used words like "gumshoe" and "dame," too.

"Show him to his car, Keats," I said, snatching the hat over the fence. The dog gleefully rounded up Jim Moss, PI, with a couple of nips to his calf and ankle.

"It's not my fault your dad's a— Ow! Quit it." Jim hopped pretty high. Normally Keats had a light touch, but not today.

"It's not my fault either," I said. "Let's forget this discussion ever happened. He can keep on running till he finds another mark."

"Maybe Daphne Newell will help Calvin," he said. "Although I thought those two had hit the rocks."

I swallowed hard. Why did worlds always need to collide around here? It couldn't possibly be a coincidence that my father's girlfriend was now a guest in my home. We shared a last name so she must know. Now I had to spend several days under the same roof hoping it never came up, especially in front of Mom.

"Jilly, I'm going to sleep in the barn for a few days," I said. "Cori wants me to be on hand to deliver the goats."

My best friend squeezed my arm. "Cori can sleep in the barn and Edna can lend her a bulletproof vest if they're coming out like shrapnel. You're sleeping in your own bed with your own pets."

"Don't worry," Edna said. "Daphne's already leaving."

She pointed to a car heading down the driveway.

"Daphne was here?" Jim asked. He was halfway to his car with Keats doing a number on his pant cuffs but he heard us. "Why?"

"Lunch with friends," I said. "Barely spoke to her."

Keats finally got Jim Moss into his car and after the sedan pulled out, I turned to Edna expectantly. "You know Daphne?"

"I know *of* Daphne just like I know everyone else in hill country. Noticed her on your farm tour during my routine surveillance, that's all. And I didn't know she was seeing Calvin, if that's what you're thinking."

I rubbed my head. "Thank goodness she left."

"There might be a little problem, though," Edna said. "I saw two people in that car, and unless I'm very much mistaken, your mother was the other one."

"What?" The word was a startled gasp.

"Why?" Jilly said.

Edna shook her head. "All I know is that someone with a red leather glove waved rather gaily. It looked like Dahlia playing queen of the town."

I rubbed my head even harder. "This isn't good at all."

"I doubt Calvin's name would come up in the short ride to town," Jilly said.

But we were already moving toward my truck en masse and Keats didn't need to herd us. Percy was sitting on the hood waiting when we got there.

"I'll call Daisy to say we'll be gone for an hour," Jilly said. "It probably won't take long to see that your mom's safe and sound at her apartment. Should I tell her about Calvin?"

"No. We'll say nothing of Calvin until the guests leave."

"Ivy. Daisy should know if she's going to be catering to Daphne. She'll be hurt you withheld that information."

Keats mumbled his agreement and I pondered for a second. Jilly would be the best person to break the news. She was a skilled diplomat. "Okay, fine. But can you do it outside so I don't need to hear?"

"Of course. I do agree we should hold off on telling your mom for now. For the sake of the guests."

"It's what Mom would want," I said. "Earlier today she asked me to be more professional in front of paying customers. That's what professionals do, right? Keep horrible family secrets to themselves?"

"They most certainly do," Edna said. "But then one day..." She made an explosive gesture with her hands. "Kaboom. It all blows up."

"Perfect business case for building a bunker, Edna," I said, as we climbed into the truck. "We'll need somewhere to hide when this news breaks."

CHAPTER FIVE

K eats managed to lean across the stick shift to rest his muzzle on my knee. He was trying to infuse me with calm from his warm brown eye but it was too big a job today.

"Daisy took it quite well," Jilly said, although I hadn't asked. "Barely said a word, actually. Although she did promise to keep it quiet."

"It may be hardest on her," Edna said. "She'll remember Calvin—and his departure—the most. Apart from your mother, of course."

I didn't respond. My tongue felt numb and my brain number. Keats let out a little whine that barely registered.

Halfway to town, however, I revived enough to glance at Edna in the backseat. "Tell me more about Daphne Newell."

"I've seen her at events now and then. Never bothered to meet her. I know too many people already and my bunker is full."

"And no one's ever mentioned she was seeing... Calvin?" I didn't want to call him my father, let alone Dad. If he was only in Clover Grove to empty our pockets, my brother could deal with him. It was all Asher's fault anyway. A couple of months ago, he'd dropped the bomb that he and Calvin were in touch.

"I hadn't heard a word about your father in years," Edna said. "If Daphne really was seeing him, she did well in keeping it off the grapevine, I'll give her that."

"Can we just call him Calvin?" I said.

"Call him whatever you like," Edna said. "Just don't call him."

"That was the plan," I said, finding a smile.

Jilly squeezed my forearm and said, "We've got your back."

"Daphne must have been hard up for dates," Edna said. "Calvin wasn't good enough for her, just like he wasn't good enough for Dahlia. Your mom was always a gadfly, but she was pretty and had plenty of options. Too young and stupid to know better."

"What unfortunate timing for Calvin to pop up," Jilly said. "We've got guests back to back this month and baby goats on the way. Extra stress you do not need."

She'd be squeezed by stress from both sides, I knew. From me and from Asher. It wasn't easy for her to be in the middle. My brother was a good man. An uncomplicated man. Yet as soon as I gave him my blessing to date my best friend he dropped a huge complication bomb into our midst.

"It's going to be so awkward with Daphne Newell staying at the inn," I said.

"Do you suppose that's a coincidence?" Jilly asked.

"I did wonder. The timing seems suspicious."

Keats rolled his blue eye up at me in a blatant, "Ya think?"

I expected Edna to wither Jilly and me with some barbs about our intellectual inadequacies but she said, "We'll have to wait and see. Calvin has kept a lot of people in the dark over the years. Daphne may need to borrow my night vision goggles to find her way out of this."

"I'm not going to be the one to show her the light," I said. "I'm staying out of it."

Edna snorted. "Yet we're driving right into it."

"We're checking on Dahlia, that's all," Jilly said. "When Daphne said she had to run home to get more photos, Dahlia asked if she could catch a ride. They were chatting like old pals so it didn't seem like they were aware they had Calvin in common."

"Maybe he used a fake name with Daphne," I said. "Like Ronnie Runaway. Still, you'd think there would be clues."

"They couldn't have been very serious," Jilly said. "You can't keep up a ruse like that for long."

"Sure you can," Edna said. "People get duped all the time."

"Maybe I should have asked Jim Moss for more information," I said. "I just didn't want to open that door."

"Give it time," Edna said. "Dirt comes out in the wash."

"Not always," I said, brushing my permanently stained overalls.

"Still, I bet it doesn't come up during your mom's ride with Daphne," Jilly said. "It's fifteen minutes tops."

"You know my mom. I bet they were still in the lane when she started her seminar on the benefits of rotational dating. By the time the car rolled up to Mom's apartment, there was at least one very flustered lady. That's my guess."

"That's my guess, too," Edna said. "Dahlia has a talent for getting people talking."

"Then she'll be very upset," Jilly said. She had Keats' hind end and all of Percy in her lap. Her hand was moving so rapidly over the cat that a cloud of orange fluff formed near his tail. In a few moments it would lift off like tumbleweed, swirl around the cab and collide with my nose. Maybe it was the way the vents were set up, or the deep yoga breaths Jilly advised, but somehow all fur clouds hit me right in the face and made me sneeze.

"Understatement," I said. "People will speak of unexplained seismic activity for years to come."

"So we need to go in strong, talk her down," Jilly said. "Should we get your sisters on board to help?"

"Daisy would be best but she's covering for us at home. Let's do a quick reconnaissance with Mom and recruit after we know what we're dealing with."

Edna cleared her throat. "I doubt Daphne will come back to the inn if the truth comes out."

"Oh my," Jilly said. "This is not going to be good for the news cycle."

"Daphne. Dahlia. Isn't it weird that their names are so similar?" I asked.

"That's just occurring to you now?" Edna said. "How about their identical hair color? Their stature? Their fondness for garish color?"

"And her tinkling laugh," I said. "Mom tinkles too, although it's usually ironic." Keats gave a discreet sneeze and I nodded. "Looks like Calvin found Mom's doppelganger."

"He has a type," Edna said. "I suppose most men do."

I thought about that. "If I'm Kellan's type, I'm in luck. There aren't many women out there who'd care to look like me."

"Correct me if I'm wrong," Edna said, "but didn't a reality TV star just model herself after you?"

I threw her a quick glare. "She was Mom's age and wore a wig with pigtails. Not even in the ballpark."

"Just saying, don't think you're so unique. When you find a good man like Chief Hotstuff, it pays to keep your eyes on the competition."

We fell silent for a few moments on Main Street. At the stoplight in front of Hill Country Designs, my friend Teri Mason's art store, I tried to read the expressions on pedestrians' faces. Did they know that my father was back? That he had a bad debt and a girlfriend identical to my mother? That I was about to step into the center of the gossip arena yet again?

Mabel Halliday was standing at the open door of her store, Miniature Mutts. Seeing us, she smiled and waved. It was just a regular smile, a normal wave. Since she was very well placed to hear every tasty tidbit, it seemed we were still in the clear.

I pulled around the corner and found parking on a side street near Mom's. For years she'd lived in a small apartment over a store. It was quiet, clean and affordable... for me, since I had footed the rent. Now my siblings helped out and she was drawing a bit of money from the salon, yet she preferred to live at the inn. The typical twists of life with my family.

"Should we run some lines together?" Jilly asked.

I shook my head. "Let's play it by ear. If she's heard, I'll leave you to handle her with the Blackwood velvet gloves. If she hasn't heard, we'll stage a family meeting to break the news later."

We walked upstairs together and knocked. There was no answer so I let myself in with my key, calling, "Mom? You here?"

It was a pointless exercise because one look at Keats told me she wasn't home. Pulling out my phone, I texted her and then tried calling. Nothing.

"Should we wait?" Jilly asked. "Do you think they went out for coffee or something?"

Keats and Percy were milling at my feet. They were both unsettled, as if sensing the seismic shift I'd predicted.

"Daphne's," I said. "I bet they went to her place to day drink and bash Calvin."

Keats mumbled encouragement to follow that line of thinking so that's what we did. I checked her address on my phone and found she lived on the outskirts of Dorset Hills, a short drive away.

"Why do families have to be so difficult?" Jilly said, once we were on the road again.

"Yours can't be as bad as mine," I said. Despite being best friends since college, I still didn't know that much about Jilly's tribe.

"You have no idea. Although I have the feeling you will before long. My gran's been calling. After not speaking to me for ten years."

"Oh? What did she want?" Focusing on Jilly's family was preferable to thinking about mine right now.

Her lips twitched in a faint smile. "I let her calls go to voicemail. I'm not ready for this yet."

"That's how I felt about... about Calvin," I said. "I knew it was coming eventually but hoped things would settle down at the farm first."

"Things will never settle down at the farm," Edna said.

Jilly turned in her seat and I knew her green eyes would be flashing in anger. "Edna, that's a terrible thing to say."

"Oh, settle your feathers, Jillian. I just meant that with animals arriving regularly there will never be a dull moment." It sounded like Edna had turned to stare out at the fields that were only now starting to green up. "There's never a good time to open the family closets and rattle the skeletons. I know this from experience."

Nearly 70 years ago, Edna's parents had perished in a fire, leaving her alone in the world. She'd done very well for herself, considering. In fact, her trauma made my father's relatively quiet departure seem mundane by comparison. Still, these events had influenced everything we'd done and become.

Keats gave another little whine and I touched his soft

ears. He would likely be making extra deposits in his therapy dog bank in the coming weeks. Lately his work had fallen more on the sheepdog side of the ledger.

"I'm okay, buddy. Everyone has family trouble. That's why we grow up and *choose* our own. Right here in this truck is my family."

"Fate brought us all together," Jilly said. "I'm grateful for that every day."

"Given what happened to me, I never expected to have children," Edna said. "And now I've got great-grand-children... with fur."

Keats gave his happy pant for the first time since we left the farm and then mumbled something else.

"What'd he say?" Edna asked.

I smirked at her over my shoulder. "He wants to know if he's in the will."

"Of course he is. Plus he's got pride of place in my bunker if that comes first."

I looked around as we drove down Daphne's street. She was so far from the city core that there were no bronze dogs. Dorset Hills was known for being the best place on earth for dog lovers and the previous mayor had commissioned dozens upon dozens of huge statues to scream that to the masses. Now there was a new mayor with a good head on her shoulders, but residents had grown attached to the monuments. Remi said neighbor-hoods did their own fundraising and petitioned to get a statue because they boosted real estate prices.

There was no sign of Daphne's car, but I parked anyway and looked at Jilly. "Maybe we should run some lines now. I was okay with playing it by ear before, but if Mom and Daphne are in there oversharing about Calvin I'm not sure I can handle it."

"We can handle it together," Jilly said. "That's what real family is for."

"And if it degenerates to fisticuffs, you know I'm armed for every occasion," Edna said.

"What weapon is right for a meeting between your mother and your deadbeat father's doppelganger girl-friend?" I asked.

"Pepper spray is my first choice in an estrogen fire," she said. I could tell she'd put some thought into it. "Then maybe I'd pull out a Dunbar blade and wave it around. Catch the light and stun them."

"Harvey Dunbar may be a superstar bladesmith, but please don't wave a sword at a guest," Jilly said. "It's bad for *our* ratings."

"Not a sword. There's a blade for every occasion, Jillian. I let Harvey Dunbar talk me into a fancy little lady dagger that practically fits in the palm of my hand. I was insulted at first, but it will have its uses."

I slid out of the truck and released Keats and Percy. The moment paws hit pavement their fur puffed. Keats' ears flattened and his tail stood straight out. Percy turned into a Hallowe'en cartoon of an electrocuted cat. "Uh-oh."

"What?" Jilly came around the truck. "Oh my. That is not good."

"It most certainly is not," Edna said, joining us. "I wish I'd brought a bigger arsenal."

After staring at each other for a moment, we spontaneously reached out and linked arms. It wasn't something we'd done before, and the human chain made it challenging to walk up the front stairs. However, we got to the front door still in formation. I used my free hand to knock and when no one answered, Edna used *her* free hand to open the screen door. I knocked again and then tried the knob.

The door opened and when there was a big enough crack, I called inside, "Daphne? Hello! It's Ivy Galloway."

Jilly leaned in, too. "Daphne! We've come to see if you need a hand with anything."

There was no answer, so I pushed open the door a bit more. Keats tried to nose his way in ahead of us, but I stopped him. "Yoo-hoo! Daphne, are you here?"

"Just go in, dagnabit," Edna said. "We don't have all day."

"I can't justify barging in without a reason, even if the door's unlocked," I said. "Worrying about Mom beating Daphne with a handbag is not a good enough reason."

Keats gave me a good enough reason. He went into a point, at least as well as he could in tight quarters. When his forepaw came up, I opened the door a little more to see what had caught his attention.

On the floor in the hallway were two red leather gloves beside the large fuchsia purse Daphne had carried earlier.

Arms still linked, we followed Keats and Percy into the house and stood together staring down at the gloves.

"Lots of people have red gloves," Jilly said. "Maybe not that precise shade. I call it 'Dahlia red.'"

"Mom was here," I said.

"Not necessarily. Maybe Daphne had cold hands and your mom loaned her the gloves. I bet that's what happened."

"Possibly," I said. "But where's Daphne? Obviously she made it home, with or without Mom."

"Her car is gone, so maybe they ran down to the Puccini Café to girl-bond over their troubles," Edna said. "I hear some of you do that."

I tore my eyes away from the gloves and looked at Keats. He had moved into another point with all his flags flying. Daphne and Mom likely weren't swapping stories over a cappuccino.

"Where's Percy, Keats?" I said. Follow the cat, find the problem, I suspected.

He gave a mumbled monologue as he led us through the living room.

"What's he saying?" Jilly asked.

"He's telling me not to freak out," I said.

"Let's not," Jilly said. "It'll be fine."

"Doubt it," Edna said, pulling pepper spray from one of many bulging pockets in her cargo pants.

Jilly was the glass-half-full one in our little family and Edna the glass-half-empty. I vacillated by the day.

We all stopped in line, blocking the entry to the dining room. There was a scattering of old photos on the hardwood floor. Among them lay Daphne Newell. She was still in the fuchsia coat she wore on our farm tour earlier. Mom must have been somewhat aghast at her pairing pink with red leather, but clashing color wasn't something Daphne needed to worry about now.

Or ever, apparently. Because Percy was standing beside her shiny brown hair and making sweeping motions with his front paw that left damp, red streaks behind. He was piling invisible kitty litter onto Daphne's head and officially pronouncing her dead.

CHAPTER SIX

The Dorset Hills Police arrived a few minutes after Kellan and his team. I'd texted my boyfriend first for emotional support, asking him to cue up his colleagues from the Dog Town jurisdiction. He must have been close by, because he got there fast, and Asher arrived moments later.

Soon Daphne's small, neat house was crowded with officers. I only had eyes for one... the tallest, darkest and handsomest of them all. Kellan Harper was Prince Charming in a uniform. Normally my heart did crazy handsprings when he walked into a room, but his expression today discouraged romantic gymnastics. He crouched with Chief Coots from Dorset Hills beside Daphne Newell, while other officers gathered to await direction.

"There are little red paw prints," Chief Coots said. "What do you make of that?"

"Well, uh..." Kellan was normally calm, cool and collected, but my pets sometimes managed to poke a pin in his professional persona. "I would guess they came from..."

A loud meow behind them made both men lose their balance. I thought Chief Coots would fall right over but he caught himself. There was no sign of Percy but I suspected he was on a dining room chair, hidden by the tablecloth, and diligently cleaning his paws of Daphne's blood.

Using one gloved index finger to lift the fabric, Chief Coots said, "Victim had a cat."

"The cat actually belongs to Miss Galloway," Kellan said. "The one who called in the emergency."

"That's Percy," I said. "And this is Keats, my dog. You might see his prints too, I'm afraid."

"How did you happen to be here, Miss Galloway?" Kellan asked.

So I was Miss Galloway today. Not even Ivy, let alone his girlfriend. My ratings had taken a huge dive after crossing jurisdictions with my crazy crime karma. I'd given Kellan the broad brushstrokes on the phone but now he wanted me to start fresh with the Dorset Hills chief. I understood protocol, but I still felt adrift in stormy seas without his support.

"Daphne Newell checked into my inn in Clover Grove this morning to begin a retreat with the Hill Country Genealogy Society," I said. "I gave them a short tour of the farm and they went inside. While I was still down at the goat pasture, Daphne left in her car. With my mother, it seems."

Asher's sandy eyebrows rose and his blue eyes

widened. "Are those Mom's red gloves?" The alarm in his voice was unmistakable.

"Possibly," I said. "She has gloves that color. Most of her wardrobe is red, actually."

Chief Coots shoved his round glasses onto the bridge of his nose to take a closer look at Asher and me. He was starting to put some pieces together. "You came to retrieve these gloves for your mother, Miss Galloway?"

"No, Chief. I had reason to think my mother—*our* mother—had an awkward and uncomfortable conversation with Ms. Newell during their drive."

"They knew each other previously?" Chief Coots said.

"They didn't," I said. "But it appears they had someone in common."

That didn't sound right and heat gathered at my collar, ready to assault my face.

Kellan leaned forward and whispered something to his colleague. Chief Coots let his glasses slide down again to stare at me. Then he said, "Clear the house, officers. All of you. Wait outside till my signal."

Kellan added, "Officer Galloway can stay." When the others had left, he said, "Continue, please."

"As far as I know my mom and Daphne Newell hadn't met till today," I said. "But apparently my—*our*—biological father knew both of them. His name is Calvin Galloway, although he may have been going by something else."

"Dad is in town?" Asher said.

The casual way he dropped that word made my throat

clench. Calvin Galloway was not my dad. "Dad" was a title you earned with care and time and attention. No matter how much contact he'd had with Asher recently, Calvin couldn't possibly have ascended to dad status.

"Calvin may or may not be around," I said. "The private investigator who visited the farm this morning didn't know for sure."

Asher took off his hat and churned his fingers through his fair hair. All five Galloway Girls had dark hair and hazel eyes in various shades of Dahlia. Asher was the golden boy, quite literally. His blonde hair had darkened a bit over time but his blue eyes were as bright as ever. "Why was a PI at the farm?" he asked.

"Officer Galloway, let me ask the questions," Kellan said. He looked at his colleague for confirmation and got a nod to proceed.

I answered without waiting for another "Miss Galloway" to hit me square in the heart. "Jim Moss, the PI, said there was a bad debt. A client had hired him to track Calvin down to collect."

"This PI thought Dad would come to you first?" Asher asked. "You won't even speak to him."

Jilly's arm was still linked with mine, as was Edna's. It probably looked strange to everyone, including Kellan. My best friend tightened the loop now. She knew how hard it would be for me to deal with the issue privately, let alone in front of the chief of a neighboring police department. I sensed she'd like to give Asher's arm a squeeze, too. We had different views on this subject, but he was entitled to his own opinions and I would try to respect that.

"He doesn't want to hang out with me, Asher," I said. "According to the PI, I looked like a soft touch for money, that's all. Otherwise, I'm sure he'd have looked you up first."

"Has he?" Kellan asked. "Looked you up?"

I shook my head. "No and thank goodness. I hope he never does."

Chief Coots stood now. "Ms. Galloway, what do you know of this Calvin's relationship with Daphne Newell?"

"Only what the PI told me. They were apparently dating at some point and then hit the rocks. When Mom caught a ride into town with Daphne, I was afraid the topic might come up. That there might be an altercation. My mother—*our* mother—has a temper."

"Was your mother still in contact with this Calvin?"

I shook my head again. "Not to my knowledge. He's never a topic of conversation at the family dinner table, I assure you. But my brother may be able to tell you more."

Asher was still churning his hair and beads of sweat had formed on his brow. "I've spoken to Dad a few times on the phone, that's all. No mention of visiting. No mention of needing money. I thought he just wanted to... reconnect."

There was a note of pain in his voice. I wanted to set Jilly free to be a girlfriend, but that would probably embarrass Asher, given the circumstances.

"So you drove here from the inn with your friends to check on Ms. Newell's safety?" Chief Coots said. "In case your mother's temper got out of hand."

This was going in the wrong direction. The direction where Mom got accused of murder. Again.

"Nothing so dramatic," I said. "We went to my mom's apartment to make sure she was okay but she wasn't there. So then we came to see if Daphne wanted to ride back to the inn with us. She had come home to collect some photos for her weekend project."

"That's what Daphne told me," Jilly said. "Our guests are working on their family trees."

"Is there a chance Ms. Newell saw the PI at your farm and got alarmed?" Chief Coots asked.

"She didn't seem alarmed when she left," Jilly said. "She was having a lovely chat with Dahlia and offered to give her a ride. That's all."

"And where is this Dahlia now?" he asked.

I shook my head and Asher did, too.

"She's not answering her phone," I said. "Probably on a date."

"It's the middle of the afternoon," Chief Coots said, frowning.

"My mom has a busy social life," I said. "She hasn't been sitting around waiting for Calvin to come back. In fact, she won't be thrilled about that news."

Chief Coots gestured to Daphne's body. "This is starting to look like a crime of passion by a jilted lover."

"Malcolm, that's unlikely," Kellan said. "This jilting took place nearly thirty years ago."

"She wasn't jilted," Asher said.

Edna raised her free hand. "I'd call getting left with six kids jilting. Or worse."

Kellan threw each of them a glare. "My point was that Mrs. Galloway likely wouldn't have any interest in—"

"Warming up the cold soup with Calvin?" Edna said. "I should think not."

"She's very popular," Jilly added. "And she doesn't waste her time looking back."

I summed it all up. "She didn't kill Daphne Newell."

"Quite right," Edna said. "If she killed anyone, it would be Calvin."

"Miss Evans." Kellan's tone was curt. "You'll have a chance to speak in due course."

"I'll speak to Malcolm when I want to," she said. "I'm sure he remembers me well."

Chief Coots unconsciously rubbed his upper arm. Another victim of the school vaccination program. "Indeed. But there's a protocol at homicide scenes, Miss Evans."

"Oh, I know. I've been at enough of them." She gave a little smirk and shrugged. "That came out wrong."

"Edna, it's no time for jokes," I said. "Daphne seemed like a lovely woman, and she was oddly similar to Mom, at least on the outside."

Chief Coots tilted his head. "Oh?"

I glanced down at the body. Keats had joined them and was sitting near Daphne's head, in the midst of the old photos. "Same size, same hair, same style sense. Even their voices were similar."

"Calvin had a type," Edna said.

Asher flinched. "Can we not talk about this?"

"We probably should have talked about Calvin long ago," I said. "Then maybe his return wouldn't have come as such a shock."

"No one was receptive when I tried," Asher said.

"You're no diplomat, Asher," Edna said. "Always blundering around like a linebacker in a china shop."

"Edna, stop," Jilly said. "This is a shock for Asher, too."

Looking around the room, I noticed the interior design for the first time. The curtains and upholstery were high-end, and the oak tables gleamed. "It seems like Daphne had money," I said. "Maybe Calvin came to talk about his cash flow problem and it went badly."

Asher swung around to face me. "Dad didn't kill this woman if that's what you're suggesting."

"Well, Mom didn't kill her either," I said.

Kellan stood up quickly, both hands raised. I realized even without Jilly's arm pinch that arguing over which parent was more likely to kill wouldn't do us any favors with Chief Coots, let alone the Dorset Hills rumor mill that dovetailed seamlessly with Clover Grove's.

"Malcolm, would you mind if I took a moment with Officer Galloway and his sister?" Kellan asked.

Great, so I'd been downgraded even further to being merely the sister of one of his officers.

"Bad idea, Harper," Chief Coots said. "Due process and all that."

"Just for a minute or two," Kellan said. "They're both overwrought."

Chief Coots stared from Asher to me and back, bushy gray eyebrows twitching. "They don't sound overwrought."

"This is how they sound when they're overwrought," Kellan said. "Besides, you know me well enough by now to be confident nothing untoward will happen."

"Which means you're calling in a favor."

Kellan smiled for the first time since he came in. "Just one. I've got a few in the bank, I believe."

His colleague nodded. "This counts as two. One for your officer and one for your girlfriend."

"None for me, Malcolm?" Edna said.

"Never enough for you, Miss Evans," he called, heading for the front door.

She sighed. "Unfortunately, that vaccination program caused many kids to lose their sense of humor too soon. If I could take it all back, I would."

"There will be time to reflect another day," Kellan said. "And that goes for you, too, Galloways. I know this has thrown you both for a loop, but our first concern needs to be Ms. Newell. With all due respect, Ivy, I ask that you go home to your guests and stay out of this."

"I can't stay out of it. Asher dragged me into it."

"All I did was speak to Dad when he reached out. There's no crime in that."

Anger percolated in my belly. "You invited Calvin out of the woodwork and now his shady activities have delivered trouble to my barn doors. One of my guests has died."

"I didn't bring him out of the woodwork," he said. "You did that yourself."

"Me! How?"

"By being a media darling, that's how. I only heard from Dad after you appeared on the news. He only looked me up because I was the easiest to find."

That forced me to recalibrate. "Well, you didn't turn him away. Like he turned us away."

Keats left the photos, circled my feet and then sat right on my boots. His high, shrill whine was almost inaudible. He hated it when I argued with family.

Crossing his uniformed arms, Asher shrugged. "I won't say I was sorry to hear from Dad. He's not what you think."

"You mean he's not a deadbeat? Because that's what I think about any man who leaves his wife and kids stranded. Deadbeat. Dead to me."

"There are two sides to every story," Asher said. "You always pride yourself on being so open-minded. Seems like a trap door shut on Dad."

"Stop calling him that." I rubbed my forehead, trying to ease the tension that often led to a migraine. "He's not our dad. He's a criminal."

Asher started to pace. "We don't know that."

"He's right," Kellan said. "We don't know that... yet. All you have is the word of one PI, and they'll say whatever they need to say if their client's pockets are deep enough."

"Calvin's a criminal," I said. "And a philanderer, too."

"You don't know that either." Asher's turns got shorter and shorter till he was nearly spinning in place. "If you mean Daphne Newell, he's entitled to date after being divorced for decades."

"They never divorced," I said. "For the record."

"*What?* She always said they did."

"Waffle words, like always. She admitted the truth recently."

My brother shook his head. "Even so, they were split. She isn't waiting for him to come home."

I looked down at Keats, drawing strength from his weight on my feet. He was telling me we'd get through this together. Even if Kellan and my family left me hanging, I would always have my dog. And Jilly, Edna and Percy.

"There is no home," I said. "But no, she isn't waiting around for a deadbeat and philanderer."

Kellan took a step toward me and stopped. "Ivy, we don't really know he's those things."

Looking away, I tried to dial back my fury. I hadn't been this angry since the night I rescued Keats. While that episode had ended well, it also showed me a side of myself I didn't particularly want to see again.

Keats nudged my fingertips and I murmured, "You're right, buddy. Not worth it."

"Calvin was on the wrong path by kindergarten," Edna said.

"This isn't your business, Miss Evans," Asher said.

"It's my business when you invite a fox into the henhouse next door," she said. "I could be at risk, too."

My brother finally tried Jilly. "Can't you help Ivy to be rational about this?"

"Asher, you're both upset and entitled to be," she said. "Let's just give things some time to settle."

"Jilly's right," Kellan said. "But for the record, there's no official evidence Calvin is in trouble. I've checked a few times."

My stomach did a twisty dive. So Kellan had been doing background searches on my father and not telling me about it. Maybe he was even discussing it with Asher. It felt like a betrayal.

Keats whined again, urging me to look down so he could transfix me and herd me away from the emotional abyss. I let him do that. Going over the edge was unfair to my dog and the people who truly loved me.

"Aren't you the least bit curious?" Asher asked. "About where he's been or what he's done?"

"Curious, no. Scared, yes. If he owes bad guys money, they'll follow him to my doorstep. I have an inn to run and people and animals to protect. I don't have the luxury of wondering how Calvin's been doing."

Asher shook his head. "Whatever he's done, he's our blood."

I felt calmer now, thanks to Keats. "In my view, relationships have to be earned, and Calvin's contributed nothing to our lives. As far as I know. If you and Kellan have come up with a different story, I'll listen."

Kellan's eyes widened, hearing the accusation between the lines. Meanwhile, Keats crept over and neatly nipped off his bootlaces. One, two, three, four black segments dropped to the floor. Percy came out from under the table and batted them around to make sure Kellan would notice.

"Hey!" he said. "You two stop that. This is a crime scene. There's no time for your games."

"We should leave you to investigate," Jilly said. "We have places to be."

"Jilly's right," Kellan said again. Jilly was scripting him now, too. "Your ark needs you, Ivy."

"Yeah," Asher said. "Ivy's way too emotional to think straight."

And Asher was way too emotional to notice Keats nipping off his bootlaces, too.

"You've said enough, Officer Galloway," Kellan said. "And you're off this case."

"What did I do?" Asher said.

"Off to highway patrol," Edna said. "Officer Road Hero."

There was a discreet knock at the door. Chief Coots was no doubt telling Kellan the clock had run out on old favors. Kellan walked over and Asher followed, pleading to be part of the investigation.

Their departure gave me a second to notice that Keats and Percy were standing among the photos on the floor. Keats mumbled for me to get a move on it, while Percy sent a few photos flying with a swish of his orange paw.

I pulled out my phone as I joined them and snapped a few photos. Hopefully that would be enough to follow whatever clue my pets found of interest. I couldn't steal evidence right from under the noses of two chiefs.

By the time Chief Coots reached us, I was ready to go. Keats circled once and managed to nip off one of his laces, too.

Then he gave me a little mumble as if to say it was the best he could do under the circumstances.

"Good job, buddy," I said, following him out. "Real family starts from the bottom up."

CHAPTER SEVEN

"Do you think we can get to your mom before the police do?" Jilly asked as we drove back to Clover Grove.

Keats was on her lap, paws on the dashboard, urging the truck on with sharp yips, as if it were a racehorse.

"Probably. I pulled out all the stops by issuing the butter tart 911. Maybe I should have done that in the first place."

Butter tart was our family "safe word." Technically it was two words, of course, but none of us challenged Mom on that when we were kids. Whenever one of us faced a particularly dire situation, all we had to do was send out the distress call and everyone would gather at a designated place. The tricky thing today was that I wanted Mom to hear the news alone first. It was the decent thing to do. So after I issued the alert to all but Asher, I sent an immediate retraction giving my sisters the all clear. Mom, however, took it seriously and answered that she was on her way to her apartment.

"That code is so handy," Jilly said. "We need our own 911."

"Yes! Just us and Gertie Rhodes," I said. "What will we call it?"

In the same moment, Jilly, Edna and I basically shouted, "Zombie 911." Keats mumbled agreement and even Percy meowed his endorsement.

"So obvious and yet so perfect," I said. "We'll have plenty of opportunity to use it, I'm sure. In the meantime, we need to handle the crisis at hand. I wonder how quickly Chief Coots will dispatch his team."

"Kellan will stall them as long as he can," Jilly said. "He's giving you a head start."

I gave a huffy sigh. "What makes you say that? There was no sign of my boyfriend today. Only Chief Harper. What did you call him, Edna?"

"Chief Haughty McSnobalot?" she said. "Or was it Chief Huffy McSniffalot?"

"Either will do. He wasn't my Kellan, that's for sure."

"It wasn't as bad as you think," Jilly said. "If you don't believe me, ask Keats."

He turned and offered a rumble that walked the fine line between agreeing with Jilly and still supporting me. My dog and my best friend were diplomats.

"See?" she said. "This is new turf for everyone. You can't entirely blame Kellan for not knowing how to react to your estranged father practically parachuting into the middle of a crime scene. He handled it like a cop, rather than a boyfriend."

"Men can't handle emotion," Edna said. "At least that was true in my day. Now some have swung too far the other way, I'm afraid. I'm not a fan of emotional inconti- nence in either gender." After a pause she added, "This is a tricky situation. No matter which way the chief stepped he was going to plant a boot in manure."

"A boot with short laces," Jilly added. We all laughed, and Keats gave a proud ha-ha-ha.

I pressed the pedal, although I was already well over the speed limit. I needed every available second to deescalate Mom. "This is all Asher's fault. Maybe Calvin came knocking because of me, but Asher didn't need to let him in. Maybe Daphne would still be alive if he hadn't."

Jilly didn't respond right away. Even a skilled diplomat had to dance lightly around landmines like this. "I truly wish he had kept the door closed, Ivy. I say that as someone who's sitting on a Pandora's box of a family. But Calvin may have shown up regardless. You're not hard to find anymore."

"It irks me to side with Asher Galloway," Edna said. "But I think men come wired with a strong drive to know their own father. He probably doesn't have the capacity to be as detached as you are. You should cut him some slack."

"Slack?" I glanced over my shoulder. "Who are you and what did you do with Edna Evans?"

"I could say the same to you. The Ivy I know doesn't let emotion get the best of her." She shrugged camou- flaged shoulders. "It's your mother coming out. I suggest you reel it back in. Become this grim reaper you brag about."

"I never bragged about being called a grim reaper."

"Maybe not out loud, but inside." Keats turned to glare at Edna and she laughed. "In my world, that's a compliment. Don't lose your edge because of your father. You'll need your wits about you for this one. It's no time to spiral into a pit of existential despair."

"I have an ark and an inn to run. There's no room for existential despair."

"Exactly. Now, notice I'm not even mocking your driving today. That's a sign of respect for your fragile condition."

"I am not fragile."

"Edna, this isn't helpful," Jilly said.

"That's where you're wrong, Jillian. My strategy is distraction and it's working. Otherwise she'd be driving us into a ditch. Am I right, Ivy?"

I sucked in a long breath. Really long. Seven beats long. "Actually, yeah. I feel better."

"I've been where you are, you see," Edna continued. "And I learned it's better to focus on the zombie right in front of you than the ones you can't see."

I laughed. "Okay. Let's take down those suckers one at a time."

"There she is... the take-no-prisoners Ivy I know. Jillian, you'd do well to follow her example if you've got wayward family."

"I'll take it under advisement," Jilly said.

"See family trouble as training," Edna said. "There's nothing better to help prepare for natural disasters."

"Or unnatural disasters," I said. "Zombies fall into that category."

"I'd rather take on a zombie than your mother right now," Edna said.

"Edna, I was thinking you might sit this one out," I said. "Jilly is best equipped for this situation. It would be great if you could go back to the inn so that Daisy can leave and see to Mom."

"Really?" She sounded crestfallen. "But I want to see how this turns out."

"We all need to play to our strengths, right? The white glove treatment is Jilly's. Yours is charging around like a superhero."

"No need to lay on the flattery," Edna said, as we parked on the side street near Mom's. "I refuse to leave without you. I'll wait here by the truck and we'll go together."

Jilly and I walked upstairs with the pets and the door opened before we even knocked. I could tell by Mom's expression that she didn't know anything. Didn't know about Calvin's return. Didn't know about Daphne's murder. Didn't know she was a suspect yet again.

And now I had to let her know all those things.

"Darling, whatever's wrong?" she asked. "I got your messages earlier but I was in the middle of something."

"In the middle of what?" I said, as Keats waltzed through the door, tail high. Percy followed, brushing against Mom's legs and making her frown. She did not like plucking pet hair from her clothing.

"I met up with a gentleman, if you must know." She looked perplexed. "Something felt terribly off today for some reason and I knew the best antidote was male company. There's a lovely man who's new in town. A piano teacher. I went to his studio and he played me some Mozart. Music really does have charms to soothe the savage breast, doesn't it?"

I cringed, despite the relief flooding through me. At least Mom would have a solid alibi.

Jilly and I kicked off our boots and trailed after Mom to her happy place, namely her wardrobe. It had once been a bedroom and was now lined with built-in closets filled with her raw material and finished creations. The corner that had housed her sewing machine was empty because her beloved pet was now at the inn. But there was still a worktable with various tools of her trade.

"What felt so off today?" I asked.

She picked up her shears and studied them. "I really don't know, darling. It started after your guests arrived. I had an unsettled feeling. What you'd call a 'bad vibe.' Percy wouldn't leave me alone. He was always underfoot and shooting out fluff. I thought it best to come back to town."

"So you caught a ride with Daphne Newell," I prompted.

"Good timing," she said. "Saved me the cab fare. She's a lovely lady." Putting the scissors down, she smiled. "Terrible sense of color and what flatters her, I'm afraid. Did you see all that pink? Looked like a unicorn invasion."

Jilly fought a snicker and won. "Did Daphne seem okay to you?" she asked. "I was surprised when she left the inn so soon."

"She said she wanted to collect more photos for her family tree book." Mom walked over to the bank of closets. "I couldn't get her off the subject fast enough. While I support your Culture Revival Project, some projects are less interesting than others."

"Genealogy seems to get a grip on people," I said. "What did you talk about instead?"

She grinned over her shoulder. "What do you think? Men, of course. The power of the rotation."

I groaned but forged on. "How did that go over?"

"She wasn't persuaded, I'm afraid. Not yet." She pulled out a red dress with feathers at the collar and shook her head. "Feathers. Can you imagine? Daphne would probably wear feathers. We didn't have much in common, but I gave her plenty to think about."

"You parted on good terms?" I asked.

"Of course. I invited her for coffee but she wanted to get back to the inn and join her friends. We agreed to meet another day." She pulled out another red dress and tipped her head appraisingly. "This is better. And Daphne will see soon enough that she should shift her focus from her emotionally unavailable man."

"Her... her *what?*"

"She has a boyfriend who's been stringing her along. Never giving her what she needs. I tried to convince her to add new men into the mix. Her man will either step up when he has worthy competition, or he'll step out." Spreading the dress on the table, she went back to the closet for seconds. "My instincts told me he was a dud, but people need to come to these things in their own good time." Swishing a skirt clipped to a hanger, she smiled. "Or so I hear. I'm trying to slow my roll, as Asher would say."

"Was she upset, Mom?" I asked. "When she dropped you off?"

"I don't think so. She squeezed my hand and her fingers were so cold I insisted she take my gloves for the rest of the ride." She draped the skirt over the dress on the table. "Just between us, it was my way of making sure she'd meet me again soon to return them. She's relatively new to the region and doesn't have many friends. That's why she joined the boring club, I suppose."

"Did she seem to know anything about you? About us?"

Mom pulled out yet another red dress. To me they looked pretty much the same except for the decorative touches.

"Why so many questions, darling?" She threw down the dress and went back for another. The cycle was picking up speed. "It's like one of your inquisitions."

"Mom. Could you stop for just a second? There's something I need to tell you."

"Are you going to share the real reason for this so-called butter tart 911?" she asked. "I hope it warrants leaving a lovely man and Mozart."

"It does, Dahlia." Jilly gently took a red satin top from Mom's hands and added it to the pile. "Just sit down for a moment."

"I don't need to sit down. Drop your truth bomb, girls. I feel it circling like a hawk over a rabbit." She turned back to the closet. "Rabbit! Yes, there's a wool dress with fur trim. I'll take that off and do something really interesting with it."

"Mom, focus. We don't have long. The truth bomb is time sensitive."

She rooted around deep in the wardrobe and emerged with the rabbit dress. "Fire, darlings!"

"Dahlia, it's about Calvin," Jilly said. "Your—your..."

"Deadbeat ex?" Mom said. Her well-manicured brows rose. "That's the only Calvin I know."

"That would be the one," I said.

"Your father?" She clutched the rabbit-trimmed dress to her throat. "What about him?"

"Calvin may be back in the area," Jilly said. "And by a strange coincidence, it appears he was seeing Daphne Newell."

Mom hugged the dress with both hands now. "Daphne's emotionally unavailable man was... was Calvin?"

I nodded. "So it would seem. Perhaps she didn't realize you had that in common."

"We had nothing in common," Mom said. "I must... I must get my gloves back. Those were the perfect shade, Ivy."

"That might be difficult," I said. "They're being taken in as evidence."

The dress dropped out of her hands and Percy moved in to scrape invisible litter over the fur collar.

"Evidence of what?" She stared at the cat. "And what is he doing?"

"Burying the remains of the truth bomb," I said. "Mom, I'm afraid Daphne died."

"Died how? Of heartbreak? Did Calvin smash her heart to pieces, too?"

"I'm afraid she was fatally stabbed. When we went there looking for you we found her. And your gloves."

Mom blinked a few times and then went back to the closet. Garments started flying over her shoulders. "I trust you believe I'm innocent of whatever you suspected me of this time."

"I do. And I'm sure the police will check your classical music alibi and clear you quickly."

"There goes a fine dating prospect." A handbag came zooming over her shoulder and I dodged. "Meanwhile I'll be tried in the court of public opinion. Over a free ride and a coincidence."

"Kellan is helping the Dorset Hills police with the investigation," Jilly said. "He'll make sure the facts come out."

"Asher." Mom turned and fired a pair of suede pumps at the wall, one after the other. "Where is he in all this? He's the one who opened the door to that man. A traitor."

"He's not a traitor." Jilly started picking up clothing and accessories. "He's trying to absorb the new information. That Calvin is back and his girlfriend—or former girlfriend—is dead. It's a lot to take in."

Mom raised another shoe as if to fire it at Jilly.

"Mom! Think twice before you throw a shoe at my best friend. Think three times, if necessary. Because I will not tolerate that." I gestured with one finger. "Nor will Keats."

Her arm stayed where it was. "There's only one side in this situation," she said.

"I wanted to think so too, but there are always other

sides. Asher has a right to his opinion and Jilly hers. The way through this is to support each other as best we can."

The shoe drifted down slowly and I nodded to Keats. When it came within range, he gently took it from her hand.

She picked up a long silk scarf and wrung it between her fingers. "Jillian, are you suggesting that Calvin had something to do with Daphne's death?"

"Not at all," Jilly said. "I'm sure it's another coincidence."

"Ivy?" Mom's gaze was as intense as I'd ever seen it. "Is that what you think? That he killed her?"

"I don't know what to think," I said, stooping to pick up some of her cast-offs. "I know he's in some trouble. I don't know if he's in enough trouble for that."

"Money trouble?" she asked.

"Apparently. Was that a thing?"

She sighed and coiled the scarf around her neck. "It was a thing. We were poorer before he left than afterwards."

"Did he gamble?" I asked. "Drink too much? Do drugs?"

"Not that I knew of." She tightened the scarf. "He was just a soft touch. Always lending money to people who never paid him back. Yet we had so many mouths to feed."

It wasn't the answer I expected and Keats gave a mumble that pretty much said, "See? You don't know everything."

"Calvin wasn't... Well, I wouldn't have thought him capable of murdering anyone. Not then." She tried to pull off the scarf but it had become knotted. "That was a long time ago."

"Let me help with that," Jilly said, approaching my mother cautiously.

Mom didn't resist when my friend unfurled the scarf. "That poor woman. She had no idea what she was getting into with Calvin."

"I'm sure she didn't," I said. "She seemed very nice."

"Nice, yes. But nice wasn't enough with Calvin, I'm afraid." She looked around the room as if seeing the carnage of clothing for the first time. "Daphne had terrible taste in clothing, but it seems we did have something in common after all. A heartbreak, perhaps."

"You recovered beautifully," Jilly said. "And raised six wonderful kids."

Mom took her hand. "I'm so sorry, darling. I could have killed you with that stiletto."

I caught Mom's eye. "You'll need to start curating your language with Chief Coots. He doesn't understand you the way Kellan does."

"Asher can run interference. If I decide to speak to him again."

"You can take your time deciding because Kellan took him off the case. He thinks Asher can't be objective."

"Of course he can't," Mom said. "None of us can."

I sighed. "Maybe not. I'm going to stay out of it, too."

Jilly and Mom both smiled in obvious relief, but Keats disagreed. He gave a little sneeze that suggested the joke would soon be on me.

"Will you come back to the inn, Dahlia?" Jilly asked. "I'll make you something nice."

Mom shook her head. "I'll clean up before the police get here and do my best not to embarrass anyone."

I pushed a load of clothes into her hands. "Daisy will be here soon, and she can drive you back later."

"I'll stay here for a while. Send Poppy over with my sewing machine. The only way I'm going to get through this is to make something beautiful. Something fabulous."

I knew she could do that. If anyone could make a silk purse out of this sow's ear of a situation, it was Dahlia Galloway.

CHAPTER EIGHT

It was always a relief to have the barn to myself. With Charlie and Poppy around so much, early mornings and late evenings were usually the only times I could call it my own. Jilly said I hid down here to avoid the inn and the guests. That was true, but she was no better. With Daisy and Mom joining her inside the house, these days she escaped to the kitchen more and more. She beat eggs and I turned manure. We were both the better for it.

Before I could burn off steam on the poop pile, I had mouths to feed and animals to bed down with lullabies. Literally in the case of Bocelli. He didn't throw back his head and join me all the time, but he still loved it when I sang to him. I warbled a little as I went about my routine and tonight I struck gold. The song resonated and he threw back his head to give a screech. It was a happy sound now, at least to my attuned ear. Clippers the miniature horse, Bocelli's best buddy, got his hooves tapping in a happy little shuffle.

Alvina, the alpaca, leaned over her pen to enjoy the

tune, but she wasn't satisfied until *my* toes were tapping and arms flapping. It had been a trying day, but I managed to find some moves for my dancing girl and by the time my performance ended, my cares had receded, too.

And so it went with the rest of the animals. Each had some personal preference I tried to indulge at bedtime. I saw it as putting money in the barnyard bank of goodwill. Even Wilma, the grumpy pig, enjoyed a back scratch. Normally she stayed outside with Byron, the Caucasian shepherd, a huge guardian dog. He was Wilma's constant companion, but his quiet authority had contributed greatly to the entire farm in a short time. Keats slept better knowing the big guy was on outdoor duty, and I slept better, too.

I left Big Mama till last. One thing I'd learned was that if I wanted animals to integrate well at Runaway Farm, I had to invest in getting to know them as individuals. This was challenging as numbers grew. On top of that, some I clicked with immediately and others, like Big Mama, I didn't. She had a pen of her own because she couldn't settle. The companions she arrived with had already moved in with the general goat population. But Big Mama was a bully goat. Big or small, she pushed them around. It was the only thing that seemed to make her happy.

Keats brought in the cows and rumbled a cynical commentary. It sounded like "a goat's a goat's a goat."

"Not true," I said. "They're all different breeds and sizes. Are you and Byron anything alike?"

He gave an indignant grumble to declare he was way above Byron's league.

"Byron is a master of his own league, which is being the big brawny bouncer. He deserves quality time and respect, and so does Big Mama."

Turning my head to look at Keats was my first mistake. Big Mama snatched my hat and retreated to a corner to enjoy her prize. The other goats would grab anything mostly in fun, but Big Mama seemed determined to ingest the indigestible.

I turned to pick up a pig poker—a long wooden pole with a brass hook on the end— before going in after my hat. Big Mama was as skilled at kicking as at head butts. In a confined space, it was a risky proposition.

Would she fall for a trade? That was my usual barnyard strategy, and my pockets were filled with a variety of treats. The problem was that I didn't know the approximate value of a light wool toque. What would Big Mama consider a fair offer? Groping in my side pocket, I found one of Jilly's homemade peanut butter and molasses oat cakes. These were a hit with many of the animals, and luckily Big Mama was one of them. She didn't stop chewing the hat, but her blue eyes, with their rectangular pupils, evaluated me. I held the oat cake on the palm of one hand, gripping the poker with the other, and backed away. After a moment of weighing her options, Big Mama came toward me.

Keats whined from outside the pen. He was being a little melodramatic. I had been in many a worse situation.

"I'm good, buddy. Don't worry."

He whined again and added a mumble to the end to say he respectfully disagreed.

There was a moment of hobby farmer hocus pocus. Big Mama dropped the hat and grabbed the oat cake. I bent quickly to seize the hat, dexterously wielding the pole to avoid knocking either of us out. While she chewed, I slipped out of the pen and closed the door.

"There, see? Even after a bad day, I can outfox a goat, buddy. Aren't you impressed?"

"Well, if he isn't, I certainly am."

I turned quickly, fumbling with the poker. The man standing behind me in the shadows had good reflexes and dodged as the hook came down.

"Whoa! Be careful how you swing that thing," he said.

I hauled in the pole and prepared myself to swing deliberately next time. "Who are you and what are you doing in my barn?"

My first thought was Jim Moss, but the man who stepped out of the shadows was considerably taller and broader. He was probably around sixty, judging by the silvering hair peeking out from his hat, but he looked fit and quite capable of taking me in a pig poker duel if it came to that. There was another poker behind him, which I hoped he hadn't noticed.

Keats whined and I glanced down quickly, expecting to see hackles up. While his flags were rising, he was more cautious than alarmed. Somehow that worried me more. There was a strange man—a big one—in our barn. Why wasn't Keats ready to banish him? Had I wounded him by calling Byron the barnyard bouncer?

Percy had a stronger opinion. He leapt from the horse stall onto the man's shoulder and then bounced off to the edge of the cow stall. The cat could get around the entire barn without a paw ever touching the floor.

The man barely flinched, which told me he'd spent a lot of time around animals.

"Take a guess," he said, in answer to my question.

Pulling out my phone, I directed the beam of the flashlight into his face, while sending Kellan and Edna a quick SOS at the same time. I already knew who it was. It was like looking into the face of my brother in about 30 years' time. This man had once been fair and his eyes were bright blue, a gene that yielded to Mom's hazel in the five Galloway Girls.

"I don't want to guess," I said. "You can't just waltz into my barn like you're welcome. Because you're not."

Keats pressed into my pant leg and whined again. Meanwhile, Percy leapt off the cow stall onto my shoulder to assume his parrot position.

"Ivy," he said. "Give me a chance to explain."

"The explanation boat sailed nearly three decades ago. The only word I want to hear from you is goodbye. Scratch that. Say nothing and go."

"Asher said you'd be like this," he said. "Whereas he's keeping an open mind."

I shrugged. "His party. Now stop talking and start walking." I shook my phone at him. "The police are on their way."

"There was no need for that. I don't mean any harm."

"I've got animals to protect, and don't think I won't.

For all I know you murdered Daphne Newell. You won't get the chance to kill anything here."

"I didn't stab Daphne, Ivy."

"And I didn't say 'stab,' Calvin. If you know that, you must have heard the news from Asher, who's off the case."

He actually smiled. "I didn't need Asher to tell me. The rumor mill is stronger than ever around here. I think three people mentioned it within an hour of its happening. And I am not to blame, Ivy."

Calvin had the same guileless expression as my brother, who'd managed to hide a few secrets, too. "Why should I believe you?"

"Because it's true and I hear you're a seeker of the truth," he said. "Daphne and I dated for awhile but it was never serious. She didn't even know my real name. What motive could I possibly have?"

I held up my hand. "You should probably save this for the two chiefs of police who are involved in the case."

"I was sorry to hear about Daphne. She was a nice lady." He turned away for a moment. "I'm afraid I bring bad luck to people."

"Sounds about right. Now you've brought your trouble to my doorstep. I have animals to protect. A business to run. I don't want your bad luck anywhere near me."

"I hear you've had some bad luck lately," he said. "It hasn't been easy for you."

His sympathy stoked the fire inside and made my face burn. "Don't even. Why did you have to drag me into this? If Asher wants to hang out with you, that's his choice."

"Asher can't help me," he said. "You can."

"The PI who showed up here today warned me you'd come looking for money. That you're on the run because of a bad debt."

"Jim Moss can spin a yarn," he said. "I'm not here for money." He glanced around for a few seconds. "I doubt you have much to spare. Running this place must take every cent you have and more."

"That's the only thing you've got right so far," I said. "So there's nothing for you here, Calvin."

"You do have something I need, and it isn't cash," he said. "I've heard the stories. You and this dog are famous, and not for farming and innkeeping. What you've accomplished is nothing short of amazing."

"My office is closed. If you need help, the chief of police will be here any minute. He's the one to ask."

"I will. But something tells me you might be even better for this job. I need to clear my name, Ivy, and it happens to be your name, too."

"And Asher's. Maybe he'll lend you a hand."

"He has to stick to the rules, whereas you have an aversion to rules." He stepped back into the light. "I probably don't get to say this, but I'm proud of you."

I took a step back too. "What I've done—what I've become—is no thanks to you."

He shrugged. "Except for half your genes?"

"I vote for nurture over nature. So I'll give most of the credit to Daisy."

"Daisy got the worst of it," he said. "But there's more

to the story than Dahlia told you, I'm sure of that." I started to speak and he cut me off. "Look, I'm not here to apologize. I know I can't make up for what happened and I won't insult you by pretending I can. All I want is some help clearing my name. As tarnished as it is, I don't want it associated with murder. Then I'll roll on again, out of your way."

"Then you'll roll back when the next disaster hits. I'm a magnet for trouble."

"Yeah, I noticed that. Blame it on the genes you don't want to acknowledge."

He walked toward me and I signaled Keats to form a fur barrier. The dog's flags were still down, which annoyed me. Keats was keeping an open mind about Calvin, but he still turned him around with subtle ease and backed him up to Big Mama's pen.

I heard sirens in the distance. "Here comes your chance to discuss your image problem with the authorities."

"Did you know I used to sleep in the barn as a kid?" he said. "Drove my mom crazy. I always tried to get Dahlia to buy a farm but she wouldn't hear of it. Luckily I've been able to earn an honest living wrangling animals."

"If your living was so honest, why are people coming after you?"

"History. The Galloways were tarnished by association with the Swensons and the web is still wide. There's a difference between people who cause trouble and people who get dragged into it. At least in my view. Your mother knew all about it, in case you're wondering."

Big Mama picked her way toward Calvin as stealthily as a cat and then snatched his black knit cap. Without it, the resemblance to Asher was even more noticeable. My brother would be happy to know he'd likely keep his hair.

"I'll let you deal with that," he said, as the sirens grew louder. "Gotta run."

He sidestepped Keats and loped to the back door. One thing I definitely didn't inherit was Calvin's grace under pressure. His movements were constrained and elegant, whereas I was the queen of pratfalls. He even managed to skirt a fresh cowflap, much to my disappointment.

"I'll be back in touch," he called. "Think about what I said."

"Sure thing," I called after him. "I can't wait to ponder our gorgeous family tree."

"Sarcasm." His voice drifted back. "That's pure Dahlia."

CHAPTER NINE

"Ivy? We should talk." Kellan looked up at me with mild trepidation after his officers and Edna had left. He wasn't so much worried about my mood as the shovelful of manure I held.

"I've told you everything," I said. "Right down to the rot at my roots."

He was going to break up with me and it was no surprise. Why would a career cop want to throw in his lot with someone like me? It was obvious now why I'd had so many collisions with criminals. Calvin's share of my genes attracted them like flies to garbage.

"Come down here and— Ouch! Hey!"

The ouch was for Keats, who gave Kellan's calf a nip through the uniform. The hey was for Percy, who landed on his shoulder with none of the usual feline grace.

"Boys, leave it." I reluctantly came down what Jilly called my stairway to heaven. Never had I needed manure therapy more, but if Kellan was breaking up with me, I'd rather take the hit with both boots planted firmly on the ground. "How are things going with Chief Coots?"

"Coots is a good guy," Kellan said. "More of a letter of the law type, but he appreciates the delicacy of this situation."

"A situation where your girlfriend's absentee father resurfaces just in time for a murder."

"And a situation where one of my best officers hasn't been fully forthcoming about his contact with said individual."

Relief surged through me at hearing that Asher had been keeping his boss in the dark, too. The thought of Kellan deliberately hiding such crucial information from me had hurt terribly.

"Asher said you knew about Calvin."

Kellan tried to detach Percy from his shoulder without success. "He told me the first time your—uh—Calvin reached out. It was before you even moved home. We did a little digging and there wasn't much to find. Calvin was a rolling stone and very good at covering his tracks. Spent a lot of time off the grid, apparently on ranches. I was satisfied he wasn't going to be a problem for Asher and our department, so I promised to keep it between us to avoid upsetting the rest of your family."

"But that was months ago and a lot has changed. You didn't think I might want to hear about this before I got blindsided?"

"I did think so, yes. So I spoke to Asher about it a few times. He didn't tell me about subsequent conversations and he promised to handle it himself. Since he'd told me about Calvin in a confidential professional capacity, I couldn't cross that line."

"Not crossing that line meant Calvin could show up and murder his old girlfriend. I wonder how Asher feels about keeping a lid on it now."

Percy seized a bit of fabric from Kellan's knitted cap in his teeth and shook it like a dead rodent. There were loose loops all over it from previous mousing expeditions.

"We don't know Calvin was involved," Kellan said. "I doubt he'd ask for your help to clear his name when he could just disappear again. He's good at that."

"Maybe he's run out of options to hide. The world isn't big enough for some criminals."

"There's work for farmhands everywhere and a culture of respecting privacy. He could vanish tomorrow and never come back."

"A girl can hope." I picked up a broom and started sweeping up loose straw. It was a job for a rake, but my hands needed to stay busy to balance the thoughts ping-ponging around my mind. "And I hope my mom's been cleared by now, with her Mozart alibi?"

He couldn't resist a grin. "Malcolm let me join that interview. I don't think I've ever seen him look quite so befuddled by a suspect's verbal dance moves. But eventually she coughed up enough convincing details."

"Thank goodness," I said. "Do you have any other credible leads on Daphne's killer?"

Kellan shook his head. "She's almost as much of a mystery as Calvin. Before she moved to Dorset Hills she was in half a dozen cities, mostly working as a personal assistant to wealthy families."

"So that's how she had money. She was paid under the table."

"Probably. Some of those families may have paid her well to keep their secrets. Chief Coots will have his hands full looking into that."

"Why did she come home? I don't buy her story about wanting to get back to her roots."

"She had enough to retire so it may have been true."

He tried to take the broom from my hands and I stepped around him quickly. "Calvin is still the most likely, no? He needed money and she probably refused to lend it to him. He said they were never serious."

"Maybe. We'll get to the bottom of it." This time he managed to grab the broom. "And by 'we' I mean the two police departments."

"Calvin asked me to help."

"And suddenly you want to give him a hand?"

"I want nothing to do with him, but the sooner he's gone, the better. He suggested he had dangerous connections. That could bring even more trouble."

"Exactly. And you can't be objective about this, Ivy. That's why I put Asher on highway patrol and that's why I'm asking you not to poke around. This may be a bigger mess than any we've come across so far."

"Yeah," I said, grabbing the broom back. "It makes manure look hygienic."

Kellan laughed for the first time since he'd arrived and more tension leaked out of me. Maybe this wasn't the site of our demise after all.

"Do you need a hug?" he asked. "Sometimes I worry I'll get stung if I make any sudden moves."

I stopped sweeping and looked up at him. "I'm sorry. Maybe you should put me on the girlfriend equivalent to highway patrol until this is over. As long as Calvin's lurking around I'll be extra prickly."

"Do I strike you as that kind of guy? The kind who steps back when the manure gets deep? Because it truly would sting if you thought so."

I sighed. "I don't believe you would. Maybe I believe you *should*. Ever since I got home your professional life has been difficult. What if dating me is a career limiting move?"

Keats had decided to intervene, circling slowly to tighten an invisible loop around us. Now there was no room to swish the broom. My face was practically in Kellan's jacket. I longed to bury my face in it, but I also wanted to do the right thing and release him from the muck of my family.

He put his hand on my shoulder and pulled me in even closer. "Then I guess I would need a new career."

"Kellan, don't say that. You love your job."

"I doubt anyone in my line of work loves their job, per se. Not seeing what we see. It's more of a calling."

"Exactly. It's your calling. You could never give that up."

"Of course I could. I'm a man of many talents, Ivy. My only true calling is right here."

He lifted his hand off my shoulder and waved it around.

"You mean the manure pile?" I joked, although my heart had begun a little shuffle worthy of Clippers. "Is it possible we share one calling?"

"Entirely possible," he said. "At least I hope so. My primary calling, in case you need it spelled out, is keeping you alive and happy. That's my hope and commitment."

Now I leaned into his coat and for the first time all day, released a full breath. I wouldn't have blamed Kellan for walking away, like Calvin had, but I was so happy he hadn't.

"Even though you know I come from bad seed? He said the Galloways were in cahoots with the Swensons."

"Back then half the county was in cahoots with the Swensons. Old Frank had something on everyone. That's how he operated. They were bootleggers and crooks."

"Still, thinking about Calvin makes me feel a little sick."

He hugged me harder. "Do you think it was all roses at my house?"

"I don't know. You don't say much about your family."

"Maybe there's a reason for that."

I waited for him to continue. When he didn't, I added, "I wish my family made it possible to say so little."

He laughed. "There are more Galloways than Harpers. I'm an only child. My dad passed long ago, as you know, and my mom moved to be with her sister in Florida."

"She'd had enough of our everlasting winter?"

"She'd had enough of our everlasting gossip. They run a craft store and do quilting bees."

"Wow. So normal. You're lucky."

"I am lucky." He kissed the top of my head. "You and

your family—human and otherwise—keep life interesting. Quilting bees wouldn't."

Suddenly he lurched away, leaving a cold draft in his wake.

"What just happened?" I asked.

"Your canine genius is done with small talk. Those little pinches on my legs leave bruises, you know. I feel sorry for sheep."

Keats gave a ha-ha-ha and drove us further apart. He liked pulling the strings on the romance. Canoodling was never going to keep a sheepdog of his talents occupied for long. But he knew I needed some stability to function at optimal levels. He had to give a little to get a little action.

"Keats, hasn't this day offered enough stimulation?" I said. "It was plenty challenging."

"Yet he still found time to take my bootlaces," Kellan said. "Now, lock up and I'll walk you to the house."

"I'll stay a bit longer," I said. "I want to hang out with Big Mama for a bit. Cori said she could drop those kids anytime."

Kellan walked over to her pen with me, shaking his head. "Kids, plural?"

"At least two, and probably the same for the other new goats. They'll be my first babies at Runaway Farm."

"Maybe the last?" he asked, hopefully.

"Breeding is definitely not in my plans." Realizing how that sounded, I quickly added, "For the goats, I mean. Or the sheep or cows, for that matter." I thought about running through the rest of the animals but he was already grinning over my blunder.

"Never mind," he said. "Just no little Wilmas, please."

"She's spayed. One of Hannah's better moves. But the way Cori drops random animals here, there's bound to be an accident or two."

He stared at Big Mama. "I bet she's uncomfortable. That's quite a load."

"Probably why she's so grumpy. But I'm going to win her over. It's my new cause."

"You do that." His smile said he was glad I had a distraction that would keep my nose out of the investigation. "I'll check in tomorrow."

I stood on tiptoe to kiss him and then gestured for Keats to show him out. Once they'd cleared the barn, I slipped into the big goat's pen to collect a partially masticated leather lump she'd dropped in the straw.

Calvin wasn't a total rock star when it came to livestock handling. Big Mama had picked his pocket, too. I was surprised she hadn't done more damage to the wallet.

"Probably tasted bitter," I told Keats, as he trotted back inside with Percy. "That's how this whole encounter tasted to me, anyway."

Keats gave a mumbled pep talk as I locked up and then led me back to the house.

"I'm not even going to look inside it till later. For now, I have to go in there and play innkeeper like nothing's happened," I said. "When life as I know it has turned upside down."

He circled behind me and delivered a little pinch to the back of my leg.

"Ow! Stop that."

That's exactly the message he was giving me: stop the self-pity. No wallowing allowed.

"Fine," I said. "Tomorrow we start with a clean slate. Let's see what mud we can fling at it."

His white tuft swished as he trotted up the stairs. According to that tail, things were about to get even more interesting.

CHAPTER TEN

The truck moved along nicely as I headed for Mandy's Country Store the next morning with Keats and Percy. After a harsh winter of terrible driving conditions, I felt far more confident about my abilities to manage this automotive monster. It was nice to have one less thing to worry about.

"Boys, I'm going to go out on a limb and say I've never needed pie more. You know that means something because I've been desperate for it on several occasions."

Keats mumbled a running commentary from the passenger seat that had nothing to do with pie, yet endorsed anything that got us moving.

"I hope it's coconut cream," I said. "It would help a tough day go down easier."

More mumbled commentary suggested I should elevate my thinking to more important issues.

"You elevate for both of us. I'm just the brawn behind your brains, and this brawn needs an optimal pie experience. I'd settle for pumpkin or pecan, but there's going to be a world of letdown if it's a fruit pie. Too much like health food."

This time Keats turned his blue eye on me and shone a light into my soul.

"Ugh. Stop that. I don't want to see what's in there and you shouldn't either."

Now he placed one paw on my leg and shot some warmth into me with his brown eye. He didn't need to mumble a thing for me to know he loved me just as I was, warty soul and all.

"Thanks, buddy. And you too, Percy." The cat had joined us in the front seat instead of lounging in the back so I must have issued an unconscious call for moral support. "I used to be like this all the time when I worked for Flordale, you know. Every day I shut off my inner light so that I could become the Grim Reaper they paid me to be. It got harder and harder to turn that light back on at the end of the day. And in the final year, it never did come on. My interior landscaping was bleak, I tell you."

Keats added his other paw to be sure to cross the T on "therapy" dog, and Percy went above and beyond with a roaring purr.

"The only thing that kept me going was Jilly, and looking back, I see she was struggling with old demons, too. I feel awful knowing I wasn't fully there for her when she needed me. But now we've got this amazing new life and look what happens. I barely get out of one quagmire and the next sucks me down. This one is the absolute worst. The quagmire of Calvin Galloway." I shook my head. "Can you believe I have to try to absolve that deadbeat? To clear his name. And mine." I touched each pet quickly. "Ours."

I expected a mumbled affirmation about my trials, but Keats still wasn't ready to write Calvin off. That unnerved me almost as much as the man himself. How could my dog take his side?

Now Keats gave a sharp yip of reproof.

"Fine, so you're not taking his side, but you've got one paw on the line. I saw how you gave him a hackles-free reception. He didn't earn that just by providing half my genes. Do you know how cheap genes are? And his are bargain basement. He did none of the high-value work of raising me."

The truck nearly stalled but I caught it in time, and Keats turned back to the dashboard to help me drive.

"Not that Mom was any great shakes, but at least she was there and wisely deputized Daisy to do the heavy lifting. Thanks to Daisy, I got a solid foundation. Thanks to Jilly, I survived the middle. Thanks to you, I got a fresh start. And thanks to Kellan, I have something to look forward to down the road."

The next mumble was noncommittal. Keats liked Kellan well enough but he wasn't ready to tie himself down yet. Playing the field was more fun, especially when committing meant closer supervision by the law.

"Obviously I'm rattled by Calvin's arrival and Daphne's passing. But we'll get things sorted out like we always do, right?"

A happy pant reassured me.

"It's just a matter of how. That's where the pie comes

in, in case you're wondering. That's usually where the first inkling comes."

Percy started kneading my leg, as if to urge me on.

"Like Edna said, the Grim Reaper of HR can handle Calvin Galloway and whatever trail of devastation he's left behind. This might even be good for me."

The blue eye gave me a skeptical squint.

"Here's how I see it. My resentment toward Calvin is a weakness. A vulnerability. I've always looked the other way when it comes up. But no more. I will use this opportunity to detox from past trauma. It's a drag on my energy that may even cloud my judgement. Therefore, by helping Calvin, I'm helping myself to become a better person and a better sleuth." I turned the truck into the store's parking lot and took my usual spot. "We're going to rise above this, and it all starts right here, with Mandy McCain's double slice."

Percy stepped into his carrier and we went inside.

"Mandy, no," I said at the counter. "No, no, no. Rhubarb is not going to cut it today. It's not even fruit. It's an ornamental plant that has no place in your fine pastry."

She laughed. "That's more drama than I expected for this time of the morning. I've never known you to turn down pie, no matter what flavor."

"Who said I'm turning it down? I'm just registering a formal complaint."

"It's spring, Ivy. A lot of people like rhubarb. It's fresh and local."

"And meant to decorate gardens unless truly desperate. I'd welcome it in a zombie uprising, for example. Here in regular pie season, it's just not right."

Mandy tapped her forehead. "Light-bulb moment... We cut you back to a single slice and then chase it with some other treats? A sampler platter. I've got a couple of new squares you'll deem more acceptable."

I took a deep breath. "Okay. One slice of decorative plant and a sampler platter. And a coffee to cleanse the palate in between."

"Deal." She gave me an indulgent smile that probably got a lot of use. Mandy dealt with plenty of "personalities" in Clover Grove. I hadn't expected to become one of them, but even my own mother called me eccentric.

While she arranged for my sugar rush, I took my favorite seat in the middle of the laminate counter overlooking the parking lot. It left room for Mandy to join me if business was slow. At this time of the morning, it usually was. On the downside, she hadn't had much time to gather intel yet.

The pie turned out to be quite acceptable. Mandy could fill pastry with gravel and I'd give it my best shot. She had taken the time to garnish the sampler platter with a scattering of violets and pansies. Counting three types of chocolate, I breathed a little easier.

"I apologize," she said, sliding onto the stool next to me. "When I heard about what happened I should have headed right into the kitchen for an emergency coconut cream session. It would probably help the pill go down easier."

"The pill of Calvin's homecoming? And Daphne's death?" I asked. "Yeah. Does everyone know?"

"Only everyone who's conscious." She offered the grimace of someone who'd felt the nasty nip of gossip in our town. "A juicy story like this will feed the beast for months to come."

"I figured as much. Any information for me yet?"

She nodded. "The private investigator in the cheap suit came in first. He was asking questions about Calvin. I tried calling but you didn't pick up."

"Must have been when I was getting mowed down by the new goat. He showed up as the guests arrived, including Daphne Newell, who didn't stay long. She went home to get more photos and you know what happened next."

"How was the Nanaimo bar?" she asked, smiling. "I've finally got the proportions just right."

"Good. I think. I'm not sure I actually chewed."

"I do know the Heimlich maneuver if something gets lodged going down."

I laughed and then pulled in a deep breath. "I try to roll with the punches but this has been a lot."

"Family," she said. "No one knows better than I do how much chaos they cause."

Myrtle McCain, Mandy's grandmother, had put her through the wringer after what I jokingly called the "homecoming murder" on my land. It took a while for us to find our way back to friendship, but it had been worth persevering.

I raised my coffee cup and clinked it against hers. "To our good genes. May they triumph."

"Did you know that Myrtle dated your great-uncle?" Mandy asked.

"I didn't even know I *had* a great-uncle."

"Sterling Fable. Calvin's mother's brother. That was back in the day when people rotated naturally. Not unlike the system your mom has in place now." She grinned at me. "Anyway, Myrtle spoke highly of him and sometimes regretted not choosing Sterling. Of course, I wouldn't be here now if she had."

I suspected that was a gentle reminder that regardless of what Calvin had done or not done, I was lucky to be here. Another reality check for the sulky sleuth. "Is this Sterling still around?"

"Not sure, but she spoke of him last year, and I thought it might be worth checking. He should know more about Calvin."

I liked how she innately knew better than to call him my father or dad. Only someone who'd had to excommunicate family grasped the nuance so quickly.

"I'll do that," I said. "And thank you."

"Who said I'm done? I can't serve you decorative plants in pie form without offering you something more interesting."

Keats came out from under the counter and stared up at her, mumbling questions.

"Slow down," she told him, laughing. "I don't know if this means anything or not, but it's a start. One day I hope to make up for what happened."

I waved my hand. "Water long under the bridge, Mandy. You've helped me so many times since then. We're friends."

She nodded, but I knew it would be awhile before

she forgave herself for withholding information that almost got Keats and me killed.

"So yesterday, some of your guests stopped here on the way to Runaway Farm. They needed to pick up some last minute art supplies. It was right before the PI showed up, actually."

"Was Daphne with them?"

Mandy nodded. "Four women. There's only that little section with stationery, right? But Daphne took a phone call and went into the frozen food aisle for privacy. Her voice got louder and I went over to see if she was okay. She apologized over and over and sounded upset. Then one of the other women called her name and told her to hurry. She hung up and by the time she came to the cash register, she was smiling like nothing happened."

"Huh. I don't suppose you got any indication of what the issue was?"

Mandy shook her head. "One of the other women got suspicious when I started rearranging the frozen peas so I couldn't keep eavesdropping."

I started to slide off my seat and she caught my arm. "There's more, Ivy. They came back a while later in two cars. Now there were two men as well, but no Daphne."

"They did? I told Daisy to keep them at the inn."

She shrugged. "They looked over my art supplies again and said they'd need to divide and conquer. There was talk of glitter and gold and silver markers and they decided to go on to Dorset Hills. I got the feeling some of them were... unsettled."

"Huh. Over Daphne's leaving, I suppose. Anyway, it puts them in the realm of suspects. They could have beaten us to her house while we stopped at Mom's apartment." Now I got up and she didn't stop me. "Have you told Kellan yet?"

"You know my policy. I give you a head start unless he asks me outright. He does turn up eventually, though."

"Might take a little longer this time, because Chief Coots from Dorset Hills is leading the investigation."

Mandy looked down at the pets. "I'd better get Keats and Percy some treats. Sounds like it could be a long day."

When she came back, Keats downed the pepperoni stick with as much dignity as I had the brownie earlier. Percy poked his head out and showed more manners.

She waved away my money and slipped a paper bag containing a few Nanaimo bars into my hands. "I feel bad about the rhubarb. I should have pulled out the big guns when I heard about Calvin."

"You've given me something far better... a place to start." I slung the strap of Percy's carrier over my shoulder. "And pie alone couldn't reconcile me to this situation. I'm going to need to throw everything I've got at it."

"Sounds messy," she said, holding open the door.

"Worse than the bog in Huckleberry Swamp," I said. "And it's ripe in spring."

Keats shook himself as if he'd been doused in pond scum and then tossed me a glare before trotting out into the sunshine.

"That'll teach you to take a liking to my blood relatives before they've earned it," I said.

Then the door closed behind us, and the sleuthing began.

CHAPTER ELEVEN

I worried about surprising Hazel Bingham so early in the morning, but she was not only up and ready to receive, but as elegant as usual. She wore a dress every day, with plenty of sparkling jewelry, and her silver hair twisted into various configurations. The very definition of a lady. As always, her face lit up when she saw Keats and me, and most especially Percy.

"What a lovely surprise," she said, leading me into the dining room. The walker she used when we first met was gone now, as was the cane. Every so often she reached out to touch the wall, or a piece of furniture, but I sensed it was more for reassurance than balance. Moving back into the Bingham manor with Michael, her nephew, had helped her heal from a broken hip and a crisis like nothing else could. "You'll join me for coffee?"

More caffeine could only help. I hadn't slept much the night before, for obvious reasons. The only problem was making sure I could find bathrooms later. I wondered if other amateur sleuths faced such prosaic challenges.

As she collected the coffee from the kitchen, I looked around the house that now surpassed its original grandeur, thanks to Michael's efforts. It was a peaceful oasis from what sometimes seemed like near-constant storms outside. In truth, incidents of the murderous kind only lasted a few days, and fate kindly gave me respite in between, but was never quite enough to recover completely.

Keats sat at my feet, mumbling a little pep talk. Normally he wouldn't indulge me, but he probably felt bad about not disliking Calvin enough for my tastes. At the end of his monologue came something that sounded like a reminder to trust him.

I met his eyes and nodded reluctantly. Maybe he did know more than I did. Maybe it would all work out.

Michael followed Hazel back into the room, carrying a tray. It held an engraved silver urn, a matching cream and sugar set and porcelain mugs adorned with spring flowers. There was also a plate of delicious goodies I wouldn't turn down despite being full already.

"I made scones this morning," he said. "I'm going to drop some off for your mom."

"That's kind of you, Michael. I'm sure she could use a little pick-me-up."

Michael was in my mom's stable of men and despite my fears that it would go off the rails and affect my friendship with Hazel, it seemed to work nicely. Neither wanted a serious relationship but they had common interests and attended events around town together. Even more surprising was the fact that she often ran into other members of her current or past rotation, and no one seemed to mind at all. It was all very civilized... until now. Calvin's arrival would probably take the fun out of dating, temporarily. Old husbands climbing out of the woodwork were never ideal, even without a murder.

"Dahlia's one tough cookie," Michael said. "She'll come through this just fine."

He left Hazel to pour the coffee and went back to the kitchen.

"I always love your visits," she said, as Percy settled into her lap. "But I suspect this one isn't just to catch up."

"Sounds like you've already heard what happened," I said, slicing into a scone. "At least my mom's version of events."

"Well, I know Calvin's back, which is sending shock waves through the community. Honestly, I expected him much sooner. In fact, I never believed he'd leave in the first place. It might surprise you to hear he was head over heels for Dahlia even after you came along. It always seemed like he couldn't quite believe his luck in landing such a prize."

I stared at her, too shocked to say a thing.

"Close your mouth, dear." Her impish grin made her look decades younger.

"You're... you're joking, right?" I tried to swallow the scone but it had turned to sawdust and I had to wash it down.

"Why would I joke about something like that?"

"It's the first I've heard of them being, you know..."

"Madly in love? I suppose that gets swept under the rug when something dramatic happens. But it was true at the time and I saw them together often. I felt simply awful when he left, but perhaps not as surprised as some."

I looked down at Keats and asked, "Do I want to know this? Can I handle it?"

He put his paw on my foot to ground me.

"I've never brought it up precisely because of those questions, Ivy. It's not up to me, and I'll stop talking right now if you'd like. But I assume you came over to access my historical files."

That made me laugh. "I did. And thank you for both sharing and caring. I may not *want* to know more, but I can't avoid the truth anymore."

"Have you seen Calvin yet?"

I nodded. "Surprise visit to the barn last night. It didn't go well."

"I would think not. He has a lot of explaining to do and that wasn't his strong suit. Dahlia had little idea what she was getting into when she started seeing him, I'm sure. He was handsome. Charming. A wonderful dancer. But there were so many red flags. His father and grandfather were both involved with Frank Swenson, you see. That was as close to organized crime as we got here. It's a cliché now, but once you got in, there really was no getting out. Not in a community this small. Your reputation never recovered."

"So Calvin's family were part of the, uh, the Clover Grove mob?"

Hazel laughed. "I suppose I've gone too far in the comparison. Back then, there was an understanding that people do things in hard times they might not do otherwise. Those were very hard times for farmers. Desperate times, actually."

"So the Galloways weren't part of the culture you've talked so much about?"

"Not the musical or drama societies, but they were very much part of the fabric of our rural society. They came out for parades or picnics. They joined every barn raising, every search for a lost child or lost cow. They were well liked, Ivy, despite having questionable connections."

"Calvin's father was the black sheep?"

"Chester, yes. And *his* father, Albert. Interestingly, it was Chester's wife who caused the most talk."

"Calvin's mother? How?"

"Polly Galloway was a beautiful woman. Intelligent. Spirited. In another day, she'd have gone far. But out here, with limited options, she took the usual path of marrying young. Your father was her only child of many to survive and she doted on him. By that time, Chester had thrown in his lot with old Frank, and I'm sure Polly worried about what would become of them."

I realized I was squeezing the china cup hard enough to break it, and set it down. "Then what happened?"

"As I said, she was a beauty, and she caught Frank's eye. Always had it, I suspect. But she wouldn't give him the time of day earlier." She sipped her coffee and her eyes lost focus for a second. "I wondered if Frank lured Chester into his web simply to manipulate Polly. Chester wasn't really savvy enough to be a career criminal, like the Swensons."

"And did Polly succumb to old Frank?"

"That's what people said. I doubt anyone knew for sure, but Chester's family became more prosperous. Calvin stayed in school and stayed out of the trouble his father got into. Then Polly died in a tragic accident—trampled by runaway horses. Calvin was about fifteen, I think. Still a boy. Chester disappeared soon after, and never returned."

"Did Calvin finish school?"

Hazel shook her head. "He was set adrift. Chester had lost the family home by then, and Calvin went from job to job, trying to find his footing. I don't know that he ever did, but that didn't stop him from marrying your mom."

I waited a few beats before pressing her. "Was Calvin drawn into the Swenson schemes?"

"If anything, he was a minor player, but still, something must have happened for him to leave like that. If it helps, I really think he wanted to do the right thing by Dahlia and the rest of you, but didn't know how."

I rubbed my temples. "So he was not only a crook, but an inept one?"

"This is where the details get sketchy. After my father passed, I didn't have the right connections to hear everything. What I *do* know is that Calvin started to look sort of haunted, and one day he was gone. I never believed the stories about other women. I saw none of that."

My head ached with what could become a killer migraine if I didn't fend it off quickly. Fumbling in my bag, I found a bottle of painkillers and washed a couple of pills down with coffee.

"With all the gossip in this town, I never heard any of this," I said.

"Dahlia tried to protect you," she said. "You're the youngest and you left town early."

"I suppose I blocked it out. I didn't want to know."

Hazel patted my hand. "We all have black sheep in the family. People we'd rather lock in the closet of memory. There are some behind me, too."

"No wonder I get into some messes, Hazel. Crime is in my genes."

"*Solving* crimes, you mean," she said. "Not committing them."

"Calvin suggested his genes made me what I am. I wanted to give him a karate kick in the kisser." I touched Keats' soft ears. "Why didn't I study martial arts?"

"Never too late to try something new. I'm proof of that." After a few moments, Hazel added, "I know this is a lot to take in, but I want you to remember that we are not our genes. We are not even our environment. We are what we choose to make of them. At least, that's my take on family. My brother was rather odd, as you know. Feared by some and reviled by others. Yet we had the same upbringing. Similar genes." She gestured around the stately room and then rested her hand on the coffee urn. "Here I am, thanks to my choices."

"I hear what you're saying. That I can triumph over a bad hand in the genetics game."

"I'm saying that you already have. You've done more good in the past year than most people do in a lifetime. No matter what hand you were dealt, you are playing it well."

She offered another scone and I shook my head. "Do you know anything about Sterling Fable? Mandy said he was Calvin's uncle."

"Sterling, yes! Polly's brother. He was a lovely man. A little too old for me, although I danced with him a time or two. He moved down the range and never came back. Last I heard he'd landed in Fleetborough. Are you going to pay him a visit?"

I nodded. "There's a reason Calvin showed up now. Maybe they stayed in touch."

"Give him my regards," she said, shooing Percy off her lap and pushing herself up from the table. "And no matter what anyone tells you, remember my words... You create your own life. Your own destiny. When you saved Keats, you started something. Look back only as long as it takes you to figure out where you're heading next."

"Solid advice," I said, following my pets to the door. "One thing I know I've done right is choose my friends wisely."

"Exactly. If you're surrounded by people and animals who care about you, you'll always do well."

Keats circled us both with his tail swishing an elaborate endorsement of her words.

"That makes me feel a whole lot better," I said.

"No need to go crazy, though," she said. "Fifty animals are plenty."

"Soon to be sixty by the looks of things. There's a trio of goats about to pop."

Now she laughed. "I do love goat's milk soap."

"If Calvin is going to scare guests away, soapmaking is my fallback plan."

"In a couple of weeks, this will be gone with the wind," she said. "I loved that movie, didn't you?"

I nodded. "I think about Scarlett O'Hara sometimes. Runaway Farm is my Tara."

"That sounds like a good discussion for the next time you come to access my mental records."

We both laughed as I ran down the stairs to the driveway. I could see the backyard from there. Normally I avoided looking at the spot where Keats and Percy had unearthed some old bones, but today I couldn't help noticing that it had been turned into a gorgeous spring garden.

Hazel was a worthy mentor. If she had turned terrible compost into flowers, I could do the same.

CHAPTER TWELVE

I'd expected Jilly to put up more of a fight, but she handed over the reins of the inn to Daisy without hesitation and joined me in the truck.

I was a little more hesitant, actually. Daisy had admitted she abandoned her post at the inn for a time the day before. Hearing about Calvin had thrown her for such a loop that she went for a long walk, she said. The cars were there when she left and when she returned, so she hadn't thought anything of it. Now she was doubly upset, but I knew she'd be more vigilant.

"Thank you for coming," I said to Jilly now. "Keats and Percy are great backup but sometimes I need my best friend riding shotgun."

"You're doing me a favor," she said. "I was glad to get away. Everyone is so upset about what happened to Daphne, yet Chief Coots asked them all to stay until the investigation is complete. They've lost interest in genealogy, I'm afraid."

"Only temporarily. They'll need the distraction of

their family trees." I glanced at her. "Do you know much about yours?"

"It's been well documented by my relatives, or so I've heard." She gave a little shudder. "I don't want to know."

I shot her a quick glance. "They produced you. It can't be that bad."

"It isn't that good." She stared out the passenger window as we got onto the highway, and I let it go. I wouldn't twist her arm if she wasn't ready to share. Instead, I started filling her in on my discussion with Hazel.

"So far, it appears that my deadbeat dad had a philandering mom who tried to protect him from the Clover Grove mob and failed. Hopefully Sterling can fill in some gaps for us."

Jilly shook her head. "It's odd to think there was anything like organized crime in a farming community."

"Right? And here we were focusing on the culture of the day. Crime tours are the way to go."

"I'd rather focus on food and the arts. Let's get this Calvin issue sorted and go back to our Culture Revival Project."

"The sooner the better." I merged onto a bigger highway and geared up smoothly. "I dropped Calvin's wallet with Kellan on the way home from Hazel's."

"After going through it first, I presume." She grinned at me. "And documenting."

"You know me too well, my friend. There were a few slobbery surprises in there, including my high school graduation photo and clippings about my promotions at Flordale."

"Really? He kept track of you that well?"

"Not just me. There were bits and pieces about all of us. Birth announcements for Daisy's kids. Asher's graduation from the police academy. And the article about my rescuing Keats."

"Huh. Is it possible he's not as horrible as he seemed?"

"Still a deadbeat. An overstuffed wallet does not a parent make."

"Poor Dahlia. Left in the lurch without so much as an explanation. All these years she's assumed it was another woman. Daisy said she's down for the count right now."

"We don't know the full story. Mom has been known to dance around the truth. Either way, Michael's scones will be just what the doctor ordered. A couple of dates and a couple of new dresses will get her back on her heels." I watched the pretty towns flick past, each looking much like the other. "She's afraid to come to the farm in case Calvin shows up again. That's one less thing to worry about."

"No real clues in his wallet?"

"Not that I could tell. There was an old pic of someone I'm guessing is his mom, the infamous Polly Fable."

"Was she as beautiful as Hazel said?"

"Grab my phone," I said. "There's a folder with all the pics."

Jilly flipped through them slowly and then exclaimed. "Oh my gosh, Ivy. She looks like you!"

"Polly? Come on. I'm the spitting image of Dahlia, just like all my sisters. We're the nesting dolls, remember?

Polly looks fair in that photo. Like Asher. In fact, she looks like a china doll. I can see why she'd catch old Frank's eye."

"Look at the horse in the background. The dog in her lap. The cat in the tree over her head. Polly Fable was the original Ivy Doolittle."

I laughed, and Keats mumbled as he stared at the phone Jilly held out for him. There was another canine comment, no doubt dissing the corgi in the photo. He didn't have much respect for any dog except Clem.

The sign for Fleetborough came too soon. Riding with my besties was the best balm for my beleaguered soul and it wasn't quite ready for another thrashing.

"What if Sterling is a crime lord or something?" I said, leaving the highway and following increasingly twisty roads to his home. "He clearly doesn't want to be easy to find."

"Plenty of us are trying to escape the past, it seems. We can't blame him for that."

"Sometimes it's the wise thing to do." I turned into his lane at last, expecting to find an old red farmhouse. Instead, it was a modern brick bungalow with spring gardens much like Hazel Bingham's.

"He can't be too scary," Jilly said. "He likes daffodils and tulips."

The old man standing on the porch didn't look like a gardener, however. He looked like a female version of my friend Gertie Rhodes, but he didn't bother to hide his rifle under a poncho, as she did. His blue-and-black checkered bathrobe billowed in the breeze over blue striped pajamas. There was a cane in his other hand that he would need to drop to fire on guests.

I stuck my head out the window before leaving the vehicle. Sometimes I was too cavalier about my own safety, let alone Jilly's.

"Hello, Mr. Fable," I called. "I'm Ivy Galloway. Hazel Bingham suggested I pay you a visit."

"Now's not a good time," he said.

"When *would* be a good time?" I asked.

"Half past never." He tossed me a grim smile. "An old man just wants his peace."

"That's what I want, too. But a disruptor of my peace showed up at my farm yesterday."

He shook his head. "I told him not to come back but he couldn't leave well enough alone."

I thought about debating whether deserting his family was "well enough," but decided against it. To get some answers, I'd need to pull out my old HR chops and deploy my secret weapon... one very few men could resist.

On cue, Jilly stuck her head out the passenger window and called, "I brought cookies for you, Mr. Fable. And some shepherd's pie. It's a popular dish at Ivy's inn."

"I've read the reviews, Toots," he said. "I know what you ladies have been doing and it isn't just entertaining. Going to get yourselves killed if you keep it up."

"Trouble seems to find me," I said.

He came to the edge of the porch. "Trouble's your last name. Might as well accept it."

My stomach sank as he confirmed my own fears about my fate. But Keats shoved his head through the window in front of me and shouted a few insults at the man.

"Stop that," I said. "It's not like you to yell."

Sterling Fable actually laughed. "You've got a knight in fur armor, I see. Bring him out so I can meet him."

We didn't give the old man time to change his mind. Keats and Percy raced up the stairs with tails flying high. Apparently Sterling's threats were mostly bluster.

After stooping to give both animals a pat, he beckoned with the rifle to follow him inside. Keats and Percy ran ahead and Jilly came behind, carrying her culinary hostess gifts.

The living room was about what I'd expected, with a brown tweed recliner and a leather couch that had seen better days. There were no pets in sight, but the gnawed coffee table legs spoke of dogs gone before.

Sterling gestured for Jilly to drop the food in the kitchen, and I took the place he assigned me on the couch. Keats and Percy didn't wait for permission to start exploring.

"Make yourselves at home," he said, to the pets, not me. I couldn't tell if he was being facetious or not.

"Pet lover?" I asked.

"Hard to avoid in my family. My sister, Polly, collected them like other girls did dolls. Never met a critter she didn't like." He pinned me with pale blue eyes that were rimmed with red. "I suppose you got that from her."

I pressed my lips together, refusing to acknowledge inheriting anything good from previous generations.

"That expression on your face?" he said. "Pure Dahlia. Holier than thou."

"Unfair," I said. "My mom had a hard life raising six kids on her own."

He shrugged. "Maybe it was better than the alternative. And no matter what she's told you, she knew what she was getting into with Calvin. The boy was lost, and she was a pretty coin for his collection."

Jilly joined me, sitting closer than she usually would. It infused me with strength.

"Hazel told me they were head over heels. Right up till he left."

"Pair of fools," Sterling said. "You don't bring six kids into the world when there's a target on your back."

"So Calvin was associating with the wrong people?"

"He'd be the first to say that. Probably did say that when he met you."

I shrugged. "I didn't want to hear it then. Or from him. Now I see it's better to know thy enemy."

"He's not the villain you imagine. Just a flawed human being like the rest of us." Sterling kicked back the recliner. "I won't pretend to approve of his decisions, but it looks like you made out alright. You've got a mouthy dog who loves you and a friend who cooks."

"And a police chief for a boyfriend," Jilly added.

"I hear you've got a cop of your own, Toots," he said. "Asher's not the sharpest knife in the drawer but he has a good heart."

"You're awfully well informed for someone who wants nothing to do with us," I said.

"I made a decision long ago to keep to myself. Easier to stay alive that way."

"You decided that after your sister took up with Frank Swenson?"

"Even before. She picked the wrong man to marry and then another wrong man to fix it."

"Two wrongs don't make Mr. Right, I guess."

Jilly applied her elbow to my ribcage but Sterling chuckled. "Smart aleck."

"Can you tell us more about Polly, Mr. Fable?" she said.

"You can call me Sterling, Toots," he said. "Since you brought cookies."

"It was my pleasure and I wanted to meet you." Jilly hauled out the smile she'd used as a headhunter with tough clients. "Ivy's so good at putting a puzzle together, but finding the first pieces that fit can be challenging."

"You might want to stay away from this puzzle, ladies. It doesn't smell so good."

"I'm used to manure," I said. "And Calvin specifically asked for my help. He's a suspect in the murder of Daphne Newell, as you probably know."

"He's innocent of that," Sterling said. "And guilty of other things, I'm sure. He didn't get the best start in life."

"But as Hazel reminded me earlier, we make our own decisions."

"I didn't recall Hazel being so snooty back in the day. She was a fine woman."

"Still is," I said. "Spoke well of you, too."

He straightened his bathrobe and grinned. "I could dance some."

"But you never married?" Jilly asked.

"Didn't work out so well for Polly. I learned my lesson."

"People say Polly had an affair with Frank Swenson," I said. "Is that true?"

Now the blue checkered shoulders shrugged. "He was crazy about her but I don't know how far things went. She had beauty and charm, and if she needed to use them to keep Calvin safe, she'd have done it. Another couple of years may have kept him out of trouble, but..."

"But she died in an accident," I said.

"Never believed it was an accident," he said. "Trampled by runaway horses? Not my sister."

I didn't say anything, so Jilly leaned forward. "Are you suggesting Frank Swenson murdered her?"

"Not Frank. He was heartbroken, and that was plain for all to see. Including his wife."

"Chester?" Jilly asked.

"Or the wronged wife?" I added.

Sterling stared out the window. "There was no investigation. The sheriff of the day looked the other way. Too messy."

"That must have been so difficult for Calvin," Jilly said.

"Yes." The word was barely a whisper. "He went from being a sheltered mama's boy to being on his own at fifteen. Barely twenty when he married."

There was a clatter in the dining room and I got up. "That's probably Percy. He likes to poke around."

"As do you, young lady. I may be old but I can still

use a computer. I've seen the trouble you get yourself into. Pure Galloway."

"Pure Galloway?" Anger percolated in my belly and shot a flare up to my face. "That's a terrible thing to say."

Jilly intervened. "Ivy's always working on the side of good."

"But not necessarily on the side of the law," he said with a chuckle. "Or so I heard."

"You can't always believe what you hear," I called from the dining room, where Percy was scaling a shelving unit and knocking framed photos as he climbed. When he caught my eye, he gave one a sharp tap with his paw. It tumbled off the shelf and I caught it before it hit the floor.

Flipping it, I saw Polly looking back at me with eerily aware eyes. In this shot, she was older and the dog at her feet looked very much like Keats. Seeing that sent a little chill down my spine. At least she had the good sense to like sheepdogs.

I ordered Percy down, set everything right, and carried the photo back to Sterling's recliner. "Polly, I presume?"

Taking it, he nodded. "On the lawn of our family home, which is long gone now. She loved to sit under that oak tree with her dogs, imagining a house full of kids and animals." He handed it back to me and sighed. "Keep it if you like. You shared the same taste in dogs, if nothing else."

I sat back down and handed the photo to Jilly. "Why do you think Calvin came back now?"

"Money trouble, no doubt."

"That's what the private investigator said. And the

reason the police think he may have murdered Daphne Newell."

Sterling shook his head. "Why would he kill Daphne? He liked her well enough, but no one took the place of your mother. More's the pity."

"You don't think much of my mom, it seems."

He raised one bushy gray eyebrow. "It's not personal. Well, I suppose it is. She was a flibbertigibbet as a girl. Marrying the right woman would have made a man out of Calvin. He needed a steady hand and wouldn't listen to me or anyone else. All it takes is one wrong deal to start down a slippery slope. That probably happened around baby number four."

"Guess he wanted to keep going till he got a boy," I said.

"Well, I'm happy they kept going or you and Asher wouldn't be around," Jilly said.

Sterling pushed the lever on the recliner and sat up. "He wanted to be surrounded by family because he'd lost his own too young. Shame it backfired."

"So sad," Jilly said. "He's been on the run for years all alone."

She might be softening toward Calvin, but not me. "We've all got to live with our choices, like Hazel said. Mine aren't always smart, either."

Keats was sitting at my knee. I touched his shoulder, trying to figure out what he was figuring out. There was more to this story than Sterling was telling me. The dog's ears were forward and his muzzle up, as if he were trying to pull details out of thin air. Since my interviewing skills were being undercut by old emotions, I'd have to count on my sidekick.

Keats gave a mumble of encouragement, and I nodded.

"What was that about?" Sterling said.

"Just wondering, Sterling... Did you give Calvin money when he came to visit yesterday?"

The old man looked startled. "What makes you think he visited me?"

"My dog says so." Keats went into a point at a loveseat opposite Jilly and me. "He sat right there."

The last traces of Sterling's smug expression had vanished. "The dog knows that?"

"He does. And for whatever reason, he doesn't have a bone to pick with Calvin. I still think he's the most likely murderer, but Keats disagrees. Eventually the dog persuades me. But it would speed things along if you gave me an idea of what Calvin is doing and why."

The recliner snapped back again. He crossed his arms and stared out the window again. "I've spent most of my life not talking about Calvin. Not talking about Polly. I had a good job, a good life. All a man needs in old age is a recliner and some nice perennials to remind him spring comes every year."

"The sooner we can resolve this, the sooner you can get back to admiring your daffodils in peace. Keats says you can help."

His eyes shifted to the dog and his mouth worked for a second as he tried to resist the spell of the sheepdog stare. "Fine," he said at last. "It's about the gold."

"What gold? Frank Swenson's? Because Keats found

all of it months ago. If Calvin is hoping for a get-rich-quick scenario he missed his chance."

"Not all of it," Sterling said. "Frank left something special for Polly. To take care of her if anything happened to him or Chester. People were always trying to kill him, you see. Failing, but trying. So he hid the treasure well and only she knew the site. I figured that's why she died, actually. Someone wanted that gold."

"Then surely the killer got it."

"Maybe. The Galloway property was ravaged by looters after her death. Rather like what's happened to Gertie Rhodes. The digging didn't stop for decades, but it did stop, so it's hard to know if they found Polly's gold or not. Calvin thinks there's still a chance."

Keats turned and his blue eye seemed to wink.

"Well, that is a credible lead, Sterling, so thank you."

"Thank your dog," he said. "He bent me to his will."

I laughed. "He's good at that." Turning to Jilly, I added, "Right, Toots?"

She laughed, too. "No one would have dared called me that in my old life, Sterling. But I don't mind it here."

He coughed up a laugh, too, and Keats joined the merriment with a ha-ha-ha.

"Full of himself, isn't he?" Sterling said.

"He's earned it. And he might again if we find this treasure. Then Calvin can deal with his troubles, you can go back to smelling the roses, and me the manure."

Getting out of the recliner, he walked us to the door. "I misspoke about Dahlia. She was a bit of a pill, but if she produced a smart cookie like you, she can't be all bad."

"Keats likes you both," I said, allowing myself to be herded out by Sterling.

Holding the door open, he said, "I mean this as a compliment, Ivy, though you may not take it that way. You remind me of my sister, Polly. She did the best she could with what she had."

I knew that quick and easy judgments closed doors on possibilities, so I patted my purse with the photo inside and smiled. "It sounds like we had animals in common. Thankfully *my* Mr. Right is also on the right side of the law."

"What's he doing with a Galloway?" Sterling asked, snickering in the doorway. "That goes for you, too, Toots. Consider yourself warned."

Keats took a dash at Sterling's pajama leg and gave it a yank. "You misspoke again, Sterling," I said, grinning as the dog led us down the stairs. "Consider yourself warned."

CHAPTER THIRTEEN

"What now, Sherlock?" Jilly said, as we drove under the arched sign over my lane that read "Runaway Far" because the "m" had long since rusted out.

"Keats and I need to transform back into farmer mode. The goat doula is coming to visit."

"Goat doula? Is there such a thing?"

"Maybe not, but I had to settle for the closest thing I could find. With our three expectant mothers, I wanted to make sure someone's on speed dial. Bridget, Cori and some of the Mafia are experienced midwives but they're often out on their unofficial business, as am I."

A familiar white van was parked outside the barn, alongside Edna's ATV.

"That's your goat doula?" Jilly said. "Gertie Rhodes?"

"She prefers 'Livestock Consultant,'" I said. "When we were searching for her missing cat recently, she told me she raised plenty of critters while Saul was alive. The treasure hunters ended all that, but she claims to have delivered nearly a hundred goats."

"Help comes from the most surprising places," Jilly said. "Normally Gertie is anxious about leaving her house for too long. How did you convince her?"

"All credit goes to Edna. She talked Gertie into hiring a security company. The Swenson gold found on her land is now paying to protect her from people looking for the Swenson gold. Things get mighty twisted in Clover Grove, don't they?"

"So twisted," Jilly said, as we pulled up beside the van. "I'm happy she can have more of a life now, even if it's delivering baby goats. She's been isolated too long."

"Now that she has a cat and a partner in prepping, she's almost cheerful. Hasn't pulled a gun on me in weeks."

Jilly laughed. "I love how that's news."

Gertie was standing at the far side of the goat pasture with Edna. Both were wearing fatigues, although Gertie had layered on a brown poncho made from alpaca wool. Her gray braid hung down her back nearly to her knees, and there was a diagonal bulge in the rear of the poncho that suggested, Minnie, her rifle, had her back. For all I knew it might be Godiva, her sword. My blade lore was as scanty as my goat lore.

Both women had been prepping for disaster long before it was a thing, or at least openly discussed. Now they egged each other on with regular target practice, fencing and other maneuvers befitting apocalyptic soldiers. Their passions in retirement certainly differed from those of most seniors, including Hazel Bingham.

"Can we be like them when we get old, Jilly?" I asked, releasing Keats and Percy from the truck.

"Armed and dangerous? I'd need some training, my friend. My current weapons of choice are a whisk and a spatula."

"There's time. They didn't start prepping in earnest till midlife, but we could consider taking up target practice."

"I'll start saving the bean cans," Jilly said.

"From boardroom to bunker in under a year," I said. "Could you ever have imagined?"

"Never. I could never in a million years have imagined our new best friends and tutors being octogenarian preppers. We were so wasted on corporate life." After a second, she added, "Just one stipulation, Ivy. No braids or ponchos."

"Edna's with you on that. She says they make you vulnerable, and not just to public ridicule. Zombies could grab Gertie and swing before she could raise her rifle. But Gertie lives on the edge."

The object under Gertie's poncho turned out to be a sledgehammer. By the time we reached her, she was taking down the fence on the far side of the pasture.

"Gertie, what are you doing?" I said. "Charlie's going to have a fit."

She stopped with the sledgehammer raised, a fearsome sight indeed. "Rule number one about goats, Ivy. Give them room to forage. And rule two? Give them distractions."

"What kind of distractions?"

She took another whack at the fence and Edna

ripped down the board. It was like they'd been dismantling perfectly good pastures together forever.

"Distractions suitable for the average dog. Because goat smarts are underestimated."

"So I should be taking the goats out on errands?" I said. "Kellan gave me heck not long ago for driving with a goat in the cab of the truck."

Gertie rolled her eyes before taking another swing. "That's just common sense. Try walking them around the property."

"You think I have time to take goats sightseeing?"

"You make time for what's important," she said. "Be good to your goats and they'll be good to you by producing a steady supply of milk. Then you can start an artisanal soap business with the Runaway Inn label."

"You're not the first to suggest it," Jilly said. "Except I'm guessing that too would take time we don't have."

"Lucky for you I'm a goat guru," Gertie said. "Used to make my own soaps and lotions and had plenty of customers. I'll get you set up." She took another whack at the fence. "But first we have to make happy goats, which takes us to rule number three."

"Which is...?"

"Build them a jungle gym," she said. "A good one. Make being a Runaway Farm goat rewarding and fun. We'll set it up right in the center of the pasture so they can't use it as an escape route. Because rule zero almost goes without saying: keep them secure. Their endless curiosity will lead them nowhere good."

"Plus their appetite," I said. "Big Mama is a pickpocket."

"She probably won't eat the booty. They mostly like the challenge."

I looked over at Big Mama, who was standing on her own by the fence. She'd stopped bullying the other goats and was now isolating herself. "Gertie, what's wrong with her? She's quite aggressive and doesn't act like the rest."

"She's ruminating, and I don't mean literally. My guess is that she trusted someone in the past and was let down. Now here she is with kids coming. Anyone would feel vulnerable." She swung her braid over her shoulder and shrugged. "You know what to do about that."

"I do?"

"Of course you do," Jilly said. "Bonding with animals is your superpower."

Edna turned from her work. "Girls, could you make us some coffee? A snack wouldn't go amiss, either. Feed both your goats and your free help well."

"It sounds like we're being dismissed," I said.

"No offense, but you're the distraction here," she replied. "Gertie and I are a well-oiled machine. The lumber for the jungle gym will be here soon. I used your card."

"You have my card?"

"Already back where I found it," she said.

"Goats aren't the only pickpockets around here," I said. "What about the midwife lessons, Gertie? Isn't that why you're here?"

"You've got a few days," she said. "We'll do a quick how-to later, and I'll walk you through the warning signs. When you see them, you call me."

"I can be here in two shakes of a goat's tail," Edna said. "As you well know."

"But have you delivered kids?" I asked.

"Human kids and plenty of them," she said. "I don't imagine this is any more challenging. Gertie?"

"A breeze in comparison," Gertie said, taking another swing at the fence. "Good practice for what's to come. Imagine delivering in a bunker, ladies."

"No thanks," Jilly said, shuddering.

Our guests had come out onto the porch to watch my friends work.

"Oops, we pulled them away from their scrapbooks," Gertie said. "There are more productive ways to spend your time than ruminating over a family tree. Besides, looking forward is the only way. Wherever you focus, you go."

Edna squinted at me. "Ivy, your sad sack face tells me you've been running in reverse all day."

"True. We ran down to Fleetborough to meet Sterling Fable."

"Ah, your great-uncle," Gertie said. "Haven't seen him in fifty years."

"How come you never mentioned him before?" I said, watching the little white goat I rescued from a TV production try to squeeze past the temporary fencing they'd set up. A sheepdog discouraged the incursion.

"Forgot about him," Gertie said, tapping her head with her free hand. "You think I can catalogue every face from this county? I've got a lot going on."

I stared at Edna. "You're the cataloguing queen. And yet I had to find out about him from Hazel Bingham."

"I would have gotten around to it," she said. "Just like you would have gotten around to telling me what you were doing this morning."

"Oh, this is how it's going to be now?"

"Always was," Edna said. "You gotta give to get, my young friends. I can't protect you if I don't know where you are. In case you need reminding, there's a killer on the loose."

"I doubt my own father will kill me," I said. "And he's still my prime suspect."

"Don't close your mind to other possibilities," she said. "Like the folks standing on your porch right now."

"Chief Coots' officers have already been over to interview the genealogy society. Nobody knows anything."

"Everyone knows something," Edna said. "Stop chasing old ghosts and focus on the new one."

"Take care of the new one and the old one will take care of itself," Gertie added.

I rolled my eyes. "You're both turning into Confucius."

"Just wise old crones," Gertie said.

"Speak for yourself," Edna said. "I'm getting younger by the day."

She did look considerably younger than when we'd met eight or so months ago. A plot against her life had brought a glow to her previously sallow cheeks and galvanized her to new physical feats. Like building a goat gym.

Jilly went up to see to the guests while Keats and I kept the goats from helping to build their new mental stimulation project. In gaps between chopping and rebuilding, I filled Edna and Gertie in on what Sterling had told me.

"I always wondered what happened with Polly," Gertie said. "The situation warranted a proper investigation, but my father said the police of the day were as corrupt as the citizens."

"Mine said the same," Edna said. "Although my family out-corrupted them all."

"Well, you're making up for it now," Gertie said. "Doing good works for goats everywhere."

"And their owners," I said. "Which leads me to a mystery gift Frank Swenson apparently hid for Polly. They may have been having an affair."

"More treasure?" Gertie heaved a gusty sigh. "Seems like Frank Swenson spent more time burying than plundering."

"Where would he bury something intended just for her?" I asked.

"I'd suggest leaving that alone," Gertie said. "Treasure hunting brings nothing but trouble."

"Oh, you know she won't leave it alone," Edna said. "Ivy's as curious as a goat and twice as stubborn."

"Let Calvin find it and move on," Gertie said. "The sooner the better."

"I have a furry treasure detector," I said, smiling at Keats. "If Calvin murdered Daphne, he doesn't deserve to find it. If he's innocent, he can take it and go."

Edna gave an exasperated sigh. "Fine. We'll all go out to the old Galloway property so that Keats can have a sniff around. If we find it, I take a cut for the bunker fund. Gold and silver will have value after the banks go bust."

"Good thinking," Gertie said, yanking out the last board. "Now stop dillydallying, old friend. Let's get this place back together before the whole world falls apart."

CHAPTER FOURTEEN

I was in the family room with the guests when Kellan arrived. Daisy had let him in and before I saw him, I felt him. It was like a heavy, dank fog fell over the room and silenced all the chatter. He was here in a professional rather than boyfriend capacity, obviously. Chief Harper on a case was a professional wet blanket. Catcher of killers, killer of fun.

He circled the room, greeting people and asking about their work. No doubt he was dissatisfied with the results of the questioning by his Dorset Hills colleagues. He was probably running his own investigation under Chief Coots' radar. Now he was the behind-the-scenes sleuth in the situation. In other words, he was getting a taste of my life.

Walt Watford beckoned him over. "Sit down and join us, Chief. I'd be happy to take you through genealogy 101 if you're interested in doing research into your own family. I'll start with my usual warning that you may not always like what you find."

"One of my ancestors was a pirate," Joanne Crayton said. "Spent years in jail before meeting the right woman and becoming respectable."

"My great-great uncle was jailed for sedition," Kathleen Nair said. "But then he met his wife and had nine children and was never in trouble again."

"That you know of yet," Walt said, laughing. "Dig a little deeper and you may find trouble. Off the books."

"My great-grandfather was shipped from England to a penal colony in Australia," Brenda Stayer said. "He was forced to marry for money to get out of debt, but that was the end of his scandalous ways."

"I'm seeing a theme here," Kellan said. "Reprobates reformed by the love of a good woman."

All the women laughed. Tittered, even. Kellan's good looks and presence more than compensated for his professional dourness. Still, it was good to see the guests perking up. They'd all wilted after the news of Daphne. Jilly and Daisy had been trying to revive them with good food and hospitality, without much success.

"You'd be surprised at how often that happened," Kathleen said. "It was one crazy exploit after another with these bad boys until they settled down with Mrs. Right."

Kellan finally smiled. "The stuff that inspires movies. I wish I saw more of those happy endings in my work. Too often it goes the other way, with crime taking a man from his family and leaving them to struggle."

The dank fog dropped over the room again. It occurred to me that what drew family historians to this work were romance, adventure and tales of triumph.

Perhaps those who encountered the miserable-ever-after stories moved on to more prosaic pastimes.

"What can you tell us about Daphne Newell, Chief Harper?" Joanne asked. She had the deep voice and authority that Walt, their mild-mannered leader, did not. "Surely something's been found by now. Ordinary people like Daphne don't just die like that."

"I blame the old boyfriend," Brenda said. "Daphne had an air of heartbreak about her. I think she wore all that pink to compensate for it."

Finn Donnelly leaned back in his chair and crossed his arms. "Money. It's always about money."

"Daphne *had* money," Brenda said. "More than the rest of us, it seemed. She had a nice house, a nice car and kept the dress shops in Dorset Hills very happy."

Joanne shrugged. "I hadn't seen a new dress or bag in some time. Maybe Finn's right and the piggy bank was empty."

"Now, now," Walt said. "It isn't fair to speculate when—"

Kathleen talked right over him. "She hadn't been herself lately. The poor thing had man and money problems. No wonder she was losing interest in her family tree."

"You could tell she wasn't committed anymore," Brenda said. "Her mind always seemed elsewhere. It brings down the spirit of the room."

"It was time for her to go," Finn said.

"Finn!" Joanne spoke first but everyone turned to stare at him. He just smirked, which made him look like a devious garden gnome come to life.

"I didn't mean it *that* way. Obviously," he said. "I meant she should find a new hobby."

Walt got up and walked over to Finn. Despite the comb-over, the taller man exuded quiet confidence. "Daphne had finished her work with us. She was ready to—"

"Do not say transition," Joanne interrupted. "I vote to ban that word from our group. After you used it the other day, she passed."

"I was going to say graduate." Walt gave her a genial smile. "She would no doubt have found new passions if—"

"Someone hadn't chopped her family tree off at the roots," Finn said. "End of Daphne, end of her line."

Joanne joined Walt in towering over Finn. "You're being disrespectful. And in front of the chief, no less." She turned to Kellan. "Why don't you say something?"

I wondered that myself. Normally Kellan was all about ending speculation.

Then I realized he was doing what I did. Just letting people chatter to see what surfaced.

"Joanne's right," he said. "Speculation is never a good idea."

"Exactly," Joanne said. "Next thing you know we'll all be accusing each other. After all, we did split up in Dorset Hills."

"There are so many good art stores there, and we all wanted different things," Kathleen said. "It would have taken all afternoon otherwise."

"Anyway, no one was gone long enough to do something like that," Brenda said.

"How long does something like that really take?" Finn said. "If you're known and trusted, I would imagine it can be quite streamlined."

"Finn!" This time every voice chimed in, including Kellan's.

"That's quite enough," he said, turning all chiefly again. "Leave the investigation to Chief Coots and his officers." He gestured around at the tables full of photos, documents and art supplies. "You have plenty to keep you busy with stories you already know."

"Exactly right," Walt said. "Back to work, everyone. We'll see these projects through to the very end."

"Do not talk about endings," Joanne said. "We're all worried we'll be next to—"

"Transition?" Finn said, pulling his garden gnome face again.

Walt and Joanne turned away, shaking their heads.

"Do pardon our manners, you two," Walt said to Kellan and me. "I suppose we're all jittery. Daphne was a bright light in our midst."

"Very bright," Kathleen muttered. "Garish."

"Geraniums," Brenda whispered. "I'll find some that very shade of fuchsia and plant them on Daphne's grave."

"That sounds like a beautiful gesture, Brenda," I said, tugging Kellan's sleeve until he followed me outside to the front porch.

"Well," he said, blinking a few times in the sunlight. "That was interesting."

"See what happens when you just let them riff? Maybe you should try it more often."

He shook his head. "I prefer an orderly interrogation, but Chief Coots has tied my hands."

"I thought your departments were working together on this."

"We should be, but he's holding the reins pretty tight."

The set of his jaw gave me a good idea why. "Is that because of your ties to Asher and me? With Calvin being the chief suspect?"

"He hasn't said. I just find myself blocked at every turn." He sighed and then added, "Malcolm's a decent cop, and he'll get the job done. Eventually."

"Well, you're doing the right thing," I said.

He glanced at me. "Which is what, exactly?"

"Poking around. Listening. Following the leads Chief Coots probably thinks are small fish."

Finally he grinned. "Being you, you mean."

I grinned back at him. "I bet my guests revealed more in that conversation than you expected. The women were jealous of Daphne's style and Finn was jealous of her money. Money that may have been running short."

"Not enough motive," he said. "How would they gain from her passing? Plus, they really didn't have enough time to pull it off, despite what Finn said. They were only in Dorset Hills for an hour or so and everyone's vouched for each other's whereabouts."

"I'm sure Chief Coots will check them all out. I still see Calvin as most likely, but hearing she may have been short of money does change things. Edna reminded me to keep an open mind."

"And I'll remind you to stay out of it. Coots won't put

up with your meddling the way I do, Ivy."

"In some ways, Coots seems lax," I said. "He lets the guests go out walking anytime they like. You never do that. Or maybe he doesn't consider them suspects either and has someone else in mind."

"We were talking about goats, right?" he asked.

I laughed. "I'm happy to change the subject, especially to goats." I gestured to the pasture. "We have much to discuss."

Charlie was on the tractor hauling a massive stump through a gap in the fence, and Poppy was working alongside Gertie and Edna as they assembled the jungle gym, complete with ramps and parapets.

"You're renovating, I see."

"That's what you do when you're expecting. It's all about stimulating their young minds, or so Gertie tells me. Welcome to my goat enrichment program."

"They need Disneyland?" He gave me one of his "where will it all end?" looks.

"Apparently I've been underserving my goats. Treating them like sheep when they're as smart as the average dog and even more curious. It's my responsibility to help them reach their full caprine potential."

"Caprine? New word of the day?"

"Part of *my* goat enrichment program," I said, leading him down to the pasture.

"I admit I'm not a huge fan of the caprine family," Kellan said. "I spend more time hunting down goat escapees than I do human criminals. Homesteaders are too lax on fencing and next thing you know there's a gang of goat thugs downtown. Last year some horned and bearded ruffians took over the square with the statue of General Clover."

General Clover was the town's official, though inadvertent, founder. He'd established Clover Grove simply by stopping briefly en route to Washington so that his wife could deliver their first child.

"I remember that. Asher told me about your single-handed intervention in a fight between rival gang leaders." I couldn't help grinning at the thought. "He said it was better than a cage match."

Kellan grinned, too. "Keats isn't the only hero in this town. Get Ash to show you the video."

A little pang in my chest made me look away. Asher and I hadn't connected much since he first dropped his news about Calvin more than a month ago. One day I hoped he could become my favorite sibling again.

I slapped on an HR smile before Kellan could see how much I missed my brother. "Gertie is going to teach us how to make goat's milk soap and lotions for the Runaway Inn brand," I said.

"Lotions. Well, that's interesting."

I could tell it was the exact opposite. Kellan's ability to feign interest in my farm musings was one of his greatest strengths as a boyfriend. He wasn't an animal person, but he was endlessly curious by nature. Rather like a goat, although he wouldn't appreciate the comparison. But taking him into the realm of soap and lotion was a step too far, it seemed, and he made an abrupt turn to get out of there.

"I heard you were down in Fleetborough this morning," he said.

"I was, yes," I said, keeping my eye on the goats. The one I rescued from the reality TV show was riding along on the stump as Charlie adjusted its position. The massive oak tree had fallen months ago, revealing gnarly, twisted roots not unlike my own family tree.

"And why were you way down there with a renovation like this underway?"

"I was exploring my family tree with Sterling Fable. My great-uncle. Did you know that my grandmother was involved with Frank Swenson, and possibly murdered?"

"Nothing was ever proven," Kellan said. "But it's in my pile of cold cases to explore when the time comes."

"It seems like the time's come," I said. "Why didn't you tell me about Polly?"

"It's old news, Ivy. Many generations of police before me decided her death was an accident."

"But you didn't believe that, or you wouldn't have added it to your pile of cold cases."

"When I took over, I reviewed decades of files and pulled out a bunch that seemed to warrant a second look. That's what detectives do." He shrugged. "Good ones, anyway. Other cases were higher priority. Some had ties to current situations, here or elsewhere."

"You just didn't want me poking around the cemetery of cold cases," I said.

"That too," he admitted. "Frank may be long dead but he's continued to cause trouble, hasn't he? For a small-town criminal, he left quite a legacy. In today's world, he'd run a global crime syndicate. He was wily and capable, and never held to account for his actions."

Kellan's lips pressed together in a grim line. For a

man of justice like him, this was a terrible wrong that could never be righted. A decades-old black mark on our community.

I touched his arm. "If you've spoken to Sterling, you know that Calvin is here to find the gold Frank buried for Polly's use. So that means her case floats up the pile, right?"

"I've heard the stories. Frank apparently left a few special stashes for people he liked."

"The ones with the riddles?" I asked.

"It was always a game with him," Kellan said, nodding. "I've only seen one of these so-called riddles. Hardly poetry, and likely unsolvable even for its recipient."

"Well, that's probably what Calvin is trying to do. Has he been questioned?"

He shook his head. "Not yet. He's lying low. But they've spoken to everyone in Daphne's small circle here. Her only interest seemed to be genealogy."

"And the murder weapon?" I asked.

"A blade," he said. "Eight inches, most likely. No sign of that yet, either."

"Calvin will know more, I'm sure of it," I said. "Sterling probably knows where he is, but he won't give him up because he's family."

"Blood is usually thicker than water," Kellan said.

"In my view, family is what you build for yourself with people who've proven they have your back."

He dropped an arm around my shoulders and pulled me close. "I suppose that means we'll be hosting aunts Gertie and Edna for years to come?"

"Most definitely." I rested my head on his chest for a moment, drawing courage to face the challenge ahead.

"Don't let them lead you into too much trouble," he said. "I can only give my full attention to the matter at hand when I'm not worrying about the traps your curiosity is leading you into. Honestly, Ivy, you're as bad as a goat."

I pulled away, laughing. "I was thinking the same about you! Only to me it's a positive. You're as *good* as a goat with your inquisitive mind. No wonder we get along so well."

He rubbed his forehead, a gesture that said he was frustrated and amused by me in equal parts. "But I'm chief goat. I carry a gun and I have a small army backing me."

"I have a small army, too, remember."

"The rogue nannies. How could I forget? Just please remember that there's a killer on the loose."

"Nanny Edna just reminded me," I said. "But if Calvin's the killer, you can relax. He asked for my help, and no matter how negligent a father he was, he isn't likely to come after me."

"That's how this kind of thing always starts out. Then someone comes after you."

"Not this time. It's different."

"It's only different until it's the same." He swept off his hat and churned his fingers through dark hair. I had to remind myself he was on duty. No matter how tempting, I never touched his hair while he was in chief mode. If he wanted to look unruly, it was a chief's prerogative. "You're not getting a billy goat, are you? They're trouble."

"We'll need to speak to my director of goat programming. You don't get milk without babies, and you don't get babies without a buck. But Cori Hogan is on your side in thinking that romance only brings strife to the hobby farmer."

"At least Cori and I agree on something. *Hey!*" Kellan jerked suddenly to one side, as if someone had yanked his strings.

Turned out that was exactly what had happened. The black-and-white puppet-master had circled around the house and crept along the side porch to seize Kellan's hat from his dangling fingertips. The dog charged down the front steps with his prize, giving it the ruthless shake that had killed many a hat before this one.

"Keats! Bring that back," I said. "The chief will get called before Council about reckless spending on headgear."

The dog pranced and sashayed, flaunting his catch. The time for serious discussion had ended, it seemed. Keats was all about the work-life balance. Or at least, balancing different kinds of work. For him, fun was mainly restricted to tormenting Kellan.

"Let's go down and christen Goat Disneyland," I said, as Keats charged ahead with the hat.

"I've got work to do," he said. "And you've got staying safe to do."

Keats appeared in the highest turret and dangled the hat over the edge. Edna and Gertie stopped working to laugh at his antics.

"Want me to get that for you, Chief?" Edna called. "It'll cost you my driver's license."

Kellan walked toward the police SUV instead. "You'll need to do a lot more than rescue a standard police issue hat to get back on the road, Miss Evans. Your crimes against the highway act are substantial."

She climbed up the goat castle with ease, took the hat and waved it. "Oh yeah? Who died and made you king, Kellan Harper?"

Keats managed to snatch the hat again and charged down the gangplank, where Gertie nabbed it. She walked over to the fence and tossed it to Kellan.

"Traitor," Edna called.

"I owe the chief a hat and far more, old friend," Gertie said. "In my bunker, it's all about strategic alliances."

"See?" I said, as Kellan opened the car door and tossed the hat onto the passenger seat. "You've got your official army, and then you've got your apocalyptic army. How many cops can say that?"

He wiped his hand on his uniformed pant leg and shook his head. "Apocalyptic nannies... Well, I'll reserve judgment till the zombie uprising. In the meantime, you owe me for another hat, Ms. Galloway."

"Now that I have a castle, I'm going by *Queen* Galloway."

"Be careful, your majesty," he said. "There's intrigue and betrayal in every court."

"Bring it on. I'll toss dissenters to the zombies."

He gave me a gorgeous smile as he drove off and I savored it, knowing that if things went as I planned, I might not see one quite like it for a while.

CHAPTER FIFTEEN

"You know that old saying, 'there's no place like home?'" I asked Keats and Percy, as we plodded through dense overgrowth that was just beginning to green up. "I don't get that vibe here. The Galloway ancestral home doesn't have any feel-good magic."

Keats mumbled his agreement. His tail was only at half mast, whereas he normally loved to explore new sites. Granted, bushwhacking wasn't his favorite way to do it.

After Gertie and Edna finished their goat castle and left, I'd decided to drive over to the property my father's family used to own. A little research had told me the home had changed hands a lot over the years and was currently empty. That was strange, because it was in a great location, about halfway between my farm and town. Once the land had been farmed for crops, but it had been left untended for so long that the forest was taking over again. That happened surprisingly quickly around here. It was like a dark force.

"Maybe it's haunted," I said. "Do you think so?"

Keats turned to give me what looked like an eye roll. I wasn't sure whether or not he believed in such things. While he clearly had capabilities other dogs did not, they were still grounded in the possible for a brilliant border collie. He was observant, vigilant and diligent. If I added a new critter at the farm, he applied himself to learning and growing. Herding Percy was like military training that wired new neural pathways daily.

The cat turned now and for a second I thought I saw a Cheshire grin. Then he blinked twice and turned back to leading us. As the smallest and most agile, he could cut his way through the bush better than Keats. I had to hand it to Percy: he loved his creature comforts but when the going got tough, he was a fluffy marmalade soldier.

"I say it's haunted," I continued. "There's a bad vibe here. And since the house has been on the market for ages, I bet Calvin's hiding out here. I figured he'd have come back for his wallet by now. I should have kept the forty bucks."

Keats gave a polite sneeze of laughter but he wasn't really in the mood for jokes. If I'd let him steer, we'd be back at the truck, which I parked in the bush near the highway. Edna was going to be annoyed I'd come without her but she had looked pretty beat by the time the goat gym was done, and I was too impatient to wait.

Trudging on, we finally made it to the house. I already knew what to expect from the real estate listing online. It had been kept up fairly well, but still had an unloved look to it.

Stepping into the open, I said, "Well, boys? Is he here?"

The dog's tail drifted slowly down and the cat's lashed a few times. Apparently, the mission was a bust. Keats was disappointed and Percy annoyed that I'd pulled him away from a busy afternoon of relaxing.

"Let's go inside," I said. "It's not breaking in when it's empty. Especially when the house belonged to your disreputable ancestors."

I varied my personal policies around trespassing to suit the situation.

Keats' tail came up and he found a genuine ha-ha-ha. Things were getting more interesting.

I expected the usual challenges, but a quick sniff around by my tuxedoed companion revealed a key under a chipped plaster gnome that really did resemble Finn Donnelly, my grumpy guest at the inn.

"Too easy, right? It's like someone's inviting us in for an open house showing."

I pulled out my phone and texted Jilly to let her know I was running late on my errands. No need to alarm her. Keats continued to behave as if the house was free from threat. At worst, I'd run into some old ghosts.

Inside, I turned on my phone light and looked around. The place had been renovated since it belonged to Chester and Polly Galloway, yet it likely still had the same basic layout, with a large dining room, a smaller living room with a massive fireplace, and what was probably a sitting room or parlor. The kitchen was outdated but well maintained, and I wondered again why the property sat vacant. Real estate was hot in Clover Grove.

Getting a foothold in Dorset Hills was out of reach for most, so we'd become both a bedroom community and a slice of homesteader paradise.

"Something's hinky," I said. "But I'm not getting old Galloway vibes. Probably for the best, I guess. Better to keep looking forward, like everyone says. Right, boys?"

The boys were indeed looking forward. Tails high, they led me up an oak staircase that had been grand once, but was now worn, chipped and dusty. Halfway up, they stopped and stared back at me. On the railing beside them a handprint had disturbed the dust... and fairly recently at that. I held my hand over it and noted that the print likely belonged to a man. Calvin had probably beaten me there and taken a trip down memory lane. Understandable, I supposed.

We walked from room to room upstairs and found nothing but a few battered pieces of furniture deemed unworthy of moving by the last homesteaders. There was no historical value in any of them, I was sure. In the last room—the smallest—I looked into the open closet and found scratches and numerals etched into the wood of the doorframe. Height markings that may have dated back to Calvin's youth. If so, someone had charted his growth right up to six feet.

The thought of someone caring enough to mark that passage—perhaps on every birthday—made my fists clench. Why hadn't he stayed to do that for us? Granted, there were barely enough doors in our house for so many kids, but a parent should find a way to commemorate accomplishments, even the mere fact of growing up.

Keats whined, jarring me out of my reverie. "Sorry,

buddy. You're right. I fell into that self-pity trap again, didn't I? If Calvin had stayed, my life would have been different, but not necessarily better. Maybe I wouldn't have been so desperate to leave town, and if I hadn't moved to Boston, I'd never have met you."

Percy gave a little mew.

"Or you, my sweet fluff." I bent over to let the cat jump onto my shoulder.

Getting my head on straight paid off immediately. If I hadn't leaned over for Percy, I wouldn't have looked under the dresser.

"Hang on a sec," I said, dropping to my knees and reaching for a small piece of paper. Part of me expected to see yellowed stationery etched with Polly's no-doubt elegant handwriting. Instead it was just regular lined paper with a few lines of writing in a nearly illegible script.

"Looks like a riddle," I said, shining the phone light on it. "Or a bit of a poem." Holding it closer I read aloud:

When I think of thee by our tree my heart grows sad and weary.

Have need of me and turn the key and soon you will be cheery.

Keats looked up at me and lifted his paw in a point. It was his way of telling me an object was significant, no matter how innocuous it might seem.

"Well, that's interesting," I said, pocketing the note. "Kellan mentioned something about Frank's riddles earlier, but this is no antique."

The white paw touched down and I assumed I was

on the right track. "Well, let's get going then. I think we've done all we can here."

Both animals scampered down the staircase, clearly anxious to shake the dust off their paws. I put the key back under the chipped gnome and started to retrace our steps to the truck.

Keats wasn't happy about heading into the bush. In fact, he circled me repeatedly to drive me to the gravel lane.

"Buddy, I hear you but I want to stay out of sight. Maybe poke around a bit more. What if there's a shed or an outbuilding where Calvin's been shacking up? Did you think of that?"

He gave a disgusted rumble. Of course, he'd thought of that and found it a waste of precious time that could be used tracking bigger and better clues.

It turned into a rare clash of wills. Normally, when Keats spoke, I listened. I knew he had his reasons for steering me differently even if I didn't understand them. But today I wanted to forge my own way, so I sidestepped the dog and kept walking into the bush.

Percy waited behind us, howling mournfully. The little orange soldier had had enough adventure for one day.

When Keats started taking little nips at my pant legs, I began evasive maneuvers, dodging and weaving. And when he circled around me and pressed me back, quite literally, I grabbed a sapling and swung around it.

There was a moment of carefree fun in the spin and I actually laughed before the cracking sound. The sapling in my hand snapped and in the same moment, the earth shifted under my boots. Suddenly, I was falling into darkness.

I landed on my side with a bone-jarring thud that reverberated through my body.

Somewhere above, Keats let out a heartrending wail.

"I'm okay, buddy," I called, before I knew that to be true. Everything hurt from the impact, but nothing sang out of broken bones. Groping in the darkness, I found a wall and got to my feet.

"Yep, I really am okay. Don't worry." I reached into my coat pocket and gasped when I discovered my phone had disappeared. "Uh-oh. Scratch that. You can worry a little because I don't have my phone. And without it, this hole could easily become my grave. Not to be overly dramatic."

Keats whined in response. In the faint light of an opening that looked to be around 10 feet above me, I could see the merest hint of his blue eye gleaming.

"I mean, what are the chances of falling into a cave on the property of my ancestors?"

Now the dog grumbled, and it was very much an "I told you so."

"Yeah, obviously it would have been smarter to listen to you. But I'm in it now. Literally. I'm going to see if I can find my phone down here. And I'm not going to panic until... Well, I'm not going to panic at all. We've been in worse predicaments, right? There's no killer down here in the ancestral Galloway cave. Just damp dank earth."

Lowering myself to one knee I groped around, trying not to think about what I might end up touching. Like a rat. Or a snake. Or just garden variety slimy slugs. There was no telling how deep or wide the space was and the phone may well be yards away.

Keats sent down an encouraging mumble and the sound formed a thin barrier between me and hysteria.

"So, I don't know if I mentioned I'm claustrophobic," I said. "That's also Asher's fault. When we were kids he'd trap me in closets or trunks or boxes. Anyplace, really. He must have had a lot of repressed anger after his father left." Percy offered an odd meow. "Yes, I have time for pop psychology. I've got nothing *but* time, apparently, since I can't find the phone."

Percy let out another, louder meow. A "pay attention, lunkhead," kind of sound.

"If you have an idea, I'm all ears, Percy."

What I noticed first was the circle of light on the dirt. It was coming from the cave's opening.

"My phone! You found it! You're both getting sardines tonight. Now, just flick it down here, Percy. Tap it from the side if you can so that the light stays on. That'll keep me from getting hit in the head."

The phone hit me in the head. And because the light went out, I couldn't see it to grab it. Luckily the thud helped me figure out its approximate landing position.

"Got it! Whoo-hoo! You're geniuses, both of you. Now let's pray there's a signal." I touched the screen and saw just one bar and worse, very little battery charge left.

The next mumble overhead was a query.

"It's not the best news, boys. Kind of like getting that one phone call from jail and the line might be dead." I reached up as high as I could in hopes of improving the signal and then pressed the number.

It rang and rang. I held my breath to the point of lightheadedness, and then finally, someone answered.

"I'm trying to take a nap, dagnabit. Building your goat castle was enough for one day, wasn't it?"

"Not really, no. I've fallen into a cave, Edna."

"I can barely hear you. I'm not forty, as much as I delude myself, and my hearing's not what it was."

I put the phone on speaker and yelled, "Using ear protection while operating a chainsaw would help."

"Are you really calling to lecture me about ear protection? Just speak up for pity's sake so I can enjoy a very well-earned grapefruit martini. I don't often indulge myself but I earned it today."

"You're going to earn it even more by getting me out of this cave, Edna."

"You're breaking up. Speak louder, dagnabit. It sounds like you said cave. Or save. Or wave? I don't have time for guessing games."

I took a chance and lowered the phone. "I fell into a cave. I'm stuck down here and I need you to come over and pull me out."

There was a moment of silence where I worried I'd lost her. Lost the signal. Lost my one chance at rescue. And then, "Is this a joke, Ivy Rose Galloway? Because we are way past that today."

"Just come and get me. I'm on the old Galloway property. Where Calvin grew up. It was last owned by—"

"I'm well aware of where Calvin grew up. There are

no caves in that region. I've crisscrossed that terrain and mapped it many times. In case of—"

"I don't have time to argue. I fell into a deep hole and my phone's dying. Just hurry, before it gets dark. Keats and Percy will come to the driveway to show you the way."

"And what exactly am I supposed to drive, Ivy? It'll take ages on my ATV and I'll need equipment."

"Call Gertie," I said. "She'll come fully equipped and you can grab a cab and meet her here."

"You're breaking up again. When we're done, turn off your phone to save your power. Send Keats to get me. And Percy, you go down and keep Ivy company. Otherwise, she's going to freak out."

"I'm not freaking out. I mean, I worry about snakes and rats and—"

"That sounds like freaking out to me. Percy, down with you. And Ivy, not another word." She sounded capable, efficient. I knew I'd made the right call. Literally.

"Don't tell—"

"Of course I won't tell Chief Hottie McSnobalot. I want to see his face when *you* tell him. Now turn off that phone."

She hung up and I left the light on long enough for Percy to slide down the slight slope of the wall until I could grab him. He instantly became my purring, furry lifeline. With him cradled in my arms, I dared to shine the light around the cave to see exactly what I was facing. My mind was full of unpleasant ideas.

As it turned out, the open space where I'd landed led to what appeared to be a long tunnel.

"Oooh boy," I said. "This is just the rotunda, and I have no interest whatsoever in exploring where that tunnel goes. If there's gold, the hobbits or dragons can keep it."

Keats panted a ha-ha-ha, which was surprising under the circumstances. I took that to mean all would be well when Gertie and Edna arrived. Even using the back trails at high speed, it would take Edna 15 minutes and Gertie 25. I probably didn't have even that much power left on my phone. It was time to conserve so that I could shine the light when they arrived. The days were getting longer but there was never much natural light in woods this dense.

"Okay, buddy," I called. "Percy and I are just going to pace around down here and sing sea shanties till you get back. I know you won't let me down. Even though I just let you down."

He mumbled something that sounded like, "apology accepted," and then he was gone. I could feel his departure, like a rubber band pulling away from my heart.

"What if that's the last time I see him? Hear that mumble?" I muttered. "He'll remember that I failed him."

I decided it was better to sit down, although the packed soil was chilly and damp. Percy settled between my crossed legs and purred, kneading my overalls to comfort me. Or himself.

"How about the sea shanties, my fluffy friend? Yay or nay?"

I expected a strident objection but he offered only a resigned meow.

And so I stroked the cat while lifting my voice to sing The Wellerman, over and over. The singing kept me from hyperventilating and eventually my heart dropped into a normal rhythm.

There was something about the old pull-together-on-the-high-seas tune that kept me grounded in this cave. It was a musical oxymoron.

Eventually a bright light appeared overhead and someone shouted, "Will you stop that infernal racket, dagnabit?"

CHAPTER SIXTEEN

I turned on my phone and directed the beam of the flashlight to the entrance of the cave. Under her camouflage hat, Edna's face looked rather spectral, but it wasn't my finest moment either. Both of us squinted as the lights conjoined to make the cave almost as bright as day.

"You probably don't want to blind me before I tie off the rope," Edna said. "Just a suggestion."

"I've never been so glad to see you, Edna," I called up. "Except maybe in the barnyard, the first time you saved my life."

"The first is always the best," she said as she cleared away some of the branches from the cave's opening. "Not to discount subsequent rescues that were equally spectacular."

"Is Keats okay?"

He stuck his muzzle under Edna's armpit and woofed triumphantly. He may not have been able to save me himself but he'd played a key role.

"Enough bragging," Edna said. "Go back to the driveway and collect Gertie when she gets here. I'm going down after Ivy and Gertie can help us both up."

"You don't need to come down here. I'll climb up the rope."

"You think I'd pass up an opportunity to check out someone else's design?"

"Design? What are you talking about?"

She swatted away the rest of the branches and I saw that the opening was actually about four feet wide. The foliage screen had made it seem much smaller.

"Your little hidey-hole is man-made," Edna said. "And covered over like some low budget Gilligan's Island episode. Or a Tarzan movie."

"Neither of which I've seen, Edna."

"Well, you haven't missed much, but they clearly inspired someone to great depths."

She disappeared for a minute or two and I heard a few "dagnabits" as she was finding a tree with the right qualities to be our ticket out. Then a thick, knotted rope dropped over the side and fell at my feet. It looked like it was fresh from one of the prepper stores she and Gertie kept in business.

"Are you saying I fell into a trap?"

"It is a trap because it wasn't properly covered, but that's not its primary function. Now, hold the rope while I come down."

Edna impressed me every single day with her fitness and dexterity, but seeing an octogenarian descend into a cave by a rope was certainly a defining moment. I could barely manage that now. Thank goodness I still had 50 years ahead to train.

"Can I go up now?" I asked. "It's felt like being stuck in a grave."

She flashed a high-powered light around and chuckled. "You'd better get used to that feeling, because what we have here isn't a cave or a trap. It's a bunker. Old-fashioned and refreshingly simple. It's damper than it should be because of inadequate sealing. But when the apocalypse comes, rain will be the least of our worries."

"Is this what *your* bunker looks like?" I asked. "Because I'm totally not okay with being trapped underground with snakes and rats and whatever else is down here."

"You'll change your tune when you see what's roaming the earth by that point," she said. "Whether it's zombies or crazed killers with souped-up machine guns. No sea shanties then."

I shuddered. It was all well and good to joke about bunkers and the zombie apocalypse, but seeing and feeling what that might actually be like made me more determined to avoid it. Keats mumbled his agreement overhead and Percy swished between my boots and Edna's. It was a silent pact to keep fighting the bad guys one by one in hopes of fending off a future so bleak.

"Let's go, Edna. Jilly's making a special dinner for our guests."

She deliberately let her light hit me in the face and I covered my eyes. "Hold onto your appetite. My payment for leaving my recliner and grapefruit martini is to poke around down here. Gertie will want to do the same, I'm sure." With a sweep of the light, she said, "Lead the way, Percy."

I thought he'd resist but his tail went up and he trotted right along. The adventures were few where Keats wasn't hogging the spotlight, literally or figuratively.

Edna followed, stooping to walk through the tunnel that was maybe five feet high.

"This is awful. I'm claustrophobic, Edna."

"Just a state of mind," she said. "Get excited about learning something."

"We'll never hear Gertie way in here."

"She'll figure it out. An underground bunker is nothing new to her."

The tunnel opened to a large chamber that could hold quite a few apocalyptic soldiers.

"How old is this place? Can you tell?"

"I'll have to do more analysis, but I'd guess at least eighty years."

"Who was prepping that long ago? Isn't that a modern thing?"

She led the way from the first cavern through another tunnel. "Think about it, Ivy. Caves have been our go-to place for safety since we emerged from them millennia ago. There's something very comforting about knowing you have one."

"It's not comforting at all to me. It's creepy. And I need my dog."

"Gertie will be down in a few minutes and you can wait for us upstairs. I'm not leaving till I've explored every last inch."

When the next cavern opened, she shone the light around. "Aha. I thought so."

Piled against one wall were tools. There were shovels in various sizes, an ax, a pick, a broom, a dustpan and tarps.

"How old are these?" I asked.

She bent to examine the equipment. "Fresh from the hardware store in town. Someone's been down here recently. I thought I saw a boot print in the first chamber."

"What's with the equipment? Is someone doing renovations?"

There was a sound behind us and I glanced quickly at Percy. His plumy tail rose not in warning but greeting.

Keats rushed into the chamber and I knelt to embrace him. Rarely had I been so happy to smell a damp, dirty dog. He grumbled and mumbled until Gertie emerged from the tunnel behind him and explained.

"I couldn't leave him up there alone," she said. "So I put him in a harness and lowered him. Don't think he liked that much, but he was a trooper."

I laughed. "Better than water, right buddy?"

Keats offered a ha-ha-ha of confirmation.

The beams from their lights made the cavern as bright as a movie set, and it felt just as fake. It was hard to believe this place had been around so long.

"Treasure hunters," Gertie said, checking out the tools. "I know the signs."

"Do you think Frank Swenson built this place?" I asked.

"He wasn't the only one hiding booty back in the

day," Gertie said. "But he was in cahoots with your father's family. They had loot to hide, but more importantly, they sometimes had to hide from those they looted."

"And probably the police of the time," I said.

Gertie shook her head. "Payoffs took care of that. Regardless, a bunker was a sensible investment in man hours even then."

Edna let Gertie take the lead after Keats and Percy as we headed into the next chamber. I felt far calmer with my canine sidekick. The white tuft of his tail fanned to tell me we were safe enough down here.

There were more tools in the next cavern, but these qualified as antiques with cracked leather and decaying wood. Dusty and disintegrating relics of a lawless time.

"This is the end of it," Gertie said. "Whatever may have been stashed here is long gone. It looks like someone beat us to the prize."

"Calvin," I said. "I bet he knew about the place from his childhood."

Gertie nodded. "Probably. But I know from experience that people will hunt and hunt till they either get lucky or drop. Just like you got lucky today."

"I dropped," I said. "Although I suppose I was lucky in not breaking my neck. Keats warned me away but I wouldn't listen."

"Maybe luckier still," Edna said. "Look at the dog now."

Keats was ahead of us in the shadows. His white tail stood straight out and when Edna moved around to throw better light, I saw his white paw had lifted in a point. He was staring at the final wall.

Taking the light from Edna, I crouched beside him. There was a little nook near the floor that barely looked big enough for a human hand. When I directed the light into it, however, silver gleamed back.

"There's something in there." Holding out my hand I said, "Screwdriver."

I wasn't at all surprised Edna had one.

It only took a second to poke out the object.

"It's a dagger," Edna said, for once stating the obvious.

"Not just *a* dagger," I said, glancing at Keats. "*The* dagger. The one that killed Daphne Newell."

CHAPTER SEVENTEEN

"You wouldn't believe it," I said, walking along the trails beyond the pastures at Runaway Farm. "It was one of the most exciting things ever to happen to me, and I'm no slouch in the thrills department."

Normally Keats would weigh in with a mumble, but he knew I wasn't addressing my comment to him. My leashed companion was caprine rather than canine. Charlie had made a goat harness so that I could offer even more enrichment to my newest guests. He had warned me against taking Big Mama out alone because she might bolt and drag me. I decided to take the risk anyway. The way she kept a wary eye on Keats told me she knew better.

"So Kellan came and gave me quite a lecture, as you can imagine, even though he was happy about the knife. I mean, if you can be happy about finding a murder weapon. I guess that's what he meant when he said no one loves police work, per se. At least we're one step closer to figuring out who's behind this. The police are going over the place with a fine-tooth comb." I shook my head. "If I never see the inside of a bunker again, that'll be okay by me. I'll take my chances on the zombies."

Big Mama let out a long bleat. She had a surprisingly deep and almost melodious voice. It was good to hear her talking, even if I didn't know what she was saying.

"Maybe you're tired of hearing about our exploits, and I don't blame you. Solving murders isn't for everyone."

Keats let out a rumble to confirm it was definitely for him and I laughed. "Not everyone shares our thirst for adventure, buddy. Big Mama is probably just glad to get out for some fresh air and exercise. Trust me, Big M, after what happened today, I really relate to how it feels to be cooped up."

I let the dog herd us to the top of a small hill and it seemed like we all sucked in deep breaths of the cool spring air. "It was so stuffy down there. I felt trapped and scared, I won't lie." Patting the goat's well-groomed side, I added, "I bet you felt the same way at your old home. If you can call it that. Cori said it was awful."

Big Mama gave another bleat. This one sounded plaintive.

"You didn't want to have your babies there. Totally get it. And while I know better than most how hard it is to trust, I hope you'll give us a chance. I don't claim to be a goat expert, but I'm a good researcher and I'll learn the ropes. One thing you should know is that I always take accountability for my mistakes when I see them. I shouldn't have assumed all goats are pretty much the same. You're an individual and we'll get to know each other one to one. It's not just about goat castles but quality time."

Keats' next grumble sounded skeptical.

"I know, buddy. It's hard to find those moments but it's important. I've made the very difficult decision to spend less time on manure and more on bonding with the livestock. After all, anyone can turn poop. It would be good for Poppy to develop pipes like mine and with some micromanagement from me, she can get the job done right."

Big Mama offered what sounded like an approving baa. Almost gentle. Clearly, I had misjudged her. Happily, there was time to course correct and open those lines of communication.

"Just one last thing. I really want to be there when you have those babies. But if I can't, I'll make sure someone is with you. You're never alone at Runaway Farm."

Keats agreed and after that, we walked in what felt like companionable silence. It replenished me even more than manure, I realized. Goat walking was my new thing.

Half an hour later, I left Big Mama ruminating contentedly in her stall as I headed up to the house.

"That's how it's done, Keats," I said. "Gotta win them over one at a time, no matter how many there are. It's a little daunting but connecting with animals is the highest reward."

The guests were already sitting down to dinner by the time I'd showered and changed. The evening felt festive after what I'd been through, so I put on a dress. That won me an approving smile from Jilly, who liked it when I went to the trouble of looking like an innkeeper rather than just a farmer.

She brought in two large serving dishes containing her upscale macaroni and cheese. While she repeatedly tested more elaborate fare on our guests, everyone seemed to want old familiars. Comfort food, taken up a notch with Jilly's judicious enhancements. No one even knew what magic she'd added, but the rapidly emptying plates attested to her gifts.

"How are your family trees shaping up?" she asked, when the tinkle of forks on china began slowing.

"Very well, I think," said Kathleen. "There is nothing more satisfying than seeing all the pieces of your personal puzzle fall into place."

I could think of plenty of more satisfying things. Like bonding with your goats. Like having your friends rescue you from a bunker. Like solving a murder. Just to name a few.

"Have you done your own family tree, Jilly?" Walt asked. His fatherly smile suggested Jilly and I were in for a lecture.

"I'm not that close to my family," Jilly said, getting up to serve second helpings. "And I'm not terribly curious about those who came before."

"Jilly," he said, "how can you know who you are without knowing where you came from?"

"Some stones are better left unturned." She laughed lightly. "But I think it's wonderful that you all take such joy in this."

"How about the Galloways, Ivy?" he said, trying me

again. "With such a large family, someone must be interested in digging into the family's past."

I handed Jilly my plate and then shook my head. "I don't know about my siblings, but it hasn't been a priority for me. As you can see, I have my hands full here."

Our guests looked at each other with obvious disappointment. They were full of zeal for their work and hoped it would be contagious. I thought about changing the subject, but a good host played to the guests' interests. Jilly had drilled that into me and normally led the way. Now she'd disappeared into the kitchen leaving me on the hook.

"Tell me what you get out of digging into your pasts," I said. "I'm really curious to know more."

"That's it, exactly," Walt said. "It's all about curiosity. About finding out what genes mixed together to cook up a unique dish like you."

Brenda giggled. "Oh, Walt, you're terrible."

"It's like holding up a mirror, Ivy," Kathleen said. "If you haven't done that work, what do you see?"

I grinned at her. "Honestly? When I look in the mirror, I see horns."

"Horns!" Brenda sounded shocked. Horrified, even.

"Horns, hooves and tails," I said. "Features vary by the day. I am my animals."

"Well, I don't even know what to say to that," Kathleen said.

"I do," Jilly said, coming back into the dining room with a sticky toffee pudding that smelled like heaven. "I say think a little bigger, Ivy. You're much more than your animals."

"You'll only know that when you start at the roots," Walt said. "Build yourself up from your very foundations. It's the most thrilling thing in the world when you unearth a new relative." He laughed before adding, "Not literally, of course. On paper only."

"Or digitally," Kathleen said. "Increasingly so these days. People just send in a sample and all kinds of secrets spill out. If your relatives are doing the same, a global family tree can sprout up in a shockingly short time."

"We're old school, though," Brenda said. "It's not about the sudden scoop. It's about the gradual piecing together. The thrill of the unexpected discovery."

"Like treasure hunting," I said. There was a hungry gleam in every eye around the table that would never be satiated by sticky toffee pudding. It was the adrenaline hit that came from finding that nugget of gold in any form. I had seen that gleam time and again, and I'm sure it was in my eye too, sometimes. I was a collector, too, of all things furry.

"That's the dream," Finn said, starting in on dessert without waiting for the rest to be served. "We all hope to find that one gem of a relative. The celebrity who can change our lives."

"Someone I know learned her grandmother was a famous singer," Brenda said. "Imagine that. They reunited and she's set for life, now."

"On the flip side, some roots long buried are rotten," Walt said. "It's important to know that, too. It can come as quite a shock."

Jilly and I both nodded. We didn't need to be told about rot at the core.

"Is that what happened with Daphne?" I asked. "I heard she was upset the day she passed."

Walt raised a hand. "Chief Coots came by again and told us not to discuss Daphne anymore. I think they're making progress in the case."

"I understand," I said. "As an innkeeper, you worry. Something happened to a guest under my roof and she fled within an hour of arrival."

"It wasn't like that," Brenda said, turning her chair a little to avoid Walt's eye. "It seemed like she just had one of those eureka moments. She wanted to go home and collect more photos. We were all going to chat about it when she got back."

"How sad she didn't get that chance," I said. "Did you sense it was a bad eureka moment or a good one?"

"Honestly, it wasn't clear," Brenda continued, as Walt tapped the table to get her attention. "Sometimes you don't know what to think when you make one of those discoveries. That's what we're here for. To support each other and offer perspective. We could all do this work alone, but putting our heads together makes it easier and more satisfying."

"I can see why," Jilly said. "You've found your birds of a feather."

"And when you lose one, it hurts," Brenda said. "Daphne was a lot of fun. At least until recently."

"Something changed?" I said. "Was it to do with this work?"

"There was no reason to think so," Kathleen said.

"She had other ghosts from her past," Joanne said. "Of the human variety."

"Don't we all," I said.

"Definitely," Jilly chimed in.

Joanne sighed. "I tried to get her to talk it out, but she was just one raw nerve the past couple of weeks. I seriously thought she'd pull out of this retreat. Maybe she should have."

"I suppose some skeletons are best left undisturbed," I said.

"Personally, I think it's always better to know," Joanne said.

"Unless the skeleton bites," Finn said. "Some do."

A loud knock at the back door made all of us jump.

"There's a skeleton out there, Finn," Walt said, laughing. "And it's coming for you."

CHAPTER EIGHTEEN

Laughter followed as I walked into the kitchen to open the door. Keats came too, acting all officious, and then dropped to his belly.

"What's up with that?" I said. "Is it Kellan? Are you readying for an ambush?"

It was an ambush all right, but nothing I'd ever experienced before.

Big Mama pushed open the door with her head and waltzed right into the kitchen. Her hooves clattered over the tiles as she sauntered to the counter and seized a whisk—Jilly's culinary tool of choice. The sticky toffee sauce it had stirred dripped onto the floor as she butted open the dining room door.

"Keats, get her," I said, although of course he was already trying to do just that. My reaction time was abysmal and even his was slow, thanks to the new environment. Herding animals with plenty of room outside was one thing. Herding them in a full dining room was another.

I grabbed two dog leashes that hung by the back door, and then slipped into my jacket. Meanwhile, a bloodcurdling scream from a guest suggested serious injury. When I joined them, however, all I could see was Kathleen pulling the sticky whisk out of her gray hair. Short and sensible now seemed very much the way to go.

"Stay calm," I said, as Big Mama clattered away into the family room. "The goat is overstimulated, that's all. Keats will herd her up and take her back down to the barn."

"What on earth is she doing in the house, Ivy?" Jilly asked. "Isn't this taking enrichment too far?"

"Our bonding exercise must have gone too well," I said, following the goat. "I can only assume she jumped out of her pen and kicked the barn door open." Then it hit me. "Oh no. The others might follow."

In the time it took me to text Edna for help, Big Mama had climbed onto one of the tables set up in the family room for the genealogy project. Surprisingly nimble for her advanced pregnancy, she hopped from table to table leaving muddy prints on their precious documents. Keats couldn't do a thing about it except follow and try to catch her eye with the mesmerizing sheepdog gaze. She paid him no heed. Exploring was definitely more enriching. When she got to the last table, however, she took a good sniff, kicked up a little flurry of photos and then hopped across to the leather couch.

"I'm trying not to scream, Ivy," Jilly said. "That's designer Italian leather, from Hannah. The nicest piece here."

"I know, I know. Go open the front door."

Keats skulked to the couch, where Big Mama stood chewing on something. He went for the element of surprise and jumped over the armrest. One nip to the lower leg and the goat was off and running again. He used all his best moves to maneuver her around the furniture.

It looked like he was winning, but then she took a sudden turn, leapt over the dog and charged at me. Her head was down and it looked like I'd be taking this hit right in the macaroni. If I chose to jump aside, she might go for the guests, who were spectating from the doorway.

"Stop that right now," I said, holding up both hands. "That is no way to behave in the house. If there's something you need, we can head down to the barn and talk there."

She stopped on a dime and simply pressed her head into my midriff. I scratched her ears and sides, murmuring sweet nothings to calm her down. One of the women cooed, "awww," while another grumbled about their work being ruined.

"I'm so sorry, everyone," I said. "This is probably her time."

"Her time for what?" Finn asked. "To wreak havoc on years of work?"

"To deliver her babies," I said. "My goat doula warned me about unpredictable behavior."

"Please, Ivy," Jilly called from the door. "Tell me she won't give birth on the leather couch."

"Not if I can help it," I said. "I hear it can happen fast, so I'd better get moving." I looped both leashes around Big Mama's neck and tried leading her to the door. The goat brakes went on, scraping over the hard-wood floor as I tugged. Keats delivered encouragement from behind but she was willing to put up with his nips to continue enjoying the comforts of the inn.

An unexpected ally joined the fray. Percy unfurled from a chair in the corner, ran lightly along the back of the couch and jumped on the goat's back. That finally startled her enough to get some forward motion. Then, with Keats basically pushing and me pulling, we got Big Mama out the front door. Outside, Percy jumped off and we escorted her down to the barn without further trouble.

Meanwhile the roar of an ATV began in the distance and Edna's custom floodlights shone out over the field. The cavalry was on the way.

Big Mama went willingly into her stall and I closed the door before checking the others. Sure enough, her friends had followed her example and bolted.

"Go help Edna," I told Keats, and he took off like a shot.

I circled Big Mama inside her stall, looking for the warning signs Gertie had told me about. Everything looked about standard for a lady goat, and the same as it had less than two hours ago.

Edna walked in with Keats and the other goats. "The good news is that I found them trying to climb into the goat pasture," she said. "They love their jungle gym that much."

"And the bad news?" I asked, folding my arms over the top of the pen.

"If I can't get a moment's downtime between 911

calls, you're going to have to put me on retainer." She stepped sideways to see Big Mama. "And more bad news? You're going to get a butt in the butt again if you don't get a move on it."

I opened the door and scooted out. "She's even crazier than usual, Edna. Do you think she's about to deliver?"

"Gertie's the goat doula. Why not call her out on a chilly night?"

I gave Edna my sweetest smile. "Because you're closer? And you said you'd delivered plenty of babies."

"Human babies, not goat babies. Sometimes we say things in hubris we regret later."

I got out my phone and went back into the pen to shoot a video to send to Gertie. "Let's get an expert opinion."

Gertie called me a few minutes later. "Honestly, Ivy, you're a full-time job."

"I said the same thing," Edna said, as I put the phone on speaker. "It's time to unionize, Gertie. Meanwhile Ivy is getting way too personal with that goat. It's indecent."

"Doesn't look like Big Mama is ready to pull the trigger based on your video," Gertie said. "Do you want me to come over to be sure?"

I did want her to come over to be sure. I wanted her to move right in until all three does had done their thing. And maybe longer. But I reminded myself that both women were over 80, even if they acted half that. No matter how animals got foisted on me, they were my responsibility, including and especially late night deliveries.

"I'll be fine," I said. "I'll sleep down here with her. Like Cori suggested."

"Go up and change first," Edna said. "You'll catch your death, and then we'll have to work even harder."

"I'm not going back in there right now," I said. "The genealogy society is a little upset about Big Mama trampling their work. Rightly so."

Edna laughed. "What a waste of time that could be better spent on target practice, or swordplay. Gertie and I are working with a master swordsman. It's surprisingly complicated to get a sword off your back and ready for business while you're running."

"Wait till we try horseback," Gertie called. "I've updated my will and made appropriate arrangements, Ivy."

"You're telling me this why?" I asked.

"You're my executor," she said. "Edna's, too."

"I don't want to think about that," I said. "Go to bed, ladies. I'm going to switch Big Mama into the larger pen and then bed down with her. I'll call if anything exciting happens."

"I have no doubt of that," Gertie said, before hanging up.

Edna looked torn about leaving but ultimately let me persuade her to go. She must have been very tired indeed to give up so easily. She'd gone above and beyond, however, and if anyone should be helping me now, it was the Rescue Mafia.

"That's what I should do," I told Big Mama as Keats saw Edna to her ATV, like the tuxedoed gentleman he was. "Cori Hogan should come over to bring these kids into the world. It's all her fault you're stuck with a doula newbie. I'm sorry about that. But I'm going to see this through myself."

It didn't take Keats long to switch up the animals and I texted Jilly to say I'd be awhile. After locking the barn door, I gathered some towels and the birthing kit, and then put up some plastic fencing to portion off a bit of the pen for my sleeping area. Then I wrapped myself in a couple of horse blankets and curled up with Keats and Percy.

Big Mama seemed content now that she had company. She pulled idly at the hay and offered a baa that sounded oddly maternal.

"It's like she's telling me to go to sleep," I said. "Like that's going to happen."

Only it did happen. The excitement of falling into a hidden bunker seemed to have tired me even more than it did my elder comrades.

Sometime later, the phone woke me up. Fumbling for the button, I said, "Hey Cori. What's up?"

"Just checking on Big Mama." There was a strange echoing sound on her end. Maybe she was in the bathroom.

"Oh yeah? It's late." I checked the phone to make sure it was, in fact, late. It felt like I'd been asleep for several days. The straw was surprisingly comfortable. It was sucking me down like the mud in the swamp, only nicer. There were sweet dreams here instead of leeches.

"Sure is," Cori said. "Goats love popping out those kids in the dead of night. You never can tell when it'll happen."

I sat up and stared at Big Mama. She was down on her side with her eyes closed. There was no sign of distress, but I wasn't facing the business end. Surely there would be some heavy breathing? She wouldn't sleep through it, would she? And if she did, what would happen to the babies? Or... what if she hadn't made it? I couldn't tell if she was breathing at all.

I jumped to my feet, wobbling drunkenly because I forgot I was wearing heels. Bracing myself on the stall, I hobbled around the partition and then right around the goat. All good. No surprise babies. Bending, I rested my hand on her side. Still breathing. I let out a long breath myself. How many times had I checked animals—especially Keats—to make sure they were doing just that? I wished they'd put up a "just sleeping" sign for the anxious hobby farmer. It was impossible to learn the ways of so many animals so fast.

At least, it felt like that now, when I was disoriented at midnight after a nap in the barn.

Keats scratched at the stall door and whined but I ignored him. There were bigger fish to fry at the moment. Percy, on the other hand, didn't wait for permission. He leapt over and disappeared.

"I'm waiting..." Cori said.

"Big Mama's fine," I said. "Not a mama yet. She's catching a little shuteye. Tired out from rampaging through the house earlier. Gave the guests something to talk about."

Cori laughed. "I heard. Edna told me you'd had a hard day's sleuthing and she worried you wouldn't notice if baby goats were popping. She wants me to spell you."

"I'm fine! No need. All good here."

"Yeah? Well, you've looked better."

"*Looked* better? Where are you?"

I turned quickly and saw the tiny trainer sitting on a bale of hay across the barn. She waved one black glove, making sure to offer a flash of neon orange middle finger.

"Howdy," she said, grinning. "You sure did look sweet sleeping in the hay with your animals. But you snored louder than any of them."

"Cori, I locked the doors. How did you get in here?"

She jumped off the bale and came over. "I have my ways."

"You have your ways into my barn?"

She shrugged. "Think of it as my barn, too. A Rescue Mafia outpost. This way we can get inside to help the animals when needed. Let's face it, Ivy, you could use backup sometimes."

"But if you have a secret way in, others may use it."

"Do I look stupid?" she asked, putting her phone away.

Most of us looked stupid sometimes, but never Cori. She was always alert and had the bright, sharp eyes of a bird. A raven, maybe.

"Hardly," I said. "Anyway, I'm awake now, and I'll set my alarm on the half hour to make sure nothing slips past me."

"Ivy, I'm here and I take orders from Edna on occasion. So, go on up to bed and come down when Aladdin crows. It's not the first time I've stood watch in this barn and it won't be the last. Plus I'm coming off a slow patch on the rescue front. My sleep bank is topped up."

Keats whined again and when I opened the door, he ran over to Cori, abasing himself with the showy greeting only she warranted.

"Do you want Keats to stay down here with you?" I asked.

She shook her head, and I saw the benefit of the gamine cut. Her shiny dark hair didn't move, whereas mine felt frizzy and full of straw.

"Clem is in the truck. I'll bring him in." She gave me an appraising glance. "I bet you looked quite nice a few hours ago."

My dress was creased and stained with heaven knows what. There was always something gooey around here and it was better not to worry about specifics. I bent over to scrape at some muck on my shoe, and that's when I saw the half-chewed remains of a photo near Big Mama's head. I grabbed both pieces and stuck them in my coat pocket to peruse later, out of Cori's sharp-eyed sight.

"I made an effort for dinner with the guests," I told her as I left the pen. "Now I remember why I don't bother."

"You don't need to impress anyone," Cori said. "People pleasing is a weakness in a hobby farmer and a potentially fatal flaw in a sleuth."

"Sounds about right," I said, walking toward the barn door, which was still locked.

Before I got there, I turned just in time to see Cori hop right over the wall and into Big Mama's pen. Grinning back at me, she called, "Can you do that?"

I had about 10 inches on Cori and was fitter than I

ever had been. But if I attempted a jump like that, it would not end well, either for me or the animal inside.

"I have other gifts," I said. Energy was flowing through my limbs now and I wondered if I'd be able to sleep once I got to bed. "Plenty of them."

"Vanity," she called after me. "The other enemy of the farmer-sleuth."

Keats offered a ha-ha-ha. He always found Cori even more amusing than she found herself.

"I'm not vain," I told him. "And you're on my side, remember? She's got her own brilliant dog and doesn't need another groupie."

I gave Cori a sprightly wave as we left, hoping she'd sense my imaginary neon orange flipping finger. Her laugh suggested she had and that made me smile, too.

It was good to have friends who'd spell you in the night, even if they called you out in the process.

CHAPTER NINETEEN

I didn't make it very far up the path before realizing I was being herded back down.

"What's the problem?" I asked Keats. "If you want to join Cori and Clem to play midwife, that's okay by me. I'm going to get some sleep."

We were right at the spot where the lights from the house and barn reached out to each other and didn't quite meet. Yet I could still see the gleam in the dog's blue eye. He wasn't interested in goat babies, it seemed. There were more pressing issues at hand.

Once he had my full attention, he mumbled a question.

"No, we cannot go for a drive, Keats. Cori would hear us leave and she's here so we can sleep, not joyride."

He circled around me again, and then took a little dive at my toes.

"Keats, come on. We'll tootle all over town in the morning if you want. I promise."

This time he went for my ankle and I jumped. Thin nylon didn't offer the protection of my overalls.

"What is with you?"

He mumbled again and something in his tone gave me pause.

"Right. You did offer advice this afternoon I ignored. I'm sorry about that, buddy. You know I usually listen."

His expression softened and became more earnest. This was important.

"Okay, fine," I said, turning to head back down the path. "It's not great timing, but I trust you. I wouldn't have fallen into a bunker today had I listened to you. On the other hand, we wouldn't have found the murder weapon."

His next mumble sounded snippy. Apparently he would have found the knife another time, when there were ropes, ladders and reinforcements to keep me safe.

"Well, everything happens for a reason," I said.

Just like this midnight ride was happening for a reason. I didn't get the memo, but Percy did. He was sitting on the hood of the truck waiting for us.

I always left a key to the truck in a hidden notch in the garage. There was nothing more irritating when you wanted to make a quick run to the feed store than finding you had to run up to the house to get the key. Okay, there were more irritating things, but most of them couldn't be solved as easily.

Cori would surely hear us leave unless she was distracted by a sudden onset of goat labor. I kept the lights off till I was halfway down the lane and resigned myself to another lecture in the morning. That was nothing new. Even Keats gave me grief.

He mumbled "quit complaining" and put his paws on the dash, ready to navigate to whatever destination pleased him.

We had covered less than a mile when the phone rang.

"Lecture number one, coming right up." I pressed talk and speaker without checking caller ID.

"Darling!" The voice boomed out, making me cringe and Keats swish his tail happily. "Swing by and pick me up, please. I'm putting on my coat now."

"Swing by? Mom, it's past midnight."

"I just came in from a date and the night's still young."

"Have you been drinking?"

"Not a drop, darling. It's a miracle with all I need to forget right now."

"Well, get some beauty sleep and I'll call you in the morning."

"You won't, though. That's the problem. I've tried you a dozen times and had to resort to getting updates from Jilly."

"There's nothing to tell, really. I thought one of the new goats was going into labor but it was a false alarm."

"After delivering six oversized babies, I don't want to talk about the miracle of birth," she said. "I'd rather hear about how you fell into that hole today."

"Jilly did not tell you that."

"No, it was your little vigilante friend, who heard it from Edna."

"Why on earth did you call Cori Hogan, Mom?"

"She called me, darling. That's how I know you're off on one of your dangerous missions. Cori said you were... How did she put it? Oh yes, *stupid tired*. And she's worried about you falling into even deeper holes. The kind you can't climb out of."

"Oh my gosh. Cori Hogan ratted me out to my mother? I can't believe it."

"Even vigilantes do the right thing sometimes. She said Edna and Gertie were even more tired and that I was the next best thing. I can't deny I was a little flattered to hear that. Cori doesn't seem like the type to splash praise around."

"Definitely not. Take the compliment and run. Anyway, I'm wide awake now and won't be out long. Keats and Percy are with me."

"That's what I'm afraid of, Ivy. Those two encourage you to do some dangerous things. You could have died in that fall today."

Keats mumbled an indignant response to my mother.

"Actually, Keats tried to stop me from that misstep, Mom. I was too stubborn to listen."

"Well, what did you find down there in the murky depths of Galloway grime?"

At least Edna and Cori hadn't spilled about that. Mom wouldn't sound as cheery if she knew about the murder weapon that had likely been hidden in the family bunker by her deadbeat ex.

"Dirt is what I found. I expect there were snakes and rats around but I didn't see any."

"There were always snakes and rats around your father, so I'm sure you're right."

"How about we pick this up in the morning, Mom? I solemnly swear to call you."

There was a long pause as she recalibrated. "You need a sidekick. A henchwoman. I have proven myself capable in a crisis."

She had, actually, but I still didn't want her along now. There would be emotions, and I was having some success with keeping them at bay. "Mom, if you're so worried, I'll turn around and go home. Call it a night."

"Do you know how many lies I've heard from you kids? I can't even count that high. But I *can* count out the numbers to call Kellan and tell him the farmer's on the move. That's what the gloved wonder told me to do."

"You wouldn't."

"Try me. I can't afford to lose my favorite daughter because she's chasing the ghost of her deadbeat father. I never thought I'd—"

She was getting herself worked up so I signaled Keats to give a sharp bark to end the tirade.

"Mom. I'm pulling up outside your apartment. If you want to ride with us, just know that my truck is a lecture free zone. I will not hesitate to put you out on the roadside and call Asher, who started all this. He's conveniently on highway patrol anyway."

Two minutes later she emerged wearing a trench coat and a fedora. Her heels were lower than usual and looked like a wedge. Someone meant spy business.

I drove through town and then, on Keats' sign, took the shortest route to Dorset Hills.

"You look... interesting, darling. There's never a bad time for a dress, but it looks like you were rolling in the hay."

"I was, actually. And it wasn't with Kellan. I had to—"

"Never mind. We're going down the maternity path again. I can feel it. I'd far rather talk about where we're going."

"To Daphne Newell's house, I would imagine. Am I right, Keats?"

He didn't bother to answer. To him, it was obvious and he had pressing things to monitor.

"I don't want to talk about her," Mom said.

"It's either Daphne or goat maternity. Because this is what I'm doing instead of holding my goat's hoof while she pushes out babies."

"The woman was obviously sad and desperate to date a man like your father. And he was obviously sad and desperate to choose someone everyone says looked like me." She threw herself back in the seat. "I don't see that at all. Daphne was letting herself go. I know it's hard work to hold the line at our age, but it's that or—"

"Not giving a hoot because zombies are after you."

"Decoy. I had too many kids to fall for ploys like that, Ivy."

"What really happened with Calvin, Mom?"

She adjusted Keats in her lap, and I saw there were two reasons for the trench coat—espionage and dress protection. "We grew apart, as so many couples do. You'll need to be careful not to let that happen with Kellan."

"Decoy," I tossed back at her. "I have too many sneaky animals to fall for ploys like that, Mom."

She stroked Keats' sleek sides with both hands before answering. "Honestly, I don't know what happened. Not entirely. I thought he still loved me, and he most certainly loved you kids. He was a good dad in the early days."

"Sterling Fable says you knew Calvin was into shady dealings."

Turning quickly, she stared at me. "You spoke to Sterling?"

"Jilly and I went down to meet him this morning. I guess yesterday now." It already felt like a lifetime ago. "I didn't even know we had family on that side." I turned the truck onto the side street where Daphne had lived. "Not that I would have cared."

"Sterling never liked me," she said, still patting the oblivious dog. "He thought I'd get Calvin in trouble. As if Calvin couldn't get himself in trouble. He was a magnet for it."

"Actually, Sterling pretty much said that himself. Calvin did, too. You were not to blame for his actions, Mom. At worst you made a poor choice in husbands. But as both Jilly and Mandy McCain said, I wouldn't be here otherwise. And I'm happy to be here. Well, on the planet, not breaking into a dead woman's house."

She reached out and squeezed my hand on the stick shift. "You have no idea how relieved I am to hear you say this. I— I chastise myself every day for my choices. Not for myself, but for you girls and your brother. I know what an impact it's had on you."

I glanced down at her hand, clenched so tightly over

mine. Mom was usually a master of denial, but it turned out she had more moments of reflection than I imagined.

"We'll all be fine, Mom," I said, trying to free my hand. I had enough trouble managing this big machine without her impeding my shifts. "After we resolve this current issue."

"The Daphne issue."

"Exactly." I pulled up to the curb a few doors down from Daphne's house and parked. Then I turned to face Mom. "Let me ask you this... Would you ever have considered Calvin capable of murder?"

At first she looked away, but when Keats squirmed around in her lap to stare too, she answered us both. "Not back then, no. Quite the contrary. I would have said he was naïve and more likely to get himself killed from not being able to manage the criminal connections he inherited from his dad."

"Sterling said you knew about his background."

"I did, at least to a degree. Like many a foolish young woman, I thought I could change him. That he'd leave all that behind when he had a family. He was very charming. Very kind to me. Very accepting. I hadn't experienced much of that growing up and then my parents disowned me over Calvin." She sighed and went back to stroking Keats. "I do regret putting young children into danger. He did the right thing in leaving, as hard as it was for us afterwards. We were the safer for it."

"He should have manned up and gotten out of the shady business to look after his family," I said.

"Like I said, he inherited trouble and as hard as he tried, he couldn't see a way out of it." Finally she smiled.

"He wasn't as clever as you, Ivy. You got your brains from me."

I laughed. "On that note, how about we do something stupid together?"

"Would you mind telling me what we're looking for?"

"That's just it. I don't know. Keats and Percy wanted to come so there's something of interest. We won't know till they tell us." This time I squeezed *her* hand. "You know the drill. Follow their lead. Don't play cowboy."

"Oh, darling," she said, opening the door. "I have no interest in playing cowboy. But I wouldn't say no to adding one to my stable."

"We've gone fifteen minutes without the subject of your rotation coming up." I slid out of the truck and released the pets. "That's a record."

"Your father's put a damper on dating this week, but it's still been my greatest comfort." She hopped out and came around the truck. "After my children, of course. The ones who *will* take my calls."

"How's everyone doing?" I asked, as Keats herded us along in the shadows. "I know Daisy and Poppy are working hard at the farm to avoid thinking about it, or talking about it, as is our family way. What about Iris and Violet?"

"Iris and I work side by side at the salon and she refuses to speak of it. Violet and Asher are incommunicado."

"It's only been a couple of days, although it feels like longer. Give everyone time to adjust."

"Of course. You know I'm a patient woman."

I couldn't help snickering and Keats gave a sneeze of laughter, too.

"Never mind," she said, before releasing a long sigh. "Calvin and I had no business making babies."

"Others have said the same," I told her as we followed the two tails up the walk.

Mom straightened her shoulders and pulled down the brim of her fedora. "Well, I'm happy we did."

CHAPTER TWENTY

E ven after the murders of recent months, most people in Clover Grove still left a key outside. I hoped the same was true in Dorset Hills, which liked to consider itself a small town despite having all the perks—and drawbacks—of a city.

Mom and I slipped around the side of the house to wait while Keats and Percy did reconnaissance out front. Coming up empty, they joined us and we made our way around the side and into the backyard. Keats worked the planters and garden while Percy climbed up the trellis and onto window sills. I was about to call it when I heard a triumphant meow. Percy leapt from the railing to what appeared to be a crab apple tree and pawed at a small nook. An object wrapped in tinfoil fell onto the grass. I opened it to find a key inside.

"Thanks, boys," I whispered. "You just made this so much easier. Breaking in would be a challenge in a dress."

"It's a skill worth acquiring," Mom said, warming to

the idea. "It adds purpose to my yoga practice. I am glad I wore a smart wedge tonight. Heels make things a little harder."

I unlocked the back door and let the dog and cat precede us into the house. The white tuft of Keats' tail was on high alert but indicated no trouble.

"We're good for a quick look around, Mom," I said. "But things could change in a second so keep your eye on that tail."

"It would help if we could turn on our phone lights."

"You mean it would help the neighbors see us and call Chief Coots. It's one thing to poke around Kellan's crime scenes and another to cross jurisdictions. He wouldn't be able to protect us."

"You're right, darling. If we're going to get arrested, it had better be for more than a midnight visit."

"How about we don't get arrested at all? Let's keep it quick and dirty."

The pets knew the drill. Percy went one way and Keats another. In the darkness, I didn't know where, exactly, but if there was anything worth seeing, they'd let me know.

Mom went into the living room where the light streamed in from the street and made visibility better. "What terrible taste in furniture," she said. "So clunky. Few people realize that image is about the whole package. It really starts at home, you know."

"Mom? Eyes open, mouth shut. Unless you find an object of interest."

"This sideboard is interesting. Antiques have their place but if they're ugly, that place is the dumpster."

"Stop it. We're not here to judge Daphne's style but to answer a burning question. Who killed her and why?"

"This sideboard is worth a look. It doesn't fit the décor and she probably kept it around for a reason."

I would have yanked her away if Keats hadn't come into the room and gone into a point beside the very sideboard in question.

"Fine," I said, yanking up my skirt so I could kneel beside it. "I'll take a look." I opened the door with one gloved hand but it was too dark inside the cabinet to see anything. "I'm going to flash the light for just one second. Can you block me?"

Mom moved behind me and opened her trench coat in a shield. I turned on my light and at first saw nothing. In the very back corner was a small white triangle. With one gloved finger, I fished out a photograph and stared at it.

"Why would Daphne have a photo of Polly Fable?" I asked.

"Your grandmother? I suppose Calvin gave it to her."

Keats mumbled something urgent. His ruff and tail were rising.

"Someone's coming, Mom. Police or worse. We've gotta run."

Sliding the photo into my coat pocket, I followed Keats' lead to the back door. Mom was so close behind that the brim of her fedora kept tapping my shoulder and startling me.

"What if they come around the back?" she asked.

"Follow Keats. He won't steer us wrong."

Unfortunately, steering us right soon had us facing

the fence on the far side of the house. There was no gate, which meant Mom and I were going over the hard way. In dresses.

"Oh no," she said, looking up. At five foot nothing, the eight foot fence was even more daunting.

"No problem for a yogi," I said. "Plus, you've got me to boost you."

"But what about the rest of you?"

"Percy can climb, and I'll pass Keats over to you. Then I'll figure the rest out."

"Turns out I was wrong, darling," she muttered as I bent over. "There is a bad time for a dress."

Thank goodness she'd worn a smart wedge instead of her usual stilettos. She left no puncture wounds behind when she boosted herself up and over. For a second, her manicured fingers clung and then she released.

"Safe," she said.

Keats herded me to a shed, where I found a folded wooden lawn chair leaning in the shadows.

"Perfect. Thanks, buddy," I said, setting it up. "Your turn."

Getting onto the chair holding the dog was quite a feat, and he wasn't at all happy about being airlifted over the fence. There was no choice; the dog only had wings in my imagination.

Mom didn't utter a word of protest as scrabbling claws descended on her. She took my most precious belonging from my hands and lowered him to the ground. Percy left his watch on the fence to join them.

I'd like to say I swung over elegantly but it was more of an awkward scramble. Never again would I leave home without a change of clothes. It was time to emulate Edna and create a customized go-kit, with boots and overalls and some tools, too. Hitching the dress up, I used the muscles farm work had given me to hoist myself over the top. I deliberately kicked down the chair before strad-dling the fence and it folded with a little snap that was nearly drowned out by the tearing sound as my hem gave way.

Normally I would have jumped off but given my footwear, chose to turn and lower myself carefully. The grass on the other side was mushy from spring rain and my heels dug into the turf.

"Slowly. Carefully," I said, letting the pets take the lead. To my surprise, Keats fell back and sent Percy ahead. It wasn't like my fearless dog to forfeit the satisfac-tion of being first. "What's going on?" I whispered. He mumbled a quick reply. "Seems like he's worried about being recognized and giving us away."

"We'd best hurry," Mom said, as Keats pushed through shrubs onto the neighbor's front lawn. She went next, pulling her sleeve over her wrist to shove back the bushes and force her way through. "Ugh. Prickly."

Indeed, my torn dress soon got snagged by thorns. The harder I tugged, the more stuck it got.

"Mom, I've got to cut my way out. Go ahead with Keats and Percy. Start the truck so we can hit it when I get there." I tossed the key over the shrubs and heard the small thud as the fob hit the ground.

No doubt the boys pointed it out, because she said, "Got it. Hurry, darling."

Keats whined at the prospect of leaving me. "Go, buddy."

This wasn't the first time I wished I'd taken Edna's advice and ordered a dagger from Harvey Dunbar, the world-renowned bladesmith who lived nearby. Tonight I had to settle for the utility knife I carried in my coat pocket beside Polly's picture. Sawing at the fabric with a short blade was slow work.

In the brief pause after breaking free, I heard movement in Daphne's back yard. Someone was setting up the chair again.

Keats was already coming back for me, as I suspected he would. He was racing in the open now, aware that our pursuer was behind Daphne's house.

I ran on the balls of my feet to avoid getting mired by my heels. I only tripped once, which was impressive, all things considered, but my hands were slick with mud when I reached the truck.

Mom had popped the passenger door and rolled down the window. "Get in. Fast," she said. "There's a car parked down the road that wasn't here when we arrived."

"Move over. You can't drive, Mom."

"I most certainly can," she said. "I learned on a stick and I'm ready to go."

Mom was known for taking out stop signs like a warrior felling villains. It wasn't an appealing prospect.

Keats hopped ahead of me into the passenger door and mumbled a direct order.

"Fine," I said, climbing in. The slit up the back of my dress made that easier. "Just a few blocks till we've lost the tail, if there is one. Then we switch."

"Buckle up, darling. I'm a little rusty, but it's like riding a bicycle."

"You never rode a bicycle."

"My mother wouldn't let me. She thought it was unladylike." She mumbled something under her breath. "It was your father who taught me to drive so we can thank him for that, if nothing else."

She slid forward on the seat to reach the pedals and I'm sure we both offered silent thanks to her smart wedges, as well. The dance between clutch and gas began with surprising grace and we rolled down the road.

"Good, Mom. Well done." I peered over my shoulder and Keats whined. "Uh-oh. I see someone running toward that car you noticed."

"Man or woman?" she asked.

"Does it matter?"

"Yes, it matters. I need to know whether to drive like a lady or not."

"I can't tell. So drive like a lady around the corner and turn off the lights. We'll find somewhere safe to switch places."

I hadn't counted on our tail picking up speed so quickly. The car's high beams were on and the pedal down. Was it Jim Moss, perhaps? He hadn't crawled out from under his rock in a few days.

"So much for ladies," Mom said, gearing up. "Hang on, now. This could be bumpy."

Instead of following the curve of the road, she drove right up over a curb, across a floral display on a median, and off the other side.

"Are you crazy?"

"He's in a sedan, darling. He can't take the curb like us. We've gained a minute."

"Mom!"

"Just keep watch on the tail and leave everything else to me."

I did as I was told, even taking photos with my phone, but that's how I missed when she turned off the road. Only when my butt lifted and my head tapped the roof did I face forward and see we were on the back trail system. "Oh my—"

"I told you to put on your seat belt. These trails haven't gotten one bit smoother. And they're never more treacherous than in spring."

"Mom, it's a maze back here. I don't even know the way back to Clover Grove."

"I do. Your father taught me that, too." She bumped along for a stretch and then took a hard left. "I thought it was useless information, but I suppose he was preparing me for this eventuality."

"Pay attention. They're still on our tail."

"Never you mind. I've got a plan."

She wove in and out, up and down, with barely a stutter. The sedan tailing us was gradually falling behind. Either their vehicle couldn't handle the terrain or the driver didn't know it well.

"What's your plan? Because my plan is to get back on the highway as soon as possible."

"Ah, there it is," she said. "Potter's Bog. It's the Bermuda Triangle of the trail system. Vehicles simply disappear without a trace."

"Be careful, please. We do not want a confrontation

out here and the dimensions of the bog could have changed."

So far, she'd exceeded my expectations but where Mom differed sharply from Edna was weaponry. If we got cornered and our tail was armed, well... the less said the better.

"It's bigger and worse than ever," she said. "I'll just give it a wide berth and then loiter for a second on the other side. He'll run up all cocky and then... boom! In he goes."

That's exactly what happened. The moment the sedan's front tires hit the bog, she took a sharp turn and then a few more until we were finally back on the highway.

"Okay," I said, pulling in a long breath. "Whew! That was truly impressive, Mom, but we need to switch over now."

"Not yet, darling." She rolled down the window. "I deserve to feel the wind in my hair. It's been ages."

"How did you do that? You're known as the worst driver in the entire county and that's certainly not what I saw tonight."

"I can't explain it, darling. There's always so much on my mind and I'm better under pressure."

"I'll say. I would have expected the opposite this week."

"Yes, it's been a hard week. Memories have been flooding over the dam I put up all those years ago. Turns out there were a few good ones, too."

She accelerated, as if trying to outrun the bad ones.

"Slow down right now. You're way over the speed limit and— Oh no!"

Mom hadn't adjusted the mirrors so she didn't see the flashing lights before Keats whimpered. Glancing over her shoulder she said, "It's all right, darling. They've already taken my license. They can't do it again."

"No, but they can impound my truck, or worse."

She pulled onto the shoulder at the wrong place and rolled up onto a curb, only to meet her old nemesis: a stop sign.

"First one I've hit from behind," she said, cheerfully. "Good thing we were barely moving. We're in for a thrashing, I'm afraid. Here's to a little fresh meat for the piranhas of gossip."

I tried to get a look at the cop as he left his vehicle but shrubs were a problem, as they had been all night. "I only hope it's not Kellan."

Keats' tail was going a mile a minute. A bad sign... for my relationship.

"Ivy Galloway, you are in so much trouble," a man called. "Get out with your hands up."

"Ignore that, darling," Mom said. "I'll handle this."

A face appeared in the window and the blue eyes that peered in were bright with amusement. The officer's smile faded fast.

"*Mom?* What the—?"

"Don't curse at your mother, Asher. Everything's fine. Now, I need you to go out to Potter's Bog immediately and pull out the sedan that was tailing us before it sinks to Middle Earth. We can talk about everything else tomorrow."

"Get out of that truck now," he said. "You're both coming with me."

As my brother perp-walked Mom to the police SUV, I circled my truck. She put up a good fight as he tried to get her into the rear, lashing out with a smart wedge. That's when I jumped behind the wheel, did a U turn and rushed home.

"Mom's right, boys," I said. "We can talk about everything tomorrow."

CHAPTER TWENTY-ONE

The lights were still on at Mandy's Country Store when I passed. "What on earth? It's nearly three a.m." I turned the truck into the lot. "I'd better check to see if she's okay."

Keats offered his opinion that Mandy was absolutely fine.

"Well then, I'd better check to see if the pie is okay. If it's under threat, I can save it."

He offered a ha-ha-ha, letting me know he was in no particular hurry to get home. Cori must be holding the fort just fine.

Pulling out my phone, I called Mandy. "You open?"

She came to the front window and laughed. "For you, sure. I could use the company."

I tucked the truck into the deepest shadows and we all went inside. Since other customers weren't around to complain, I let Percy roam freely. The cat was a trooper about his carrier, but he'd earned his freedom tonight.

"What are you doing here at this hour?" I asked.

"Use your nose," she said, smiling.

"You're baking? Did you stay late or come early?"

"Couldn't sleep so I decided to get a jump on things." She looked me up and down and while her delicate eyebrows rose, she didn't comment on the dire state of my attire.

"Mandy, it's not a great idea to be here alone in the night. I don't need to remind you that there's—"

"A killer on the loose. I know. That's why I couldn't sleep. It brings back such terrible memories, Ivy. When that happens, all I can do is bake them out."

I sat down on my usual stool and nodded. "I get it. That's when I turn to manure management. This smells so much better."

"I forget my troubles by turning this place into my test kitchen. I've tried out a couple of new recipes if you want to be my guinea pig."

"You bet I do. And I'll take a double espresso, if you don't mind."

"You'll be up the rest of the night."

"The ship's sailed on this one," I said. "I've got a goat warming up to deliver and Cori Hogan is spelling me. I'll take something along to thank her."

She was gone a few minutes and I stared out into the night, waiting for Asher or Kellan to pass. One of them would come to dress me down, and frankly, I deserved it. The coffee and sugar would help me roll with the punches.

A few vehicles passed, none with cherries on top, unlike the cheesecake tart Mandy delivered.

"Too sweet in my opinion," she said. "But you could probably use a blood sugar spike around now."

I thought about using the fork she provided, but just picked it up with my fingers. No one was around to watch. As I chewed the creamy treat, I couldn't help smiling. "You are a gift from the heavens, Mandy McCain."

Her pale cheeks flushed and she shook her head. "If that were true, I wouldn't spend my nights worrying about the past."

I swallowed another bite before saying, "Just stop. I mean, don't stop baking. Ever. But stop beating yourself up over what's in the rearview mirror. If you're looking back, you'll hit something."

"Did you hit something?" Mandy asked. "Because I'm pretty sure I see a dent in your fender that wasn't there two days ago."

I chugged the coffee before answering. "Blame that on Mom. I was up to no good and she drove getaway. You heard it first here."

Mandy's eyes widened. "Oh my. You'll be the talk of this counter for days to come."

"I can't help giving, Mandy. I'm a philanthropist."

"Let me get you another coffee," she said. "And some of my kitchen-sink cookies."

"Kitchen sink?" I called after her.

"I just threw everything in to see how it worked out."

"I'll take one of your world class Nanaimo bars, too. You did get the proportions exactly right."

Keats whined to get my attention. The treats won that competition, and when I finally followed his point, headlights were already coming into view.

"Not high enough for a police SUV," I said. "Something we should worry about?"

He panted an urgent yes-yes-yes. I picked up my phone in case I needed it.

A car passed Mandy's store going far too fast to get a good photo, but I tried anyway. It looked like a very dirty sedan. One that had just dragged itself out of a bog, perhaps.

"At least the driver didn't have time to notice the truck," I said. "Should we go after it, Keats?"

His tail drooped. It was either too late or too dangerous to have any luck with pursuit.

"What just happened?" Mandy asked.

"Someone was following us earlier, which is why we got into a situation. Do you have any idea what Calvin's been driving since he got back? He hid his wheels when he visited."

She shook her head. "Most people pass through this store, but Calvin hasn't."

"Strange," I said. "Because he's the only one in a hundred-mile radius who can resist your pie."

"Guess you didn't inherit your sweet tooth from him," she said, with a smile.

"No, but it looks like I've inherited other traits, as much as I'd like to pretend otherwise."

"I hear you. Myrtle runs through my veins, remember. At least she passed on her head for business."

"You'll surpass her by far," I said. "Have you thought of franchising?"

She nodded. "Someday. Not till I can sleep through the night again. More worries I don't need."

"Gotcha." I hopped off the stool. "I'd better get going. Do you mind if I use the restroom first? Saves me going inside and waking people when I get home."

"Of course. I'll get your takeout ready."

The mirror told me Mandy's eyebrows had been kind. I looked like I'd been dragged behind a runaway llama and chewed up by... well, coyotes, since none of my animals would commit such crimes against what had once been a pretty dress.

"Have I ever looked worse?" I said, not to my reflection, but Keats, who'd come into the restroom with me. There were no boundaries in our relationship and no point pretending otherwise.

He mumbled an affirmative. I had, in fact, looked worse.

"I suppose. After getting attacked, maybe."

His next mumble was kinder, affirming that he loved me no matter how I looked.

"I appreciate that, buddy. If I want to survive to the apocalypse, I had better cut vanity loose right now, like Cori said. Did you notice Mom managed to look good despite the fence climbing and the killer hedge? How does she do that?"

"You okay in there?" Mandy asked, outside the door.

I tried squashing my bushy hair down with damp fingers and called, "Crazy as always, Mandy."

We came pretty close to hugging each other as she saw me out but remembered in time that we weren't really the type. Percy gave her ankles a lovely swish, though.

"The pie's always here for you," she called through the glass.

I gave her a wave. True friendship was about more than hugs. It was about pie and secrets and late night oversharing. I was lucky to have Mandy in my life even though I'd almost died because of her.

CHAPTER TWENTY-TWO

After Cori left, I curled up in the straw and flipped through my phone, trying to find clues among all the photos I'd gathered lately. There were enough for a small family album but I couldn't see a pattern. My mind was spinning, but eventually it gave up the fight and tossed me into the abyss of sleep.

The crow of a rooster woke me. Or at least a reasonable parody thereof. I opened my eyes to find Kellan standing with his arms crossed over the side of the pen. Keats' tail swished in the straw but he didn't get up.

"Hey," I said, without moving. "Do you see any goat babies?"

He took a good look at Big Mama and shook his head. "No babies. She's still huge." After a second he added, "Goats don't eat their young, do they?"

"No. I've never understood the biology behind that. It seems counterproductive. But just so you know, goats do sometimes eat the placenta."

"Did you really need to tell me that?"

"It's a public service announcement. She might do it at any moment. Wouldn't you rather be warned?"

"No, Ivy, although I'd love to be warned about other things. Like when you're about to break into a crime scene, for example. Especially if I need to account for it to a colleague in a different jurisdiction." He swept off his hat and ran a hand through his perfect hair. "But, no, I do not need to be warned about goats eating placentas. Shall we establish some guidelines around warnings? So we're clear on both sides?"

"Sure," I said. "How about we go inside and draw them up over coffee? Seems like Big Mama plans to hold onto those babies a bit longer."

"As much as I'd love a coffee, I think we should chat down here. No need for the guests to hear about what you were doing last night."

Normally this was where I'd bob and weave, play a little cat and mouse, but Kellan sounded pretty sure of himself. Mom must have spilled.

"Did someone see me somewhere I shouldn't be?" I threw back the blankets and got up. The act was about as graceful as a downed horse scrambling to its feet. I was hobbled by my outfit, and stiff and sore from cumulative adventures. Keats circled me, trying to keep me on my pins.

"Yeah, actually. Daphne Newell's neighbor watched as you and a small man in a trench coat and fedora climbed a fence. He even got some video of you thrashing in his hedge. It sounded like he enjoyed that a little too much and seeing your dress, I know why."

Looking down at my disheveled outfit, my face

started to burn. Dating the most handsome man in all of hill country set the bar too high for this farmer. I'd asked Cori to lend me the spare clothes she kept in her truck for emergency rescues and she'd just laughed. They wouldn't have fit me anyway. She was no bigger than my mother—the supposed small man in a fedora. If Mom heard that description, she'd never settle for a smart wedge again.

"That hedge is a great security system," I said. "Had to cut myself out. What else did this guy see?"

"He saw you run to your truck. Got a pic of your plates. Said the short guy drove getaway."

Okay, so there was no proof I was *inside* the house, or he'd say so. That might downgrade Kellan's lecture from a hurricane to a tropical storm.

"Cori Hogan could be mistaken for a small guy," I said. "If she wore a fedora."

There was a small chance Asher had covered for Mom. It was worth a try.

"Possibly. But Cori's road record is surprisingly clear, given her recreational activities. And yes, I've checked." Percy jumped onto the wall of the pen and stepped onto Kellan's shoulder to head butt his cheek. It was nice of the cat to serve as a fluffy storm wall. "You know whose record *isn't* clean, though? Your mother's. The stop signs all breathed a huge sigh of relief when we suspended her license. Yet another one died last night."

"Rumors of its death have been greatly exaggerated," I said. "It was just listing a little. Like it went on a bender with all the other road signs."

He pressed his lips together, either in frustration or to

keep from laughing. I hoped for the latter. Sometimes if I could make him laugh, he'd relent. Percy did his best to elevate the mood with purring I could hear nearly two yards away. Turning up the woo, he started licking Kellan's morning stubble with a rough tongue. The chief hadn't been home to bed either, but unlike me, he looked cuter than ever.

"Come back after brushing those teeth, Percy," Kellan said. "I suppose you and your canine conspirator told Ivy she needed to break into a crime scene?"

If he interviewed the pets, it was always a positive sign. Keats chimed in with some mumbles, taking his share of the blame.

"They did," I said. "Cori spelled me on midwife duty and I was trying to head up to bed when these two suggested a drive."

"And then you thought, 'Why not take Dahlia along? She's super skilled and we can have some mother-daughter bonding time.' Is that how your thought process worked?"

I gave a snort of laughter. "Not exactly. Cori heard me leave and ratted me out to Mom, who pulled one of her tantrums and insisted on coming along to protect me."

"To protect you? Dahlia?"

Trying to run a hand through matted hair, I gave up. "I thought the same, I won't lie. But the fact is, she did help. When Keats told us someone was coming, Mom turned into a pro spy, going over the fence and through that killer shrub with ease. Granted, she did wear smart wedges instead of heels."

"And how did she come to be at the wheel of the huge truck you have trouble handling yourself?"

"I was stuck in the hedge and she was just supposed to get it running. By the time I freed myself, she was running all right." I came a little closer and leaned against the pen on the opposite side of him. Hopefully my morning breath was better than Percy's. "Here's where it gets strange, Kellan. Mom was great behind the wheel. Great with the stick. Great with navigating the trails. She purposely lost our tail at Potter's Bog. It was like being in an alternate universe."

He closed his eyes. "I don't want to think about what could have happened back there."

"But it didn't and we're fine," I said. "Any luck finding the car?"

"Already gone when Asher got there."

"I figured. I think it passed when I stopped at Mandy's store afterwards."

"Mandy was in the store at that hour?"

"She's in the night owl club, too. Anyway, Keats didn't like the looks of one car that passed and it seemed to be covered in mud. I'll send you all the pics in case you can match the plates. My money's on Calvin. I don't see how anyone else could have escaped Potter's Bog so fast."

"It wasn't Calvin," Kellan said. "I have officers watching him."

That made me blink but I kept going. "He could find a way. Didn't he manage to stay hidden for decades?"

"Not from me," Kellan said. "I knew where he was and when he moved on. At least most of the time. Then I'd catch up to him again."

"You tracked him for years? Even before you lived here?"

"Monitored, not tracked. I try to keep tabs on people like him, but there was no professional reason to reveal his whereabouts. On the personal side... you made it quite clear that you didn't want to know."

I stared at him. "I would have wanted to know so that I could at least prepare for his arrival."

"Well, you didn't put that in the boyfriend handbook. Whenever his name came up you got upset. I put a lot of thought into it, Ivy, especially since Asher felt differently. It wasn't easy being caught in the middle."

I hadn't had enough sleep for this conversation. It could wait. "Moving on. Are you positive Calvin didn't give you the slip last night?"

"Positive. He didn't murder Daphne Newell, either."

"He has a credible alibi? I don't believe it."

"I could show you video footage, but you'll have to take my word for it. Hopefully that still counts for something."

"Of course it does. But you might want to double-check that footage. Anything can be faked these days."

"In the big leagues, yes. We're not in the big leagues." He tired of Percy's ministrations and dropped the cat gently inside the pen. "There were several captures of Calvin on security feeds the day of Daphne's death. He took a long stroll down memory lane. He was at the high school and the sports stadium. Then he drove over to the Palais Royale in Dorset Hills and we got a shot of him there."

"The Palais Royale? Why?"

Kellan shrugged. "It was the social hub back in his day. And it's where he took your mom on their first date."

I shuddered. "I don't think I want to hear more."

Percy jumped back onto the wall and then onto Kellan's shoulder. Meanwhile, Keats pressed against my shins.

"See?" Kellan said. "That's why it gets confusing for me as a boyfriend. As a cop, it's more straightforward. Your recklessness last night was alarming. You and Dahlia could have died in Potter's Bog."

"She said she drives better under pressure. And apparently a stick makes all the difference." I couldn't meet his eyes. "Calvin taught her to drive and navigate the trails. You learn something new every day."

"If you keep an open mind, that's true. You've been blinded by emotion." He leaned over to rest his hand on my shoulder and I backed out of reach. "It's completely understandable, but it doesn't mesh well with amateur sleuthing. Or professional, for that matter. Objectivity is key."

"I'm still objective," I said.

Keats added a few comments of his own... and for once he agreed with Kellan.

"If you don't believe me, believe Keats," Kellan said.

"You two are chatting now?"

"Only when it comes to your welfare. Then, somehow, we have a meeting of minds."

I turned to the goat and sighed. "If not Calvin, then whom? Jim Moss, maybe? The genealogy people? You and Chief Coots must have other suspects."

"We might, yeah. But I'm not sharing anything more

with you right now. Letting Dahlia drive getaway... I mean, honestly, Ivy. I often turn a blind eye to your exploits with Jilly, Edna and Gertie, but I will not stand by while your mother pilots a weapon of mass destruction."

I glanced at him now. "And you're saying *my* mind's closed?"

"She took out another stop sign. It could as easily have been a citizen."

I glanced around and gave a little scream. "Oh my gosh! It's happening. Kellan, it's happening!"

"What's happening?" His frustration gave way to alarm.

"Big Mama. She's— There's—" I gestured to her hind end, from which something like a bubble was emerging. Inside I could see two little hooves. The big goat was on her side and barely panting, although there were ripples running across her abdomen. This was one stoic goat. "Grab the towels," I said, gesturing to the stack on a shelf beside him.

"Should we call someone? Gertie? Cori? A veterinarian?"

"I've got it covered. I've watched the videos ten times over. Pretty much all I have to do is catch the kid, make sure it can breathe, take care of the cord and rub it down. Big Mama should do the rest."

I knelt beside the goat and readied myself, as if to receive a football.

"Should I lock out the dog and cat?" Kellan asked, opening the door of the pen.

"Good idea, yeah."

It took him so long I started to think it was a stalling tactic, but it was never easy getting Keats to leave my side and Percy was able to leap out of reach.

Finally, he came back and knelt beside me.

"You don't have to watch," I said. "This won't be a stroll in the garden."

"Believe it or not, I've delivered babies. On the roadside, when the mom-to-be didn't make it to the hospital on time."

"Oh. Well, then. You're going to be a huge asset in the midwife department."

"You'll do fine," he said, reassuringly. "Your instincts with animals are superb."

His confidence buoyed me, and luckily Big Mama had it all covered anyway. It probably wasn't her first baby rodeo.

The first kid emerged so quickly I thought about Edna's comment that they shot out like bullets. After making sure the wee thing was able to breathe, I didn't dally in cleaning it up and tying off, snipping and disinfecting the cord. The kid appeared to be nearly black, with eerie blue eyes like its mother. And Keats. And even Fleecy, Edna's cat. I was surrounded by eerie blue eyes, but only the goats had rectangular pupils.

"It's so small," I said. "Poor little thing."

"It's fine," Kellan said. "Look at it trying to stand already."

The kid couldn't coordinate its spindly legs but it was certainly trying.

"You massage him with the towel and turn away," I said.

"Turn away? Why now?"

"If she wants to eat the placenta, I'm going to let her."

"Oh, I'll watch. I bet it's like a zombie eating a human brain," he said.

"Probably. As Edna would say, it's great training for the apocalypse. If you can handle it."

He squared his shoulders. "I can handle anything you and this goat throw at me."

I laughed and then sighed. Lectures aside, how did I get so lucky?

The next kid was a tan and brown, also with blue eyes, but Big Mama wasn't done. She eventually pushed out a third and just as I started to relax, a fourth arrived. The last one seemed impossibly tiny. No wonder Big Mama had been so grumpy. What a load!

Kellan and I worked beautifully together, saying little until Big Mama was on her feet and busy licking the last kid and murmuring soft, throaty maas. As each baby wobbled and hobbled toward the milk bar, my spirits lifted. Kellan had a huge grin on his face, too.

We sat holding hands and helping out where needed, until Gertie arrived. She leaned over the pen and beamed. "What a beautiful sight. It's almost enough to give me hope for the world."

"Then hang up your rifle," Kellan said, getting to his feet.

"I said almost, Chief. No need to get crazy."

She shooed us out and I walked Kellan to his car. By now he looked a little worse for wear, too, and I was less embarrassed about hugging him.

"Can you do something for me?" he asked, taking a

step back.

"Shower? Brush my teeth?"

He shook his head, smiling. "You look good to me, like always." He pulled a baggie out of his pocket. "Can you take this to Calvin?"

I stared at the bagged wallet and then backed up a few steps. "Why? You know where he is, so you can drop it off."

"Ivy, you're going to need to confront him at some point. Otherwise, it'll chew you up from the inside. I know this from experience."

Keats was sitting at Kellan's feet, staring up at me. He mumbled something rather elaborate and I sighed.

"He agreed with me again, didn't he?" Kellan asked, grinning.

Turning up his blue eye, Keats added a sassy "don't get used to it" mumble.

Percy sat on Kellan's other side, blinking solemnly.

"Clearly, I'm outnumbered," I said.

Kellan gestured to the barn. "Vastly so. And increasing by the hour. Congrats on your new kids, farmer Ivy."

"We make a good team," I said, as he climbed into the car.

"You're just realizing that now?"

I watched till the police SUV disappeared around a curve in the lane and then looked down at the boys. "That went better than expected. And yet people always say having kids won't keep your relationship together."

Keats gave a sneeze of a chuckle. It sounded like he was just indulging me, but I was quite happy to take it.

CHAPTER TWENTY-THREE

"Are you sure you want me to come?" Jilly asked, following me down to the truck.

"Two hundred percent sure," I said. "Maybe more. The big question is how much will I owe you for it?"

"Zero. Even less," she said. "I'm honored you'll let me be your second."

That made me laugh. "It's not a duel. At least I hope not. Just an incredibly awkward encounter. Something I'm doing because Kellan wants me to."

"That's not the only reason," Jilly said, scooping up Percy along the way. He rode contentedly in her arms, whereas with me, he always had to assume his parrot pose on my shoulder. He was Jilly's baby and my second head. I wasn't sure what that said but it probably wasn't a compliment. "You want to put this tension behind you, too. I know it."

"Maybe. It's been a little distracting. Kellan basically said it's undermining my ability to sleuth."

"Which means more because he doesn't really want

you to sleuth in the first place. That's Kellan the boyfriend talking. He's worried about you."

"I admit letting Mom drive wasn't my wisest move. It'll cost me the moral high ground in future family squabbles. I've always been fully confident that my judgment was better than any blood relative's."

Jilly laughed as she circled the truck but her smile was gone by the time she'd buckled up. "Asher hasn't been himself, either. He's barely called since Calvin came back."

"Like me, he got spanked for poor judgment," I said, sending Keats into the back seat. "Highway patrol is the cop dungeon. Bringing Mom in may have scored back a few points."

"Poor guy." She raised her hand. "Now, you know full well I am on your side, and that I asked Asher to stand down on Calvin. But I still feel sorry for your brother. He was older when Calvin left. He remembers more. Missed him more."

I slid behind the wheel and sat for a second. Keats rested his muzzle on my shoulder and I touched his ears with my fingers. The little ritual grounded me, as always.

"That's true for all of them, I guess. Daisy, Iris and Violet were old enough to realize we were better off without him, but I'm sure they felt the loss more too. I only have a few hazy memories of Calvin. More have surfaced this week. It's Pandora's box, like you said."

"Everyone processes at a different rate," Jilly said. "You'll all need to be patient with each other. Keep an open heart if you can."

She squeezed my arm and the double hit of affection

from my two besties filled me with enough courage to turn the key in the ignition. "I'm going to try. So, how about we get this out of the way?"

"The sooner the better. It's a lot to carry."

I pulled Calvin's wallet out of the front pocket of my overalls and stuck it in the coffee holder. "It *is* a lot to carry. He stuffed that thing so full of photos and clippings the stitches are coming out."

"That's got to say something, right?"

A few days ago I might have snapped at her, but today I just shrugged and started rolling down the lane. "Wouldn't it have been easier to just call home?"

"You'd think, but we can't be inside his head. This was all his stuff, not yours. Remember that. You were only kids."

"And why replace Mom with a lookalike?" I glanced at her. "Don't tell me men have a type because you are unlike anyone Asher's ever dated before. And I'm quite sure Kellan's exes were not crazy hobby farmers who got dragged through muck."

Her laugh was warmer, and Keats chimed in with a hearty pant.

"I bet Kellan never dated anyone seriously after you split in college," she said. "He used his work as a way to block everyone out."

"You think?" I turned right onto the highway, heading away from town. "Then maybe I can stop worrying that he's comparing me to sweet, domesticated women who know the steps to every dance and always say the right thing."

"You, my friend, can deliver baby goats and catch

killers. You're a cut above everyone else in every way that counts and Kellan Harper knows it."

"Yah," Keats said.

Jilly and I both turned instantly, and the truck bumped onto the shoulder. I caught myself just before hitting a road sign and joining Mom in ignominy.

"Did he just...?" I started.

"Say yah?" she finished. "It sure sounded like it."

The dog gave a regular ha-ha-ha pant and we both shook our heads.

Getting the truck righted, I said, "I'm delirious from lack of sleep."

"Well, what's my excuse? We both heard it."

I eased back onto the highway and drove more carefully. "You have good reason to be delirious enough to hear a dog speak. Ever since you left Boston, it's been one crazy event after another. And through it all, you support not only me and my animals but my entire family. No one else would take on the Galloways, Jilly. You are worth all the gold buried under this town."

"I consider it an honor and a privilege." She cast another questioning look at Keats and shook her head again. "Now, where is Calvin hiding out? In that bunker on his old property or something worse?"

"The Big Snooze Motel just up the road, apparently. It wouldn't have taken much legwork to find him."

"But you didn't want to find him. That was the point."

"I suppose. I just wanted to pin him for murder without ever speaking to him again. That seemed about what he deserved for being a derelict dad."

"Dad! Did you hear that, Keats? She actually used the d-word."

"Not for reals," I said. "I doubt we'll ever get to that status. But I would like to clear this big ugly shadow named Calvin from my unconscious and step out of the way if the rest of my family wants to have a relationship with him. He can come to your wedding, if you like. I will not protest."

Jilly just laughed. "Horse before cart. Asher has me on ice right now."

"He's just processing in his man cave. More specifically, his squad car. Pulling Mom over was probably the most exciting thing to happen in his highway hero career."

"I only wish you'd videoed the whole thing."

"Asher did, with the police cam. That's why Kellan was so upset. Mom was going like stink when he clocked us. Shame about the stop sign."

"The universe was sending a message," Jilly said. "Stop. Look around. Appreciate what we all have."

"I did exactly that afterwards. I stopped at Mandy's to appreciate her and then came home and appreciated the sweetest little goats on the planet. They're all girls, by the way. Does. Makers of milk and ultimately, more kids. New side hustle, coming right up."

"Runaway Farm products are the next frontier," she said. "Enough merchandise and we won't have to worry about scaring guests off."

"We'd have to sell a lot of soap."

"Expensive soap with lavender and herbs. I'll plant a garden soon."

"The future is bright, Jilly. All we have to do is reunite Calvin with his wallet and encourage him on his way. Then I'll figure out who murdered Daphne and prove to Kellan that my brain is functioning at maximum capacity once more."

"It sounded like he's getting pretty close on this one, didn't it?" she asked.

I shook my head. "Not close enough. Chief Coots is hobbling Kellan's investigation. If he were on the cusp of solving anything he wouldn't hang around playing midwife."

"Not to mention family mediator," she added, slyly.

"That too. In fact, all signs point to his needing my help. And for that to happen, I'll have to put Calvin in a nice tidy box in the back of my mental closet, where I never need think of him again."

"That sounds more like repression, whereas I'm here to help you have a conversation with him."

"My plan was to dump the wallet and run."

"The dump and run ploy turns around later and chases you," she said. "There's no need to unleash everything today. Just lift the lid and let off a bit of steam. Got it?"

"Got it. Release a bit of steam and turn back into Sherlock."

"Perfect. I'm proud of you."

Keats leaned on my shoulder again and said he was proud of me, too. This time it came out as a regular mumble, and I think Jilly was probably as relieved as I was to hear it. We had enough to worry about without a genius dog *actually* talking.

CHAPTER TWENTY-FOUR

C alvin looked older and smaller standing in the motel doorway than he had in my barn. I wouldn't have thought it possible for him to age and shrink so fast if I hadn't seen the exact opposite happen with Edna Evans. She'd gone from an old lady in a recliner to an ATV-riding warrior. Miracles did happen around Clover Grove and not all of them involved a certain sheepdog. Sometimes they worked with you and sometimes against you. It seemed like my father's past was dragging him down, even without a murder conviction.

"Ivy. I hoped you'd come," he said.

My good intentions evaporated instantly, replaced by annoyance. Jilly squeezed my elbow and Keats leaned against my leg. I truly wanted to put this angst behind me but I wasn't ready to forgive just yet.

"Chief Harper asked me to bring back your wallet," I said, offering the baggie. "I'm sorry my goat stole it."

"I'm sorry I let her." He took it and then crossed his arms, leaning against the door frame instead of inviting us in. "I was so focused on getting your help that I left myself open to caprine capers."

"Turns out you didn't need my help anyway. The chief said they're satisfied with your alibi. I guess you're free to go."

"I'm not going anywhere till Daphne's killer has been found. We were never serious but she was a good woman and didn't deserve this."

Meaning he probably still had some treasure hunting to do. It was the real reason he'd come back, after all.

"The police will get to the bottom of it soon."

"Never did have much confidence in police," he said. "With the possible exception of Chief Harper and your brother. When I was young, all they ever did was turn a blind eye. They left my mom and me exposed to bootleggers and crooks, including my own father and grandfather. She had to ally herself with the biggest criminal this town has ever seen to protect us."

"I heard about Polly," I said. "From Sterling."

"He said you'd visited." Calvin reached out to shake Jilly's hand, since I had neglected to introduce them. "He also said Asher was a lucky man, Jilly."

"I've had a warm welcome into the Galloway clan," she said. "I'd love to hear more about your mother. Polly sounds like a resourceful woman, and charming, too."

He brightened and nodded. "She was always fun, no matter what was going on. And there was always something going on. Her biggest mistake was marrying my father."

"Because he was a crook," I said.

"Because he was an *incompetent* crook. He never got

a job done right and that put everyone at risk. Frank Swenson only kept him around because Polly asked. But that didn't stop others from trying. He was always coming home with a black eye or split lip."

"What a difficult childhood," Jilly said.

"She did her best to shield me from the worst, and I didn't know the cost for years. Sometimes we'd go over and stay with her parents where there were plenty of animals. Those were the happiest times." He turned to me. "Have you seen the old homestead?"

"The Fable home? No. I thought it had been knocked down."

"There's a legion hall on the property now, but part of the house is still standing."

"Why don't we go see it?" Jilly asked.

I turned, glaring, and she just gave me a smile that said she knew what was good for me. Keats mumbled his endorsement of the plan.

"I'd like to show you," Calvin said. "I took Iris and Violet the other day. Asher had already been on his own."

My inner hackles rose again but a couple of deep breaths drove them down. Iris and Violet were allowed to make their own choices and didn't need to tell me about them. If I hoped to free myself from this shackle, I had to make peace with everything I'd shoved into the mental closet that had Calvin's name on it. Soon he would leave Clover Grove, but I'd be here forever and my siblings were an important part of my life.

"Sounds good," I said. "I know where the legion hall is. We'll meet you there."

There was no one in the parking lot when we arrived,

but Calvin still parked what was likely a rental sedan in the bushes. I did the same with the truck. And despite Kellan's assurances that Calvin was innocent, I took a close look at the car to make sure it wasn't caked with mud from Potter's Bog. It was clean, but not straight-from-the-car-wash clean. I was a little disappointed, but not surprised. If he had followed us, he would likely have kept up with Mom.

"Follow me," he said, forcing his way through bushes nearly as prickly and fierce as those near Daphne's house.

It wasn't long before Percy and Keats circled and got ahead of him to forge the path.

"These two are something else," he said. "It's like they've been here before."

"They haven't," I said. "But they usually know best."

Keats mumbled something loud enough to drift back to me: *Always.*

"You've been told," Calvin said. "He's a dog with opinions."

The fact that he admired my animals unnerved me. Was I going to end up liking Calvin against my will? It was an unspoken rule that anyone Keats liked, I liked. I couldn't change that rule at whim. Trusting the dog without conditions pretty much kept me alive.

Again Keats rumbled. It sounded like, "remember that," and I laughed.

"Are you having a conversation with your dog?" Calvin asked.

"He's got plenty to say. I understand some of it."

"My mother was like that," he said. "She always kept sheepdogs. Border collies, blue heelers, corgis and more.

She chatted to them all day and they seemed to answer back, too."

"How interesting," Jilly said from behind me. I didn't dare look back at her because of the bushes, but I knew there was a little smirk on her face.

"It was embarrassing sometimes," Calvin added. "Because she didn't just do it at home. When we walked through town with Champ, her lead dog, it was like she couldn't make a decision without consulting him first. 'Where should we go first, Champ? How does it look in the grocery store, Champ? Any concerns about the hardware store, Champ?'" After a few seconds, he went on, "She talked more to that dog than to me. And definitely more than to my father."

"Sounds like he was keeping her safe," I said. "Like Keats does me."

"What happened to Champ?" Jilly asked. "After she passed?"

"He died with her, I'm afraid. Trying to save her. As if a sheepdog could stop a pair of runaway horses."

My eyes filled with tears and words died in my throat.

"That is so sad," Jilly said. "Tragic."

It was tragic and I had no doubt whatsoever that Keats would do the same. It was a timely reminder to listen when he persuaded me against what I wanted to do. Maybe Champ had tried to warn Polly that day and she ignored him. She sounded just as stubborn as me.

There was a yip up ahead. Keats was telling me to stay focused. That this wasn't just a walk down memory lane. There was more to learn here.

"It was for the best," Calvin finally continued. "Champ would have died of grief otherwise. They were inseparable. Seems like you and Keats may be like that, too."

"We are," I said. "He's pretty much the best thing that ever happened to me."

After a minute, he said, "You want to hear something strange? Champ had one blue eye, too."

"Really? That is a coincidence," Jilly said. "Right, Ivy?"

The news shocked me into silence again, and a particularly nasty branch whacked me in the face while I tried to digest the information. It seemed like more than an eerie coincidence. A portend of some kind.

Finally we emerged at the old Fable home. Unlike the Galloway house, it had pretty much fallen to ruin. The roof and some of the walls had caved in, and the porch was just a bunch of jagged boards that stuck out like fangs.

"Why is it such a wreck?" I asked, standing on the sloping, mossy stones of the front walk. "Nearly every other old house in Clover Grove has been so well preserved. Even your father's home."

"After Mom's death, people said it was haunted. They'd always believed she was having an affair with Frank Swenson, and now they said she was a witch, too, because of her eccentric behavior. Either way, no one wanted the land, although they were happy enough to dig it up in the unrelenting hunger for gold. Sterling ultimately sold it to the legion, and they built their own hall."

"Was she?" I asked. "Having an affair with Frank Swenson?"

He shook his head. "Not to my knowledge. He loved her, I'm sure of that, but I don't think she ever gave in. My father didn't make her happy, but Frank wouldn't have, either."

I walked around, taking everything in. There was an old weathervane stuck in the lowest branches of a large oak tree.

"Can you get that, Percy?" I asked.

The marmalade cat was already on his way up the trunk, and when he reached the branch he waited for us to stand back before knocking it off. Picking up the twisted metal, I smiled. There were four rusty goats on it instead of roosters.

"So you talk to cats, too?" Calvin said, sounding bemused.

"Sure, and about sixty other animals. People think I'm crazy, too."

"Huh," he said. "Then I guess your mother was right that six was our lucky number. I wanted to stop at five. It was a lot of kids and with my reputation, I had trouble holding down a job."

Words turned to dust in my throat again. No kid wants to hear she was unwanted, even when she's old enough to have kids of her own.

As always, Jilly stepped in when I stumbled. "That's a lot of mouths to feed at any time," she said.

"Dahlia didn't need to twist my arm too hard. As an only child, I loved having a full house. It was just the practicalities. We were young when we got started.

Neither one of us was prepared for so much responsibility so soon."

I didn't want to hear this, so I shifted into neutral and let Jilly drive the conversation. After all, she was doing this for Asher, too. For the good of the entire family.

"What happened, if you don't mind my asking?" she said. "I mean, with Dahlia. Everyone seems to think you two were good together."

"Revisionist history," he said. "No one thought so at the time. They said she was too good for me. That I'd be her downfall. It wears on a man's pride when people expect him to fail his family." He broke a branch off the oak tree and snapped it in two. "But they weren't wrong."

"Dahlia survived," Jilly reminded him. "Everyone survived."

"Because I left," he said. "There were people after me. People who wanted to collect on my father's debts and thought I had the money to pay them."

"Why would they think that?"

"Frank's so-called treasures. He had put something aside for my mom, in case my dad... disappeared. But if Frank provided for her, she didn't collect before she died. My dad left soon after, either by his own steam or Frank's." He looked up at the old house. "I came here to stay with my grandparents when I was fifteen. Wasn't really wanted, I'm afraid. I was seen as my father's son, and I turned into him, eventually. Funny how that happens."

"It doesn't sound to me like that's what happened," Jilly continued. "You left, rather than drag your family into danger. Were you even involved in crime?"

"Just enough to stay alive," he said. "And never after I left. The web here had expanded with the generations and it seemed everywhere I turned there was pressure to do the wrong thing."

"It sounds like this town is built on a lawless foundation," I said. "Since Frank was part of a founding family."

"No wonder there's still so much trouble," Jilly added. "It's baked into the mix."

"True," he said. "It was hard to avoid. And crime is even more dangerous when you're no good at it, which I wasn't. So I turned into a rolling stone, waiting for my father's enemies to die off so that I could come back. I only took the chance after seeing what Ivy had accomplished here and right away a dirtbag stuck out one hand for money. The other had a gun."

"Jim Moss' client, I presume? Who is it?"

"The less you know the safer you are. I thought maybe it was my time to find this treasure of Polly's. Clear the so-called debt and help out the family." He scuffed the soil with one boot. "I didn't expect to be welcomed with open arms. I was never able to send enough, but I did what I could."

"Mom said you sent nothing. Zero. Nada."

He frowned. "Asher told me that, too. I sent plenty. Sometimes she cashed the checks, mostly she didn't. Seems like she preferred to be a martyr at the mini mart."

I almost laughed but nipped it back. Mom *had* been a martyr at the mini mart, until she got fired from that job, too. She never let on there was another source of income. It would have made things easier, especially for Daisy. But desperation had given me the life I had now.

Perhaps my siblings would come to the same sort of realization.

"Dahlia did her best," Jilly said. "Obviously there was more to the story than Ivy and the others knew."

"I never deceived Dahlia, and I asked her to come with me. But being on the run with six kids wouldn't have gone well."

Finally I spoke. "There must have been another way. But even if you had to go, there were phones. Postcards. Email eventually."

He went back to scuffing the dirt. "It's what your mother wanted. What she thought was for the best and would keep you safer. I respected her wishes."

Keats had had enough conversation and nudged my leg to get me moving. I circled the house with the weathervane dangling from my fingertips, and Calvin and Jilly followed.

"Have you had any luck with Polly's treasure?" I asked.

"No, and I've combed this property and the Galloways' many times, both before I left and again this week. Treasure hunting makes you crazy."

"It may have been reclaimed by Frank," I said. "Or found by others. There are success stories I know about, and probably more that I don't."

"I heard that from the chief." I looked back and saw a grim smile on his face. "Never did like those Langman sisters. Glad you set them right, Ivy."

"Oh, they're not done yet," I said. "Edna Evans says they're like cockroaches."

"Agreed. But I honestly don't think they'd kill anyone."

Keats mumbled his dissenting opinion.

"Really?" Calvin said. "They're that bad?"

Jilly and I glanced at each other. Calvin had just had a direct exchange with my dog without noticing it.

Finally Jilly turned and raised the question she knew I'd been wanting to ask. "Calvin, do you have any idea what happened to Daphne Newell? It seems coincidental that she'd be killed the week of your homecoming."

He raised empty hands and then twisted them together. "We hadn't been in touch for ages. I worried she'd get too attached and things between us were never going to get serious."

"Is that all?" Jilly asked.

"I don't think anyone would kill her to get at me, if that's what you're thinking. She lived in another state when we met so no one here knew about it. I was surprised she moved back."

I looked down at Keats, who was staring at Calvin intently with his blue eye. There was more to this story, even if Calvin wasn't fully aware of it. "Did Daphne know about the treasure Frank hid for Polly?"

"Not from me." He gave a heavy sigh. "She did ask a lot of questions, though. Maybe the rumor mill reached her. In my day, gossip traveled like wind over the hills."

"Still does," I said. "It's magic."

"Black magic," Jilly said.

Keats looked from me to Calvin and back. That's when I realized Calvin may have been played.

"This is going to sound strange," I said. "But do you happen to know if Daphne was a natural brunette?"

"Blonde," he said. "She said she wanted to try something different."

"Maybe she thought you had a type," I said. "Like Mom."

He laughed. "Dahlia is one of a kind. The exception to all the rules."

"And a threat to stop signs everywhere," I said, as Keats gathered us up to go back.

"She still knocking them off?" Calvin said. "I accused her of doing that on purpose. There was a decent driver under all that attitude."

"At least she still knows her way around Potter's Bog," I said, glancing back at him. "Thank you for that."

He smiled, and although I couldn't quite bring myself to return it, I didn't scowl either.

Keats pranced around with a ha-ha-ha. He was proud of me again.

"Thanks, buddy," I muttered. "Me too. But we've got more work to do."

"Be careful," Calvin called.

I wasn't sure whether he was warning me about our footing or had overheard my words to Keats. Either way, he was right.

CHAPTER TWENTY-FIVE

On the way home from our family reunion, Keats began pacing in the back seat. Percy moved into Jilly's lap to avoid the paw traffic.

"What's up with him?" she asked.

I shrugged. "I've got a strange feeling, too. It's like when Mom said she sensed a hawk circling overhead."

Jilly crossed her arms and hugged herself. "We're the bunnies, I presume?"

"Not necessarily. But I'd better stay focused today. Thanks to you, there's a little less steam clouding my vision."

When we were nearly at the farm, Keats stuck his head between the seats and woofed.

"What now?" Jilly asked.

"He wants to keep going. I think he's looking for something. Let's see where this leads."

I rolled down the rear window partway. Maybe some fresh air would speed his search.

He stuck his entire head out, and it wasn't long

before the white paw came up—not just in a point, but an enthusiastic clawing of the glass. His tail was issuing a bristly alarm at the same time.

We were half a mile past Edna's driveway at this point, and there was thick brush on either side of the highway.

"I don't suppose we could just call this one in?" Jilly said, as I pulled onto the shoulder.

I grinned at her. "Let me get Chief Coots on the horn. Tell him my dog is getting a bad vibe off the bushes. Let's just take a quick peek first, if you don't mind."

"I do mind. I'd rather face down the ghost of dads past than a killer in the bush. Can't we at least call Edna to come bearing arms?"

Studying Keats, I shook my head. "He's not *that* worried, according to the ruff report. Why don't I take a look and you can stay in the truck with Percy?"

"As if. I'm registering my objections, but I'd never let you go into the woods alone." She zipped up her jacket. "I've never been outdoorsy but I'd hoped Mother Nature would be welcoming here. Instead, there's always this quiet menace."

"Never mind, Goldilocks. Keats has you covered, and Edna can be here in about five minutes. Six if she dithers over whether to bring sword or crossbow."

Jilly laughed as we set off, and I congratulated myself on brightening the mood. Keats steered us along the gravel shoulder for a stretch until we saw tire tracks leaving the highway and heading straight into the bush. I figured it was yet another entry point to the trail system, but the trees didn't yield to the familiar old ruts.

Instead, there were just the broken branches of forced entry. No vehicle would get far this way. Not even a tank.

Keats urged us on with excited mumbles until I saw the glint of glass and metal ahead.

"It's a car," Jilly said. "A brown sedan."

"Gray, I think. But it's covered in a whole lot of muck. Methinks this car was lucky to escape Clover Grove's very own Bermuda Triangle last night."

Snapping some photos, I shot them over to Kellan.

"Any idea who owns it?" Jilly asked.

I bent over to peer inside. "Owned. Past tense. There's a fuchsia mitten in the passenger footwell and a fuchsia scarf on the back seat. Daphne's car has been missing."

"So the big question is who stole it," Jilly said.

"And the *other* big question is why is it hidden within walking distance of Runaway Farm?"

AFTER CHECKING in on the guests, I headed down to the barn to visit Big Mama and family. Charlie was doing the chores, while Poppy sat cross-legged in the nursery pen with a kid in her lap.

"Why is Charlie shoveling while you're sitting?" I asked. "I pay you to make his life easier, Pops. So that he'll never ever retire."

"I'm worried about the babies," she said. "Only two can nurse at one time and it isn't fair. This one is the smallest and can't compete. So I'm making sure she gets her chance, even though Charlie says it's survival of the fittest."

Sometimes Charlie's practical sensibilities clashed with my save-them-all attitude. It was nice to see Poppy stepping in to become chief goat advocate. Of all my siblings, she'd been least interested in Runaway Farm when I got here. In eight months, she'd transformed. Maybe not as much as Edna, but Poppy hadn't been through a near-death experience. Yet. As a confirmed daredevil, it was bound to happen sometime.

"Families aren't always sweet, are they?" I said.

She glanced at me and frowned. "I haven't been to see Calvin, if that's what you're asking. The others are falling all over him."

"It's not like that, Pops. Well, maybe for Asher. I think they just want to put bad feelings behind them."

"It was hard enough coming fourth in line without his leaving," she said, avoiding my eyes. "At least there were a few scraps of attention for me while he was here."

Ah. No wonder she was so worried about the fourth baby goat. She was the fourth kid in our family. It probably wasn't as bad as being the sixth and coming after the golden boy, but it wasn't ideal either.

I thought about Jilly's words and then shared them. "The weight of what happened is a lot to carry, Poppy. You might want to talk to Calvin while he's still in town. Let off some steam and reduce the pressure inside. On Jilly's advice, I did that today and feel a lot better."

Keats mumbled that he thought of it first, and I laughed.

"You two are crazy," she said, gesturing between us.

"Don't even. I heard you pep-talking this brood when I came in. That's what happens on Runaway Farm."

"Well, I hope they listen. They need to pull together."

"Good advice," I said. "And you're going to need to learn how to pull, too. Literally. Charlie said milking is too hard on his back, so that's going to be your job."

"Milking? In the morning?" Poppy tended to clock in late and I hadn't made a fuss over it. I wasn't the Grim Reaper of HR anymore and wanted her to find her own footing. Like Mom, she'd cycled through many jobs and moved around a lot, too. But if she wanted to be a full-fledged part of our team, it was time for more structure.

"Eight a.m., like clockwork," I said. "Welcome to our dairy. Gertie's going to teach you the ins and outs of milking and soapmaking, and Jilly will market the products."

I expected a fight, but she looked down at the little doe in her lap. "Can I keep this one?"

"All of them. I was hoping for girls."

"You're going to need a bigger ark," Charlie called from the horse stall.

It was becoming a common refrain. "Working on it, Charlie. The universe will provide."

"So far all it's providing is trouble and manure," he said. "And then more manure."

We were all laughing as I left the barn. There were half a dozen things on my to-do list, but I had the feeling I should be someplace else.

Keats evidently shared that feeling, because he herded me back to the truck, where Percy was fending off the morning chill by reclining on the hood in a frail sunbeam.

"Where to, boys?" I asked, as they jumped inside. "Can we do some good today? Because I feel like I've been a little selfish lately. I never did enough navel gazing in my old life, and now I've shifted too far the other way. Somewhere in the middle lies peace of mind."

Keats mumbled a dissenting opinion. Perhaps peace was the enemy of crime-solving.

"We need some balance, my tuxedoed friend," I said. "We may share sheepdog personalities, but this pace is harder to sustain for me than for you."

Paws on the dashboard, he gave a ha-ha-ha.

"Braggart. You're practically still a pup. Just you wait."

I watched for his sign and then turned left onto the highway. Then he tapped on the passenger window and I made a right onto a road I hadn't tried before. There was a handful of homes with large gardens, chicken coops and golden retrievers in the yard. Homesteaders. They had all the perks of farming without the harsh realities.

At the end of the road, Keats signaled a turn that appeared to lead directly into the bush. Soon the entry widened to become another way into the secret trail system. It was nearly grown over. The homesteaders clearly didn't venture far afield.

"Bootleggers and crooks," I said. "We have them to thank for these trails, boys. But we also have them to thank for needing them. Today was an eye-opener, wasn't it? Calvin shed some light on the town's shady past."

Keats nudged my phone in the console and I took the hint.

"Good idea. I'll let Jilly know we're on another fool's errand. Maybe you'd like to tell her yourself, since you're branching into human language."

He mumbled a smart aleck remark that I didn't try to understand. It sounded like an insider dog joke.

This path was more circuitous than many but less treacherous than some. Happily there were no tire-sucking bogs lying in ambush.

I wasn't particularly surprised to see the red roof of the legion hall ahead of us. Our exploration of the Fable homestead a few hours ago had been cursory because of the awkward family dynamics. Keats was wise to suggest another poke around.

After parking in the same place, I updated Jilly again. "Kellan would be so impressed with my precautions," I said. "I guess that talk with Calvin did a lot of good. After an abscess drains, there's relief and clarity."

I grabbed my backpack from the bed of the truck and used it as a shield to push through the savage brush until we reached the decaying remains of the Fable home. I hadn't sensed much of anything on the Galloway property, but here I did. It was like Polly reached out across the divide with cold fingers and brushed my forehead. Maybe she was clearing out the rest of my mental weeds.

"Obviously, I shared something in common with my grandmother," I said. "Good taste in dogs with one blue eye, for starters. She stood right where I am with her Champ. Can you believe it?" A shiver ran up my spine.

"Now I understand the genealogy society a little better. I feel roots under this earth."

Keats didn't waste time on reflection. He was following Percy up the splintered remains of the front stairs.

"Careful," I called. "Looks like it could crumble with a sneeze."

I wished I'd thought to bring along the weathervane from the truck. It had felt like a talisman.

"At least I have better taste in men than Polly had," I said, starting to circle the house again. "She liked the bad boys, it seems. Mind you, it sounds like it was harder to tell the difference in those days, and women had fewer choices."

Coming back to the front of the house, I sat down on a mossy stump to stare at it. I was missing something. An idea tickled the corners of my consciousness and it was time to look past the family politics that had clouded my view.

"It's in the photos," I said. "The old photos."

Keats came down from the porch and brushed against my shins, mumbling the whole time. It was quite a monologue but he went too fast for me to understand.

"Slow down, buddy. Give me a chance to catch up."

I pulled out my phone and started examining the small collection. At a glance, I could see there was a record of Polly's life in images, from girlhood to a woman not much older than I was now.

Enlarging the photo Percy had first flicked to my attention, I studied the home depicted there. It wasn't a mansion by any means. Just a regular white house with darker gables. Looking from the photo to the house before me, I saw one of those gables, chipped and black, lying on the ground. I hadn't seen another old house quite like this in Clover Grove, where red brick was more common. In the photo, a weathervane stood on the roof. The image became blurry the more I stretched it, but I thought I saw goats rather than roosters.

"Why would Daphne Newell have a photo of the Fable home on her dining room floor, and a photo of Polly hidden in her sideboard?" I said. "Was she doing some work on Calvin's family tree? Maybe that was her way of getting closer to him. Or, more likely, closer to Polly's treasure."

There was the photo from my father's wallet. Another from Sterling. And the one that Big Mama had seized and spit out in two pieces. There had to be a reason this record of Polly's life had fallen into my hands.

Keats rumbled something that sounded like, "keep going."

"Maybe one of her buddies from the genealogy group found out what she was researching. They all have that crazed look of treasure hunters. Or maybe she had a partner in crime who turned on her when she got too close. Greed would be motive enough. But if so, which one? And did any of them find the gold?"

Keats nudged my hand. The one with the phone. There was more homework ahead.

Flipping through my camera roll, I studied the shots of Polly in front of this house with generations of pets showing the passage of time as much as her face and clothing.

"Champ," I said. "We're looking for Champ."

There was a whine of encouragement. The photo from Daphne's cabinet was of Polly when she was my age or older. This time she had one arm around the oak tree, pressing her cheek to its trunk with what looked like a coy smile. A border collie leaned into her leg, and the dog seemed to be smiling, too. It was hard to tell from the grainy black and white image which eye was blue.

The most recent photo of Polly with Champ was the one Big Mama had stolen from the table in the family room. Unfortunately, it was also torn and chewed. In one half, Polly's hands were clasped over her heart. In the other, Champ stared up at her. They were separated forever soon after, I presumed.

"Heartbreaking," I said. "This may have been their last photo together. Even their last time here together at the home she clearly loved."

Percy got into my lap to head butt my chest. I thought the cat just wanted to get me moving, but it prompted me to grope around inside my pocket for the fragments of the original photo. Flipping the halves, I saw a few words on the back that I had missed before. Faded, well masticated words. I could only pick out a few of them. Just enough to know they were the same as the words on the note under the dresser in the Galloway home.

The riddle. Frank had written the riddle on the photo. And the photo had been in possession of Daphne or someone else who'd been scrapbooking in my family room.

"*When I think of thee by our tree my heart grows sad and weary,*" I recited. "The oak tree! It's in every photo, boys. She loved that tree. Look at her hands clenched over her heart. That's a clue. I feel it."

I took a new photo of the partial image and blew it up as much as I could. "There's something on the tree. Over her head. That's where Champ is looking, too."

Keats gave a little yip and then a nip to my pant cuff. Time to get moving.

By the time he'd herded me to the old oak, Percy was on his way up. I was last to the party, as usual.

"I see it," I said, backing away again. "It's so much higher now that the tree's grown. I can't tell what it is." Zooming in with my camera lens, I snapped a photo. The image showed a blurry image of a heart carved into the tree. Inside were the initials PF + F. The "S" for Swenson was gone, if it had ever existed.

"Okay, so Frank showed his love in the old-fashioned way, with a pocketknife. And Polly's smile says that actually meant something to her."

Keats herded me around the wide base of the tree. On the opposite side from the heart—the one facing the bush—was a large, blackened hole. The trunk had been struck hard by lightning long ago, yet the tree survived.

Percy found his way to a branch near the hole and gave me a purr-meow.

"Oh no. I'm going to have to join you up there, aren't I?"

Glancing down, I met Keats' intense, blue stare.

"I don't like heights, boys." The dog mumbled something. "I don't like caves, either. You are correct. Is it so wrong to want my boots planted on the grass?"

Sighing, I went back around the house where I'd seen

a ladder. It looked almost as old as the oak tree and had no business supporting a sturdy farmer. Luckily, there was a length of rope in my backpack, which I'd begun transforming into my personal go-kit.

After propping the rickety ladder against the tree, I collected the rope and tossed it over the branch where Percy had sat. He was above it now, keeping out of the way.

I looped the rope around my waist and did some mental calculations about the length. If I got it right, the rope would catch and swing me. I might lose my breakfast, but not a vital organ.

"We've pretty much done this before, remember? At the Bingham manor. It ended well then. I mean, if you consider discovering human remains ending well. It solved an old mystery and brought peace to Hazel. What are the odds of doing the same again today?"

Keats mumbled that the odds weren't too bad. His tail was up, although his ears were twitching forward and back. When his ears moved like that, I got moving. Time might be short.

I put one boot on the bottom rung, testing it.

"I guess this beats scuba diving for sunken treasure, right?"

The dog gave an assertive yes to that and I laughed. He hated water, yet it was probably only a matter of time before we found ourselves in that very predicament. There were only so many places to hide secrets.

"All right then, up I go, and fast. The longer I think about it the worse it will get."

I counted myself lucky that most of the rungs held up

under my work boots. One snapped completely, however, and two others gave ominous cracks. I'd be going down a lot faster than I went up and breakfast was most definitely in peril, if not my spleen.

The ladder barely reached the hole in the tree. It was as if Mother Nature had decreed, "You got here just in time."

Keats whined below and I called, "All good, buddy. I'll just straddle this big branch and peek inside."

My phone lit up the large crater and revealed a metal box. I reached in to grab it, and my fingers tingled as I touched its rusted sides. I had no doubt that this had belonged to Polly once. Whatever it contained, she'd meant for it to land in the hands of her descendants.

"I should wait till I climb down to open it," I said, examining it from all sides. "My utility clippers will snap that little padlock easily. It's so rusty I could almost break it with my fingers."

Keats whined again, voting for climbing down before cracking open the family vault. But I couldn't resist. Just one quick peek to satisfy my curiosity.

It was a bit of a balancing act, trying to grab my clippers from my side pocket while holding the box and clenching the bough between my knees. In the end, I put the box back in the hole and then clutched the trunk with one arm while leaning in to seize the loop of the lock and twist.

As predicted, it snapped easily. I lifted the lid and then swapped out the clippers for my phone so I could look inside.

What I saw took my breath away for a minute. It

wasn't gold, but it was most certainly a treasure in terms of family history. There was an old leather-bound diary, a red velvet bag that felt like it held jewelry, and a square of cardboard, which depicted a map. It had faded with time but I was sure we could find whatever Polly, and likely Frank, had wanted to share.

Now, Keats' tone changed from pleading to urgent. His ruff was up and his ears down. Someone was coming, and it wasn't a friend. Meanwhile, I was literally stuck up a tree while my defender paced below.

I did the only thing I could under the circumstances —texted my army. Then I prepared to make what would surely be the least elegant exit of all time.

CHAPTER TWENTY-SIX

The ladder hadn't made any promises on the way up but I had expected it to stick around. As I started to turn on the branch, however, the ladder made a run for it. Keats darted away when it fell. His howl came from distress over my being far out of range of his interventions. Percy, still above me, offered an eerie yowl of his own.

"Quiet, boys," I said. "Keats, go hide behind the house. We're just going to wait this one out. Maybe Calvin's come back for another poke around. Chances are good no one will look up and see the stranded hobby farmer perched like a turkey vulture."

Keats didn't leave easily. It took another couple of exhortations before he finally crept to the side of the house, tail still bristling. Calvin had never elicited such a reaction before so I knew the intruder likely wasn't him. There were worse things than awkward family reunions, it seemed.

I stared over the clearing in the direction of my truck.

My entire body prickled now and my brain geared up, making calculations and connections. If I had enough time, the answers would fall into place one by one. Pressure always helped... as long as it didn't tip me over. There was a long way to fall today, rope or no rope.

So Daphne Newell was looking into our family tree. Her colleagues in the genealogy society had suggested a heartbreak, but also that she needed money. What if the heartbreak wasn't over Calvin at all? What if her true love was someone on the genealogy team, who'd decided he loved the idea of keeping all the treasure more than Daphne herself? Mandy had said she overheard an argument. That Daphne was upset. Perhaps her partner had decided to cut her out of the picture—permanently—and take her photos. She'd successfully hidden one in the sideboard. Perhaps there had been even more.

With only two men in the group, it narrowed the playing field. My money was on Finn Donnelly. He made no bones about wanting to find a fortune in a family tree. Apparently it didn't matter if it was someone else's. On the other hand, Finn was repugnant, at least to me. Exactly how far would Daphne go for money? At least Walt was pleasant, although he was probably about 20 years her senior.

The two men had driven to Dorset Hills in the same car just before Daphne died. Both had opportunity and motive. There hadn't been much of a window, however, so again, my vote was for the younger, spryer man. It was hard to imagine Walt jumping into a cab, murdering Daphne and driving her car back to downtown Dorset

Hills to meet up with his crew in such a short time. But anything was possible when someone was gold-addled.

Daphne's car was key to the whole operation. The daily walks—sanctioned by Chief Coots—gave the killer a chance to case out the Galloway home and hide the murder weapon in the bunker. And then he used the car to follow me to Daphne's house last night and returned it to the bushes while I ate cheesecake at Mandy's.

Keats gave a low rumble from his hiding place. I don't know if the sound really carried, or if I just felt it in my soul. I was about to get confirmation that Daphne was never interested in my father and was primarily in love with the idea of what was inside this tree. All I could do now was hope that these roots, the physical ones, would protect one more family secret.

The man who emerged from the bushes was wearing a hat with a brim and a red-checkered jacket. Instead of the treasure hunter's usual shovel, he carried something far more terrifying... a chainsaw. Clearly, I wasn't the only one who'd put two and tree together. I may have reached the treasure first, but that's where my advantage ended. The way the brim of his hat swiveled warily told me he'd likely seen my truck and knew to expect me. Help was on the way, but my heart thundered so that I couldn't hear sirens, let alone the roar of Edna's ATV.

"There's time," I whispered. "An old oak doesn't fall in an instant."

In the distance, Keats rumbled again. Encouraging me to hang tight. That was the biggest challenge. My arm only reached a third of the way around the tree trunk and it suddenly felt boneless. I was clinging with spaghetti.

The lumberjack walked across the clearing and finally tipped back his head. It wasn't Finn Donnelly but Walt Watford. Apparently the genial head of the genealogy society had conspired not only against Daphne, but my father. My family.

It took less time than I'd hoped for him to spot me. His eyes bulged and his mouth gaped, but like all the coldblooded killers I'd met, he recovered quickly. A feral smile curved into place and his eyes narrowed as he assessed my predicament.

"Hey there, Ivy," he said. "So you do have an interest in your family tree after all."

I pulled in a couple of slow, deep breaths and pressed the record button on my phone. The only way I was getting out of this was to keep him talking. So I sent an internal memo to the former Grim Reaper of HR. She'd helped me out of many binds before, perhaps none quite so uncomfortable as straddling a tree.

"You sure did," I said. "You're an inspiration, Walt."

"Was it something I said?" he asked.

I nodded. "It was everything you said. I thought about all the years I'd avoided thinking about my family and realized it was a mistake. What I didn't know left me exposed."

"I've never seen someone more exposed than you are right now. Although there wasn't much of your dress left when you ran away from Daphne's house last night. Your short sidekick sure can drive."

"My mom," I said, laughing. "Possibly the biggest surprise of many this week. You did well, considering. The police have Daphne's car, by the way."

The chainsaw dipped sharply. I'd surprised him. Hopefully enough to make him realize he didn't have time to play arborist today.

"I'd forgotten how bad the trails get in spring," he said.

"Mom said the same. I'm glad you gave her that little pick-me-up. It's been a tough week for her, what with Calvin popping up."

"For all of us," he said. "If he'd stayed gone it wouldn't have come to this. Daphne and I had a plan, but she lost her nerve, I'm afraid. I think she had a soft spot for Calvin."

"I'm assuming you had a soft spot for Daphne?"

"Soft enough. She was a stellar researcher. One of the best I've met. But at the end, she said it was Calvin's treasure to find. Well, I didn't come this far to abandon the hunt."

"She knew about the hazards of digging into old secrets," I said. "You all said the same thing."

"Sometimes we strike gold. Other times, compost. That's where you'll end up, I'm afraid."

"Maybe not," I said. "I get awfully lucky sometimes."

He laughed. "I've heard. Not this time. You'll fall on your own sword. Or in this case, my chainsaw."

"Sounds messy. I can think of better ways to go. You made it pretty easy for Daphne. I bet she didn't see it coming."

He shrugged. "I wish it hadn't gone that way, but like you said, she knew the risks. When she saw all the photos of this house in my family collection, she realized I had much more at stake than her. That's why she left the inn."

My brain did a few quick turns around the clues and came up empty. "I don't get it. Why would you have so many photos of my ancestral home?"

"If you'd done your homework, you'd know about a little branch on your family tree that you missed. The branch with the wavy line."

"Wavy line?"

"It's the symbol that signifies illegitimate offspring. Chester Galloway, your grandfather, had a few waves, one of them being me."

"Really? How nice to meet more family. You'll excuse me if I don't come down for a hug. Sometimes it's better to keep family at a distance, right?"

"You know all about that, I guess."

"My father and I rebuilt some burned bridges this morning," I said. "Right here on this property. You can do it, too. Blood is blood, right?"

"Blood is good," he said. "But gold is better. And I intend to take what should be mine. We lived a rough life, Mom and me. Chester refused to divorce his wife like he promised. But Mom got her hands on some of their family photos, in case I could find the treasure everyone talked about even then."

"There was something special about Polly," I said. "That's why Frank Swenson was looking out for her. And she was looking out for her child."

"Calvin's a petty crook," he said. "An inept one at that."

"Inept, maybe. Crook, no. At least not according to

Chief Harper. My father has a record of no more than the usual mischief of youth. Whereas *you're* a murderer. Poor Daphne."

"Like I said, Daphne knew what she was doing. At first she was happy to go undercover and find out more from your dad. But when she heard he was coming back here, she changed her mind."

"She took back the photos she'd found," I said. "When she left the inn."

The brim of his hat bobbed an affirmative. "We were so close to finding what you've just discovered. But I couldn't risk her sharing the photos or riddle with Calvin."

Finally I heard a faint rumble in the distance. Edna. If I could keep him talking just 10 minutes longer, I'd be okay.

"That's when you brought Finn into the scheme? I assume he covered for you in exchange for a cut of this." I slapped the tree. "He seemed oddly blasé about the whole thing."

"It was already done when I told him and he rolled with it," Walt said. "His silence was reasonably priced and allowed me to get the car hidden. I needed it."

"Are you going to give Finn a fair slice of the pie? I asked.

His laugh was as hollow as this tree. "Fair enough to keep his big mouth shut, I suppose. But fair is in the eye of whoever holds the chainsaw."

"Walt, wait," I said. "Here's the thing. While I have no interest in treasure, per se, I find myself fascinated by my grandmother. We had something in common and I want to know more. You lit the fire."

"And now it'll burn you up."

"What I found is mine," I said. "It's meant for me— for my family—not you. Chester Galloway left us nothing but a bad name, apparently. Polly Fable tried to be more generous."

"I've heard enough," he said. "I hoped you'd go as quietly as Daphne, but it's about to get very noisy."

He set the chainsaw on the ground and yanked the cord. It didn't start on the first pull or even the second, and I prayed it was out of gas. One more pull got it roaring, however, and he straightened to use both hands to put on safety goggles.

There was a movement across the clearing. I hoped for Edna, but instead, saw the silvery blonde hair of my father. He looked up and caught my eye, surprised but not shocked. He expected to find me here... just not *up* here.

He gave me a sign that he was going to tackle Walt. I shook my head and drew my finger across my throat for good measure. The chainsaw was a worthy opponent.

I had a better idea. Equally dangerous, but better. I glanced up at Percy and then to the side of the house where Keats had emerged to fix me with his blue eye. My furry soldiers were ready.

"Be careful," I said.

Neither pet could hear my voice over the chainsaw. I couldn't hear it myself. But they knew. Keats gave the merest swish of his white tuft and Percy's mouth opened in a soundless battle cry.

I gathered up the slack in the rope, hand over hand. Then I pulled myself up into a squat on the bough. There was no time for second guessing. Walt was bending over to lift the saw. Another moment and I'd run the risk of being sliced up like deli meat. "Bombs away!"

I pushed off sideways, feeling a horrible midair pause before the sudden drop began. The rope burned my palms as it unfurled. If I'd planned better, the arc of my swing would have been smaller. Walt had enough time to see me coming and straighten up with the chainsaw. Fortunately, he couldn't lift it high enough in time.

Gripping the rope tight, I lifted both boots as I swung forward and kicked him hard in the gut. I worried he'd fall on his own chainsaw—something I definitely did not want to see—but it took an arc of its own and dropped to the grass. He tumbled onto his back.

I landed a couple of yards away, upright by some miracle. Now all I had to do was keep Walt from grabbing the saw again.

A black-and-white streak shot across the yard just seconds before an orange bullet landed. Even the chainsaw couldn't drown out Walt's screams as Keats knocked off his hat and Percy delivered his classic 20-claw head massage to Walt's comb-over.

As the downed man tried to fight off my pets, Calvin grabbed the chainsaw and advanced on him. Walt scrabbled backward, but within a few yards, bumped into camouflaged pant legs. Edna never got a chance to unleash her artillery because the police were fanning out behind her.

It was over.

My father turned off the chainsaw and in the strange, heavy silence that followed, I said, "Percy, come. I'm going back up there to get—"

"You will do no such thing, young lady," Calvin said, making a sweeping gesture to one officer running toward us. "That's what brothers are for."

CHAPTER TWENTY-SEVEN

W hile the police dealt with Walt and dispersed to collect Finn Donnelly, Edna and Calvin escorted me back to the truck, where I sat down on the damp earth to open the box again.

"Look," I said, displaying the contents to Calvin. I took out the diary and gently flipped through the pages. My palms were raw from the rope but my fingertips did the walking. "Polly told her whole story here."

"We'll look at it later," he said. "Let's get you home."

I stared at the map. "We're not going home yet. There's a map."

"Kellan can take care of that," he said.

Edna bent to peer at the diary. "Calvin, you're welcome to look the other way if you like. Ivy and I are going to meet up with Gertie Rhodes to check things out."

"It'll wait for tomorrow," he said, opening the door of my truck and pointing.

"Or maybe it won't," I said, letting Edna help me to

my feet. "Your mother wanted us to find this and I'm not letting it get away."

"I'll drive," Edna said. "You've had quite a shock, Ivy."

"Nice try," I said. "I'm already in the doghouse over letting Mom drive the truck."

"That was pure lunacy," she said, walking around the truck to the passenger side.

"Dahlia's great in the back forty," Calvin called after her. "Utterly fearless."

Edna stared at him over the flatbed. "How about you, Calvin? Are you fearless? Follow or not, it's your choice."

He followed, bumping over the rutted trails in his sedan during a very twisty ride to the old Galloway homestead. Gertie was already parked and leaning against her van when we pulled up with Calvin close behind.

"Well, if it isn't Calvin Galloway," she said. "Living on the lam must have treated you well because you haven't changed much."

"Hey, Gertie," he said, grinning. "I didn't think a braid could grow that long. Or is it one of those clip-ons?"

Gertie straightened and let Minnie poke out from the folds of her poncho. "Pardon me?"

Calvin's grin didn't falter. "I said your hair looks lovely."

"Gertie, let it go," Edna said. "He was first on the scene to help Ivy and he didn't mess up."

"You called him?" I asked.

Edna shrugged. "He was closest and knew the best route. Daisy gave me his number."

"Ivy didn't need my help," he said. "That swing was something out of a Tarzan movie. Or Gilligan's Island."

"Ivy doesn't remember those shows," Edna said. "But since you do, you're going to love what we have to show you today."

I wasn't thrilled about going back down into the Galloway family bunker, despite having a team with me. Hanging from a tree branch was infinitely preferable. Still, I lowered Keats into the hole in a harness and then climbed down the ladder Gertie had set up in the entrance.

"You do the honors," she said, handing me a flashlight. "Keats was trying to tell us last time, but we didn't listen."

"Finding the murder weapon muddied the signs," I said. "Better late than never, right buddy?"

He mumbled a sassy response and trotted ahead of me into the tunnel system. Calvin delivered animated commentary from the end of the line until Edna stopped him.

"Silence, young man. I'll brief you on bunker etiquette later."

When we reached the last chamber, where Keats had found the dagger in the notch, the dog went into a point and stared straight ahead at what looked like any of the other mud walls.

"There's something behind it," I said, as Gertie and Edna flashed their lights around.

"False wall, most likely," Edna said. "Common bunker ploy."

"Sounds dangerous," Calvin said. "We should leave that to experts."

The lights swung around together and pinned him in their beam.

"We are bunker experts," Gertie said. "I defy you to find better in this region."

"Don't deny us the money shot, Calvin," Edna added. "We've been through a lot with your daughter."

"But what if the structure collapses and we're trapped down here?" he said.

"Do I look worried?" Edna asked.

I raised my hand. "You never look worried. That's not a good indicator."

"Worry ages you faster," she said, and both women chuckled. "So then ask someone who *is* a good indicator. Does Keats look worried?"

On the contrary, Keats was starting to dig at the wall himself. Percy sat back and let him do the dirty work. The white paws quickly grew dusty.

"That's good, buddy, but let the bunker experts take it from here, okay?"

Edna handed me her flashlight and pulled a knife with a fancy handle from one of her side pockets. "Harvey Dunbar would not approve of using a fine piece of workmanship on a job like this, but if I'm right about what Keats has exposed, it'll get the job done nicely."

I squatted to peek at the small space the dog had cleared. The layer of dried mud concealed a wooden door.

A few gentle, strategic taps of Edna's dagger brought

the false mud wall crumbling down. Behind it, there was indeed a wooden door set in a wood frame.

"Now for the million dollar question," Gertie said. "Will it open?"

That took more careful work by both women, but in due course, they stood back to let me do the honors.

"You found the place," Edna said. "The hard way."

I looked at Calvin, because he was the one Polly was thinking about when she hid that map in the tree. Not me.

He shrugged and said, "It's your party. I'm just along for the ride."

I pried at a little groove along the edge and the door opened with a groan. Age hadn't been as kind to the wood as it had to my friends.

Shining the light inside, I followed the beam on hands and knees.

"Trunks," I called, sitting back on my heels as Keats and Percy examined each one. "Three of them."

Both animals agreed on one, but all had heavy padlocks.

"I don't suppose anyone has a bolt cutter?" I called.

"Of course we do," Edna said. "It's in the prepper manifesto."

Gertie slid the tool in beside me. "Bigger would be better, but it'll work if you give it some English."

In fact, it took sweat and contortions, but finally I got the right angle and the lock snapped.

"Oh wow," I called back, even before the lid was fully open. "Someone just got rich."

"Rich is good," Gertie said. "But the discovery is what counts. Savor the moment, Ivy."

I hugged the boys. We'd had so many terrible moments of discovery together. Stumbling—literally—into a good one was a very welcome change.

After snapping some photos, I backed out and let Gertie and Edna open another trunk and Calvin the third. While they savored their moment, I went back through the tunnels and followed Percy up the ladder slowly. Then I pulled Keats up in his harness. Afterwards, the two animals frolicked in the first wildflowers, sensing we'd come to the end of this particular journey.

Eventually I called Kellan and told him what we'd found. It was just fate that my phone died while he was in the middle of what was shaping up to be a fine rant. He could recap the highlights for me later. For now, I just wanted to enjoy the fresh air.

"So now you've joined the buried treasure club with Gertie," Edna said, as they climbed out of the bunker one by one. "It's quite exclusive."

"I don't want it," I said. "It's Frank Swenson's dirty money."

"Don't be so sure of that," Calvin said. "I doubt my mother would have accepted the proceeds of crime, as desperate as she may have been."

"What a life she could have had with this," Edna said. "Such a shame she never got to enjoy it."

"You keep it, Calvin," I said. "Pay off Jim Moss' client. It's your chance to start over."

He shoved clenched fists into his pockets. "It's too late to start over. That ship has sailed."

Edna gave a dismissive cluck. "I started over in my eighties, and I'm making up for lost time."

"It's true," Gertie said. "We're the poster girls for late life transformation."

The two old friends cackled and shoved each other playfully.

"Zombies, beware," I said, as we gave each other high fives.

Calvin stared at us, as if assessing whether we had full control of our faculties. Collectively, we may have only had faculties for one in that moment.

Then he shrugged. "Let's see what the chief says."

I nodded. "And let's see what Polly's diary says. If the money's dirty, we give it to worthy causes. There's plenty of it and we'll make sure it does some good."

"That's how we roll, here in the treasure capital of hill country," Gertie said. She'd donated the majority of her share of Frank's treasure to a community center everyone in town could enjoy.

"Now *there's* a marketing hook that could beat Dog Town any day of the week," I said. "Unfortunately, we'd be swarmed."

"Surely that's the last of the gold," Gertie said, shuddering. "Frank must have spent years allocating his spoils to the ground."

"He lived past ninety," Edna said. "Still charming the old ladies. But he left his wife and never married again. No one held a candle to Polly, it seems."

Now that there was plenty of good news in the bank, I told my father the bad news. "Walt said he's your stepbrother. Your father's illegitimate son."

He sighed. "It doesn't surprise me, unfortunately. I think that's partly why Frank thought he could lure my mother away. But she had that till-death-do-we-part mentality."

"After Polly passed, Chester could have hooked up with Walt's mother but he didn't."

"I got the sense he blamed himself and appreciated her more after she was gone. He went downhill fast."

"Drank himself to death," Edna said. "From what I heard."

"You don't think Chester killed Polly?" I asked.

Edna looked at Gertie and then shook her head. "No offense, Calvin, but your dad didn't have smarts or horse sense. I don't think he could have pulled off a plan like that."

"If there even was a plan," he said.

"There was," I said, watching Keats give Calvin an appraising stare with his blue eye. "Keats says so."

"And how would your dog know? That was a long time ago."

I shrugged. "He knows things. We don't really question how."

"I've spent my whole life around farm animals and I don't buy this woo-woo stuff, Ivy."

"Guess it skipped a generation," I said, smiling.

"Calvin, we all come in as skeptics," Edna said. "Keats and Percy will turn you into a believer."

"I'm not sticking around long enough for that to happen," he said.

Edna gave him a stare intended to chill him to the bone. "Suit yourself. But when you get a second chance like this, I believe it's your moral responsibility to make good use of it."

"Ivy needs help in her goat dairy," Gertie said. "Since you're bragging about your farm know-how."

"It wasn't bragging. Just facts."

"There you go, Ivy," Gertie said. "Goat expertise from someone who has time on his hands, unlike me."

"Really?" Calvin said. "You're that busy?"

"I am, yes. Edna, too. When the world as we know it collapses, we'll be ready."

"Prepping is a full-time job," I said.

"I want a bunker just like this," Edna said. "Very well built, especially for the day."

Gertie took a look at me and said, "Go home, Ivy. You're wilting. Edna, can you ride along and then be a doll and swing back with some coffee? The cops may be a while."

Calvin and Gertie were bickering before we were even out of earshot.

"Do you trust him?" Edna asked.

"Mostly." I smiled as Keats and Percy resumed their chase through the trees. "But I trust Gertie and Minnie more."

"Smart girl," she said, patting my shoulder. "Polly would have been proud of you."

CHAPTER TWENTY-EIGHT

The spring sunshine finally delivered a warm kiss on the day everyone gathered for the barn-raising. Technically, it was a "big shed" raising, but it was still exciting. In the week or so since the revelations at the Fable and Galloway homes, Charlie had cleared and fenced more land with help from Calvin and Poppy to accommodate our growing goat population. I wasn't sure how I felt about having my father around so much, but I was too busy to waste more angst on it.

Mom had continued to avoid Runaway Farm and I hoped it would stay that way until things calmed down. If Calvin stuck around Clover Grove, their meeting was inevitable, but delaying it was in everyone's best interests. And if there was one thing you could normally count on with Mom it was skipping out on hard physical labor. No doubt when she was good and ready to see Calvin, she'd be wearing her very best red dress and killer heels.

My family was full of surprises, however, and when

Asher's truck rolled up the lane, there was a flash of red from the passenger seat.

"Oh no," I said to Jilly, who was setting out coffee and platters of food on a table in the parking area. "I just wanted a nice old-fashioned barn-raising. Full of community spirit."

Indeed, dozens of friends had shown up, including the entire Rescue Mafia. Cori had flipped Kellan the orange-fingered glove twice already, but I noticed they'd also opted to move lumber together. I supposed that was the very definition of keeping your enemies close.

"It'll be fine," Jilly said. "I've been talking your mom through this. She wants to be here for you today. Without drama."

"This is Dahlia we're talking about," I said. "She only has one setting, and it's drama."

"Give her a chance. You're giving Calvin a chance."

"I wouldn't say that. He's just here all the time. He didn't ask me so I couldn't say no."

Jilly laughed. "I guess he's trying to make up for nearly getting you chopped up for firewood."

"Not to mention being gone for decades." I eyed him through the steam from my coffee cup. "It'll take more than goat whispering."

His bragging had been justified. The goats adored him, and he spent many an hour just sitting in their castle hanging out in the sunshine. He'd even slept in the barn for a couple of nights to be on hand to deliver the last of the kids.

There was one goat, however, who preferred me to him. She was standing behind me now, nibbling on the fingers of my free hand. Big Mama wanted to be patted constantly. In fact, she was needier than both cat and dog combined. On the bright side, that meant she could be trusted out of her pen and I took her for strolls without the kids, where we chatted about the weather like regular farmers. Keats didn't like this at all but he had plenty to supervise in these busy days. I turned and scratched Big Mama's ears, as an excuse not to watch Mom make her entrance. But it was useless. I had to turn back.

And what an entrance it was...

Asher jogged around the truck and opened the door to help her down. He set out a little stool and she slid gracefully out of the passenger seat. I expected fancy attire, but she was wearing her one pair of jeans, a light red jacket and... work boots. Her hair and makeup were dialed down to a six on the glamor scale. One hand came up in a royal wave. On it was a brand-new red leather glove.

"Do you see that?" I asked. "Mom's got steel toes. I hope she doesn't plan to do any kicking."

"You should talk," Kellan said, coming over to sling an arm around my shoulder. I knew he was there to offer support in the face of this dreadfully awkward reunion. "She's probably jealous of your Tarzan move. Walt Watford was glad to be taken into custody to escape you."

"I do what I can to make your job easier, Chief," I said, managing a grin. "I hope Chief Coots was disappointed."

"He was. You know I don't gloat but... thanks for that." Kellan moved out in front of me to block my view.

"Just look at me right now. Not them. It's better that way."

I did as he suggested. "So you've put Polly's cold case to rest?"

He nodded. "Walt confirmed the testament in Polly's diary. She was being targeted by his mother, who hoped that by getting Polly out of the picture, Chester would choose them and share the fortune she thought he had. Meanwhile the key to that fortune had died with Polly."

"Such a shame," Jilly said. "And what's to become of the money?"

"At the end of the investigation it will likely belong to Calvin. It's worth a lot in today's currency. But that won't happen till I've crossed every single T. Something always comes up with Frank Swenson. I honestly wish I'd met the man because he was a brilliant criminal."

"And Polly was genuinely happy about accepting this gift from him?" Jilly asked.

"Apparently so," I said. "Her diary claims it was earned through his legitimate ventures, which were also successful. There was no need for him to work on the dark side."

"He just liked the challenge," Kellan said. "Wanted more."

"Wanted what he couldn't have, most of all," I said. "It sounded like Polly was very clear with him that they could be nothing but friends. But she did love Frank. I could read that much between the lines of her diary."

"It's always complicated," Jilly said.

"It's never complicated," Edna said, coming up

behind us. "So how about you folks stop overanalyzing and roll up your sleeves?"

"Where are my... my parents?" I asked, turning. The word didn't fall easily from my lips, and might never.

Edna pointed to where Keats was supervising their reunion. White tuft swishing gently, he herded them closer and closer until they were about a yard apart. Then he moved into the middle, creating a furry wall to protect each party from... complications.

"See? All good. Gertie and I will babysit them all day and make sure neither one gives you a moment's trouble." She tipped her head. "I wonder if Calvin's vaccinations are up to date. He's been on the run a good while."

I laughed. "I leave them in your capable hands, Edna. Thank you."

She jogged off and Kellan dropped a kiss on my cheek before doing the same.

Jilly took a deep breath. "Ivy, there's something I need to tell you."

"You're engaged?" I asked.

She shook her head. "Romance is the last thing on my mind right now. I've got family trouble, too."

"Your gran?"

"My gran. And if you can manage without me for a week or two, I'd like to run down and visit."

"Of course, but I thought you two were on the outs."

"We are. After seeing you Galloways get things sorted, I was inspired to try."

She looked out at Asher, who was working alongside Charlie, Kellan, Cori and Poppy on the foundation of the new goat barn. As always, he sensed her eyes on him and looked up with a wide smile. My brother and I hadn't spoken about what happened yet, but I was confident we'd be able to put all of this behind us. Sometimes it was better to let the dust settle before stirring it up again.

Jilly returned the smile but it faded as soon as he turned back to his work.

"Is your grandmother okay?" I asked. "Is she ill?"

"It's hard to know with her. She's not... She's not normal, Ivy."

I laughed. "And my family is?"

"Compared to mine, yes. There are true eccentrics in my mom's line, and they consider *me* the odd one. I'm the black sheep of the family. I wasn't sorry to leave them behind, and I asked them not to contact me."

"But your gran keeps reaching out."

"There's trouble in her retirement community. She doesn't feel safe." She sighed. "And she's probably not."

"Well, we'd better run down there and see what's going on. You, me, Keats and Percy. We're good at sorting out trouble, no?"

"I can't ask you to do that," Jilly said. "It'll be dangerous."

"And what we face together in Clover Grove isn't?"

She ran her fingers through her curly hair and turned it into frizz. "It's different dangerous."

"Different sounds like a vacation to me. Different dangerous by the sea." Keats had arrived by my side and Percy set his paws against Jilly's leg in a request to be rocked like a baby. "What do you say, boys? Should we go kick some butt in the retirement community?"

"Not the pets," she said, picking up Percy. "It's one

thing for me to put you in harm's way, but quite another for..."

Keats cut her off with a sharp, decisive yap.

"The dog has spoken," I said. "We're a team. I'll get Edna to oversee things here and we'll take a road trip. I thought I'd never ever get a vacation."

"It's not going to be fun," Jilly said, trying to tame her hair again.

"Oh, it will be, my friend. We make everything fun."

At last, she smiled. "Somehow, we do."

Keats circled and tightened his invisible loop to pull us into a hug until Percy yowled in protest.

"It'll be fine," I said, when the dog let us part. "We'll be back on Runaway Farm alive and well in no time."

Keats gave an enthusiastic wag that welcomed the adventure ahead and Jilly finally caved.

"Okay, then. The sooner we leave the better." She looked around at the milling crowds of people and animals. "I want to get it over with and come home to my real family."

"So long, Clover Grove," I said, as we walked over to join the workers. "Hope you're still standing when we get back."

Have you joined Ellen Riggs' author newsletter at **Ellenriggs.com**? You'll receive two stories free, including *The Cat and the Riddle*, which is EXCLUSIVE to subscribers. The story takes place after *Swine and Punishment* and sets the stage for a future novel. Don't miss out! Plus, of course you'll see some great photos of my adorable dogs.

While you're waiting on the next *Bought-the-Farm* book, if you would be so kind as to leave a review of this one, that would be amazing! Reviews help stoke the fires of creativity.

RUNAWAY FARM & INN RECIPES

Mandy's World Class Nanaimo Bars

First Layer:

- 1 cup graham wafer crumbs
- 1 cup unsweetened flaked coconut
- 1/2 cup finely chopped pecans
- 1/3 cup cocoa
- 1/4 cup sugar
- 1/4 tsp salt
- 1/3 cup butter, melted
- 1 egg, beaten
- 1 tsp vanilla

Middle layer:

- 1/3 cup unsalted butter, softened
- 2 tbsp custard powder
- 3 tbsp milk
- 1 tsp vanilla
- pinch salt
- 2 cups icing sugar

Glaze:

- 3/4 cup Belgian semi-sweet chocolate, roughly chopped
- 2 tbsp butter

Instructions

- Heat oven to 350°F. Line an 8-inch pan with parchment paper, with ends hanging over sides of the pan.
- Stir together graham crumbs, coconut, walnuts, cocoa, sugar and salt. Add butter, beaten egg and vanilla, stirring to combine. Press firmly into prepared pan.
- Bake until firm, about 10-12 minutes. Set aside to cool.
- For the middle layer, mix butter and custard powder in a large bowl with a mixer. Add milk, vanilla and salt and mix to incorporate. Add icing sugar in two additions, mixing until light and fluffy. Spread over bottom layer. Refrigerate for an hour.
- Melt chocolate and butter together. Spread chocolate glaze over middle layer.

Chill for 30 minutes. Remove from pan using parchment edges and cut into squares.

More Books by Ellen Riggs

Bought-the-Farm Cozy Mystery Series

- *A Dog with Two Tales (prequel)*

- *Dogcatcher in the Rye*
- *Dark Side of the Moo*
- *A Streak of Bad Cluck*
- *Till the Cat Lady Sings*
- *Alpaca Lies*
- *Twas the Bite Before Christmas*
- *Swine and Punishment*
- *The Cat and the Riddle* **(Newsletter Exclusive)**
- *Don't Rock the Goat*
- *Swan with the Wind*
- *How to Get a Neigh with Murder*
- *Tweet Revenge*

Books by Ellen Riggs and Sandy Rideout

Dog Town Series

- *Ready or Not in Dog Town* (The Beginning)
- *Bitter and Sweet in Dog Town* (Labor Day)
- *A Match Made in Dog Town* (Thanksgiving)
- *Lost and Found in Dog Town* (Christmas)
- *Calm and Bright in Dog Town* (Christmas)
- *Tried and True in Dog Town* (New Year's)
- *Yours and Mine in Dog Town* (Valentine's Day)
- *Nine Lives in Dog Town* (Easter)

- *Great and Small in Dog Town* (Memorial Day)
- *Bold and Blue in Dog Town* (Independence Day)
- *Better or Worse in Dog Town* (Labor Day)

Boxed Sets:

- *Mischief in Dog Town - Books 1-3*
- *Mischief in Dog Town - Books 4-7*
- *Mischief in Dog Town - Books 8-10*